**“I want you to do me a favor,” Jenna said.**

Out of the corner of her eye she saw Tito turn and look at her. “Sure,” he said. “Anything.”

“Please don’t talk to Halley about any of this. The whole thing with Chase. I’d appreciate it if you’d leave it alone.”

“All right,” said Tito, and Jenna knew he meant it. Of course he wouldn’t press Halley for information about the abusive ex-con father she’d had to run away from. And he wouldn’t press Jenna either if she didn’t want him to. He would be discreet. He would respect her boundaries. He’d go on being the friend and coworker that she needed, and not push for more, because that was the kind of man he was.

A barrier had come down today. Jenna had suffered a hull breach, and things wouldn’t be quite the same. She had to preserve the distance she had left, keep a buffer of privacy around herself and Halley. That was the only way to keep them safe.

Dear Reader,

There's a special kind of comfort in those beloved food and drink establishments where the staff know you by name. Over the years I've been blessed with many of these—Gerald's Donut in Oklahoma City, where my grandmother used to take me on weekends; Richard's Restaurant in Harlingen, where I first learned the joy of being a "regular"; and the Starbucks in Lake Dallas where I used to go to write while my daughters were in ballet. Naturally, such places are always finding a way into my stories.

Tito's Bar has been a favorite gathering place for the residents of Limestone Springs all the way back to the first Truly Texas book. A big reason for that is Tito himself. He's always available to listen to people's troubles and offer counsel while serving them drinks.

Jenna's been hanging around for a few books now, too. She's capable and dependable, but nobody knows much about her life before she came to Limestone Springs.

I'm excited to finally bring Tito and Jenna out of the background and give them a love story of their own. I hope you enjoy it.

*Kit*

# HEARTWARMING

## *Hill Country Home*

---

*Kit Hawthorne*

If you purchased this book without a cover you should be aware that this book is stolen property. It was reported as "unsold and destroyed" to the publisher, and neither the author nor the publisher has received any payment for this "stripped book."

PLEASE RECYCLE
THIS PRODUCT IS RECYCLABLE
Recycling programs for this product may not exist in your area.

ISBN-13: 978-1-335-47560-2

Hill Country Home

Copyright © 2023 by Brandi Midkiff

All rights reserved. No part of this book may be used or reproduced in any manner whatsoever without written permission except in the case of brief quotations embodied in critical articles and reviews.

This is a work of fiction. Names, characters, places and incidents are either the product of the author's imagination or are used fictitiously. Any resemblance to actual persons, living or dead, businesses, companies, events or locales is entirely coincidental.

For questions and comments about the quality of this book, please contact us at CustomerService@Harlequin.com.

Harlequin Enterprises ULC
22 Adelaide St. West, 41st Floor
Toronto, Ontario M5H 4E3, Canada
www.Harlequin.com

**Printed in U.S.A.**

**Kit Hawthorne** makes her home in south central Texas on her husband's ancestral farm, which has been in the family for seven generations. When not writing, she can be found reading, drawing, sewing, quilting, reupholstering furniture, playing Irish penny whistle, refinishing old wood, cooking huge amounts of food for the pressure canner, or wrangling various dogs, cats, horses, and people.

**Books by Kit Hawthorne**

***Truly Texas***

*Her Valentine Cowboy*
*Snowbound with the Rancher*
*Hill Country Promise*
*The Texan's Secret Son*
*Coming Home to Texas*
*Hill Country Secret*

Visit the Author Profile page
at Harlequin.com for more titles.

To my mom, who taught me by example the meaning of grace.

**Acknowledgments**

Many thanks to those who answered my questions about working in restaurants, breweries and bars, particularly my husband, Greg, and my daughter Grace. There's a whole lot that goes on behind the scenes to keep things running smoothly so customers can come in and feel comfortable, whether they're sipping coffee while working on their laptops or kicking back with a beer and a burger at the end of a long day.

Thanks also to David Martin for information about Formula 1 racing and flashy sports cars, and to my cousin Colby Langford for his help with police procedure. As always, many thanks to my critique partners Mary Johnson, Cheryl Crouch, David Martin, Janalyn Knight, Willa Blair and Nellie Krauss, and to my editor, Johanna Raisanen, for their invaluable insight and encouragement.

# *CHAPTER ONE*

LALO'S KITCHEN WAS really hopping tonight, with every booth and table full and the back patio crammed to capacity. A crowd stood closely packed just inside the glass front of the old downtown building, waiting to be seated. Seemed as though the entire town of Limestone Springs had unanimously selected that evening to dine at Lalo's. Beyond the pass-through, Tito's Bar was doing a brisk business as well.

Jenna Hamlin balanced a loaded tray high above her head as she threaded her way through the crowded room. One of her servers had called in sick that afternoon. Luke, the other manager, had come in on his evening off to pitch in and was now busily bussing tables, but the wait staff was still spread way too thin.

She reached the guy sitting alone at the

two-top over by the exposed brick wall and brought her tray down to waist level.

"Here you are, sir," she said, setting the glass in front of him. "One sweet tea. And your loaded nachos should be out in a few minutes."

Her mind was already racing two or three steps ahead. She had two entrées and a basket of cheese curds to deliver to the couple at the next table, and drink orders to take from the party of four that had just been seated in the corner booth. So when the guy asked her a question, it threw her off her rhythm.

She stopped in midstep and turned back around. "I'm sorry?" she asked.

He spoke up, louder this time. "I said, *did you stick your finger in my tea?*"

Then he sat back and smirked.

Slowly his meaning broke over her. He looked so pleased with himself, with his round blue eyes and toothy grin—as if he'd said something clever, as if Jenna ought to be flattered by the suggestion that she could sweeten tea with the touch of her finger.

Jenna had seen this guy before in Lalo's Kitchen. He had one of those names made of initials—C.J. or T.J. or something. He liked to talk, especially to the female wait staff. Only a few days earlier, Jenna had watched Veronica, one of her part-timers, trying desperately to get away from him, a forced smile pasted on her face, as he droned on and on.

*I didn't want to be rude*, Veronica had told Jenna after finally making her escape. *He is a customer, after all.*

*That's why he thinks he can get away with it*, Jenna had replied. *He's taking advantage of that customer-is-always-right crap and using the power imbalance to gratify his ego. Don't let him get away with that. Be polite but firm, and if that doesn't work, come get me or Luke, or even Tito from next door. We'll back you up.*

Veronica had looked doubtful. She was young yet, only a senior in high school. Jenna was thirty-two, with years of experience waiting tables and tending bar during college, as well as other experience with men who abused power.

Now was her time to shine, to put all that wisdom into practice.

She gave Sweet Tea Guy a quick, cool smile, just enough to show that she got the joke without implying that she thought it was funny. “No, sir,” she said. “Our sweet tea is sweetened with a simple syrup made from cane sugar.”

His grin widened. “But why go to all that trouble when you can sweeten it yourself?” He waited a beat, then added, “You know. Because you’re so sweet.”

Either he was too obtuse to take a hint, or he simply didn’t care. It amounted to the same thing.

Jenna pushed down the rising wave of annoyance. She didn’t want to appease the guy, but she also didn’t want to lose her cool. Getting mad would just give him power over her. She would be polite, unruffled, firm.

“No, sir,” she said again. “That wouldn’t work, and it wouldn’t be sanitary. Is there anything else I can do for you?”

“Well, you can sit down here with me, and smile at me while I drink it,” said Sweet Tea Guy. “Make it go down easier.”

Jenna didn’t dignify this with a reply.

“Enjoy your drink,” she said, then turned and walked away.

She delivered the entrées and cheese curds to the other table, took the drink orders at the booth, cleared some dirty dishes and took them to the washing station, narrowly avoiding a collision with Lalo Mendoza, the restaurant's owner. Lalo was the cousin of Tito Mendoza, who owned the bar next door. Like Luke, Lalo had come in this evening to help, but unlike Luke, he was merely getting in the way without contributing anything, standing around with his hands on his hips and a worried expression on his face. Jenna finessed her way past him, then headed back to the break room to check on Halley.

Any time Jenna was at Lalo's Kitchen, Halley was there too—which meant Halley was there for roughly half her waking hours in any given week. Between rush times, when the dining room was mostly empty, Halley sat out front, reading, doing her schoolwork, wiping down tables, wrapping silverware. But whenever the dining room started to fill up, Jenna sent her to the break room, which not only freed up valuable table space but also kept Halley away from obnoxious customers like Sweet Tea Guy.

The situation wasn't ideal, but there were worse alternatives. At age twelve, Halley was legally old enough to stay home by herself while Jenna worked, but there was no way on God's green earth that Jenna was letting Halley get farther away from her than sprinting distance. That was how it had been for the past year and a half, and how it would continue for the foreseeable future.

The building that now housed Lalo's Kitchen had once been a law office, but that had been eight years ago, well before Jenna's time. She'd only ever known it in its present form, beautifully renovated in a pleasant blend of modern comfort and retro style. The exposed brick wall on the left side of the big open dining room continued down a long hallway that made a straight shot to the back of the building, with doorways on the right. Jenna went down the hallway, backing against the wall to make way for Clint, another part-time server, who was carrying a loaded tray to the dining room. She passed the kitchen, where Abel, the cook, was lifting a metal basket of fragrant, glistening sweet potato fries out of the deep fryer. Next came the two restrooms, followed by a third door, topped by a sign that said Employees Only. This led to a passageway connecting Lalo's Kitchen to Tito's Bar, with access to two break rooms, two offices, and a closet of cleaning supplies shared by both businesses.

Jenna entered the passageway, then opened the door to the break room belonging to Lalo's Kitchen.

It was a small but comfortable space, with a narrow fridge shoehorned in at the end of a wall of efficient cabinetry. Leftover cake from Clint's birthday stood on the counter next to a stack of disposable plates. Another wall was taken up by two rows of cubbies with employees' names written on labels in Veronica's pretty hand-lettering script. There was even a cubby for Halley, filled with schoolbooks, notebooks, sketchbooks and leisure reading.

But Halley herself was nowhere in sight.

Jenna backed up through the Employees Only door, which hadn't yet shut behind her. The restroom doors were both slightly ajar, and the lights were off.

She turned the other way, looking down the remainder of the hallway to the glass back door. She'd never liked that door. It led to the patio, the space of which was divided by vine-covered columns and trellises into lots of cozy little room-like areas. Anyone could slip in from there while Jenna was occupied in the front and reach the break room without her ever knowing.

A sound from the passageway made her jump. There was Halley, coming out of the break room of Tito's Bar, holding a canned soda in one hand and a paperback book in the other, with one finger marking her place.

Jenna hadn't had time to build up much of a panic, but her knees went weak with relief and she had to lean against a wall.

"What were you doing in there?" she asked, fear sharpening her voice.

Halley tossed back her straight blond hair. "Tito told me he got me some of those sodas I like, so I went to his break room to get one."

A quiver of irritation ran down Jenna's spine. She didn't like for Halley to go into areas that properly belonged to the bar, at least during business hours. Besides the safety issues, she felt sensitive about bringing up a child so close to a bar.

Of course, Tito's wasn't really a *bar* bar. Yes, it did have the word *bar* right there in the name—Tito's Bar. But it stood right next to Lalo's Kitchen, with a big pass-through doorway connecting the two businesses about halfway down the connecting wall, which gave it the vibe of a bar and grill, or even a European tavern, rather than a straight-up bar. You could bring your craft beer from Tito's over to your table at Lalo's, or take your burger from Lalo's to your spot at Tito's, and pay for your purchases at either cash register. And as Tito himself often said, people who were willing to pay eight dollars for a beer generally weren't looking to get drunk. Still, the place did sell hard liquor, and have the occasional three-sheets-to-the-wind customer.

"You know, we have a full selection of craft sodas on tap right here in the restaurant that you can drink for free," Jenna said.

Halley shrugged. "I like these ones from H-E-B. Tito got them just for me. But the box they come in is too deep to fit in our break room fridge. So he put them in *his* break room fridge and said I could come get one anytime I want."

"Take a few out at a time and keep them in our fridge," said Jenna. "I don't want you going back and forth between the restaurant and the bar."

"But Tito's fridge is, like, twelve feet away from ours!"

"It's in a different building. Anyway, I don't want you leaving the break room at all without asking me first."

They were rash words, and she knew she'd made a mistake the instant she heard them coming out of her mouth. Halley stared at her in disbelief. "Seriously? You want me to ask permission every time I go to the restroom? That doesn't even make sense. I'd have to leave the break room to begin with before I could find you in the dining room to ask permission. And that's if you're even *in* the dining room. Sometimes you fill in at bartending, which means I'd have to go to the bar to track you down—and you don't want me to go into the bar."

Jenna's head swam. She didn't have time to quibble over semantics; she had to get back to work. But she couldn't walk away without fixing this.

"You don't have to ask permission to go to the restroom," she said. "But for everything else, find me and ask first."

"What do you mean, *everything else*? You

just told me to stay out of Tito's break room. Where else am I going to go?"

Jenna sighed. "Look, I know it doesn't seem fair for you to be stuck in the break room for hours on end. But that's how it has to be right now."

"Why?" Halley asked.

"What do you mean, why? You know why. You can't be too careful."

"Yes, you can."

Halley wasn't whining or cajoling. She was as cool and composed as Jenna had been with Sweet Tea Guy.

"*What* did you say?" Jenna asked, putting some starch in her tone, in a last-ditch hope that Halley would back down.

Halley did not back down.

"I said yes, you can. You *can* be too careful. If you're so afraid of crowds that you never leave your house, or so scared of doctors that you refuse to go to the hospital when you're hurt, or so worried about food poisoning that you never eat food and end up starving to death, then you're too careful. I'm just saying."

She was right, of course. It was exactly the sort of thing Jenna would have said to her own mother at that age, in pretty much the exact same words.

Jenna stared at Halley, and Halley stared right back. When had Halley gotten so *tall*? She was almost eye to eye with Jenna now. It was almost like looking in a mirror. That hair, those cheekbones, that hard set to her chin, were eerily like Jenna's own.

The unflinching gaze of the bright blue eyes, though—that was all Chase.

Jenna drew herself up as tall as she could. "This isn't that and you know it. I just want you safe, Kara. Okay?"

"Halley."

"What?"

"I'm not Kara, I'm Halley."

Jenna shut her eyes. She wanted to scream. What was happening? How had this situation gotten so far outside of her control?

"I know," she said. "I'm sorry. Just be safe, okay, Halley?"

"Okay, Mother," Halley said with a tiny sigh.

She managed to pack a lot of subtext into that sentence, foremost of which was, *You're not my mother.* Halley had never said those words to Jenna, not out loud, but Jenna could feel them in the air.

Halley had started calling Jenna Mother when she was four years old, long before either of them could have possibly suspected that Jenna would one day be her legal guardian. Halley had gone on calling Kara Mom, but by some odd child logic, she'd found this other word that meant the same thing and decided to use it for Jenna. Kara hadn't liked it much, but she hadn't been able to stop Halley from doing it, and eight years later Halley was still calling Jenna Mother. Sometimes the name had a warm, affectionate feel to it. Other times, like now, it sounded formal and stiff.

Halley went to the correct, Jenna-approved break room and closed the door behind her. The whole thing was surreal, as if Jenna were watching herself at that age, shutting her bedroom door in her own mother's face.

Somehow she'd never envisioned Halley going through a back-talking, authority-challenging stage. Halley was supposed to be immune to all that. She'd seen so many ugly things at such an early age that she was supposed to be grateful just to be in a stable environment, and happy to follow the rules because they were there for her protection.

She used to cling to Jenna whenever Kara came to pick her up, her voice shrill with desperation. *No, please! Don't let her take me away. I want to stay with you!*

It had been like ripping her heart out to let Kara pry off those clinging little arms and take Halley back to the house the two of them had shared with Chase—a dank, disorderly, comfortless house full of brooding silences and ugly outbursts.

Halley didn't cling to Jenna anymore. There was no need now that the two of them were together all the time. The stable, peaceful home life with a predictable schedule, no yelling and plenty of food in the fridge was now the everyday life. Maybe it had lost its value now that there was no horrible alternative to compare it to. Maybe it was confining and dull.

That could spell trouble. Halley wasn't even a teenager yet, but she would be soon. And sometimes teenagers did terrible things.

Jenna shook her head hard. What mattered was that she'd gotten Halley far away from the bad stuff. She'd changed their names, covered their tracks and started a whole new life for them several states away. If Halley started giving her a little lip, well, Jenna could deal with that.

She got back to the dining room just in time to see Clint bring Sweet Tea Guy his order of nachos. Sweet Tea Guy didn't look pleased about exchanging Jenna with Clint, but there was nothing he could do about it. In another twenty minutes—half an hour, tops—he'd be gone.

But he didn't leave. And as the evening passed and the crowd thinned, he moved on from sweet tea to beer.

*Never mind,* Jenna thought as she served and bussed tables. *You can't stay here forever. I can wait you out.*

One of the big TVs was rebroadcasting the Monaco Grand Prix. Jenna's dad used to watch Formula 1 racing, and when she was little she'd watch with him sometimes, curled up next to him in his big armchair. The Monaco Grand Prix was a notorious street circuit race, with very little room for passing, and no room at all for driver error. Jenna watched a red Alfa Romeo careening through the streets, skimming walls and buildings with mere millimeters to spare.

The sight flooded her with memories of another Alfa Romeo, also red, driven by a broodingly handsome boy with his left hand resting carelessly on the steering wheel and his right arm stretched out along the seat back, warm against Jenna's shoulders. That one had been a street car, not a race car, but with enough power in its engine to reach glorious adrenaline-spiking speeds with no trouble at all, hugging the turns of narrow country roads through the Blue Ridge foothills. She'd loved those drives—windows down, music cranked up, the world rushing by as the boy at the wheel gave her that heart-melting James Dean smile. Now the memory made her sick.

She closed out a party of seven, and after they left she saw Luke wiping down Sweet Tea Guy's table. Yay! Gone at last.

"Looks like things are finally calming down," Luke told her. He was tough-looking, with his strong build and full beard, but with the kindest eyes Jenna had ever seen. "I'm going to head home."

"Okay. Thanks for coming in."

"No problem. Have you finished making out next week's schedule?"

"Not yet. I'll get it sent out tomorrow."

"All right." He started to go, then turned back. "Almost forgot. The chalkboard got messed up tonight. I think someone spilled a beer on it. I know Veronica usually does the chalkboard art, but she's gone home. Do you think Halley might want to give it a go? She's always drawing, and she's really good."

Jenna smiled. "I'll ask her. I'm sure she'll be happy to try her hand."

"Great. See you next week."

As she watched him leave, she sent up a quick prayer of thanksgiving that this most excellent of bosses was back on the job. Some months earlier, Luke had gotten fed up with Lalo's constant micromanaging and undermining and had actually quit without notice, just taken off his apron and walked out the door, right in the middle of a dinner rush. It had been a pretty dramatic thing for mild-mannered Luke to do, but as it turned out, he'd also been dumped by his girl and was at the end of his rope.

That had been the beginning of a busy

and stressful time in Jenna's work life. To Lalo's credit, he'd pitched in, doing his best to take over Luke's duties, but he hadn't done them very well. He'd have done better to give Jenna more responsibility to help, which as it turned out was one of the many things Luke had wanted him to do all along, but he hadn't. It was as if Lalo had to prove that he knew best.

Lalo did not know best.

It was sorely trying for Jenna, being lectured on how to do her job by someone who knew far less than she did about what that job actually entailed. The part-time employees weren't being managed properly; they slacked off, playing fast and loose with the schedule. Afraid to hold them accountable, Lalo tried instead to make them all happy by demanding more from his reliable employees. It was a case of the squeaky wheels getting all the grease, and the smooth-running, reliable wheels having their bearings ground down under excess strain.

Lalo's Kitchen had gone noticeably downhill. Food quality suffered, service got slower and sloppier, and the place always seemed to look dirty. Every day, Jenna heard from longtime customers complaining about the decline. They missed Luke, and his dog, Porter, and the way things had been under his management, and they weren't shy about saying so. Slowly, those longtime customers started dropping away.

Jenna liked to think that the final straw had been when she'd given Lalo her two weeks' notice. She hadn't wanted to leave the place that had been a major factor in bringing her to Limestone Springs to begin with, but it wasn't the same place anymore, and she'd said so. Lalo had replied, *Hold that thought*, and taken out his cell phone and called Luke right then and there, and begged him to come back. Luke had agreed to return only if certain demands were met, one of which was that Jenna get moved up to management. Lalo had complied. Since then, he'd mostly kept out of the way and let his managers manage. The customers had come back as well, revenue went up, and everything was better.

By closing time, Lalo's Kitchen had cleared out completely, and Tito's Bar was mostly empty. Standard policy for both restaurant and bar was to not rush customers out right at closing time. As long as they were behaving themselves, they could stay while the workers cleaned around them, and as long as they weren't drunk, Tito would go on serving them.

Jenna stood in the pass-through between the bar and the restaurant, leaning her shoulder against the casing as she faced the bar. It was quieter now, quiet enough to hear the music being piped into both spaces—a carefully crafted mix of hits and lesser-known favorites from the past few decades. Tito was in charge of playlists, and he took the responsibility very seriously. He knew exactly what to play to foster whichever mood he wanted to cultivate in the customers.

He was standing behind the bar now, slender and straight in his snowy white shirt and black vest, his perfect posture making him appear taller than he was. He always wore black and white at work. Jenna didn't know if he even had any other clothes. Light from the overhead pendant fixture shone on his hair, making it look impossibly glossy, like polished ebony.

His dark eyes swept over his domain. Long tables and benches ran almost the full length of the room. They were empty now except for one stein of beer on the table closest to the pass-through.

Jenna liked Tito's face, with its high forehead and cheekbones tapering to a long chin covered by a neatly trimmed beard, its thick black eyebrows and deep-set dark eyes, its wide, sensitive mouth. It was a thoughtful, intelligent, inquisitive face, with a look of query and searching about it—a responsive, mobile face, capable of being quirked into a rich variety of comical expressions. He was graceful and deliberate in movement, whether pouring a drink or running a damp cloth across the sparkling-clean surface of the bar top. At the end of the night, when he was counting money, he always put on a pair of old-fashioned gold-rimmed spectacles that perched unevenly on the end of his long bony nose, and looked at Jenna over the tops of them with his forehead all wrinkled up.

Everyone liked and trusted Tito. Customers confided in him, spilling out their troubles over their drinks. It was a stereotype, the sympathetic bartender, but justified in his case. There was something about him that inspired confidence, something deeply compassionate but also thoroughly rational, a razor-sharp intellect softened by self-deprecating humor and a sincere interest in other people.

Jenna understood the draw. She felt it herself. It would be so easy to confide in Tito, pouring out the whole messy history of how she and Halley had come to Limestone Springs, sharing the doubts that wracked her day and night, appealing to him for the wisdom and insight she knew he'd be happy to share, if only she'd ask.

But that could never happen. Her secrets had to stay secrets. She had to keep her new life, and Halley's, airtight. She couldn't afford to slip up.

Tito's eyes met Jenna's, and he smiled at her. It was the easy, casual smile of a good friend, but it sent a peculiar flutter through her heart. She smiled back.

She was about to turn around and head back to her own duties when someone appeared just beyond Tito, out of the hallway that ran along the far wall to the restrooms. It was Sweet Tea Guy. He crossed in front of the bar to the table closest to where Jenna was standing, picked up the beer stein and raised it to her, his grin as goofy as ever.

Jenna felt her own smile wilt.

Ordinarily, Jenna liked working closing shifts. She and Halley were both night owls, and homeschooling gave them the freedom to set their own hours. Her favorite time of day was after the last customer had left and the doors had been locked—especially on nights when Tito was closing, too.

And now here was Sweet Tea Guy, refusing to leave, ruining everything, the way inebriated guys always did.

Minutes passed. The part-timers did their end-of-shift cleaning tasks and went home. Luke left for the night, and so did Lalo. And still Sweet Tea Guy sat stubbornly in his spot, clutching his drink, refusing to budge.

Jenna went back to the break room. Halley was sitting on the tiny sofa with a book, her coltish legs bent at sharp angles. She looked up expectantly as the door opened.

"Sorry, you can't come out yet," Jenna said. "Some diehard is out here taking his time. He got a little inappropriate with me earlier, and I don't want you in the dining room until he leaves."

Halley scowled. “Can’t you throw him out?”

“Not yet. We’ll clean around him for as long as we can and hope he takes the hint and leaves on his own before it comes to that.”

Halley let out a long, exasperated sigh—whether at Sweet Tea Guy for being so inconsiderate, or at Jenna for not throwing him out, or at Jenna for being so protective, was impossible to tell.

“It shouldn’t be much longer,” Jenna said with an optimism she did not feel. “Tito just switched the playlist over to indie pop.”

Indie pop, according to Tito, was the genre to play when you wanted lingering customers to wind down and clear out. Ordinarily it worked like a charm, but Jenna suspected Sweet Tea Guy might be a tougher nut to crack.

“Lock the door behind me,” she said.

Halley gave her an incredulous look.

“Do it,” said Jenna. “I’ll come get you when he’s gone.”

Halley clomped over to the door and pushed it shut.

As soon as she heard the dry click of the

lock, Jenna shut her eyes and leaned her forehead against the door, suddenly exhausted.

Then she opened the door to the supply closet and started loading her cleaning cart. A clipboard hung from a hook on the side, with a checklist for all the tasks to be done at closing, and spaces for the closer to initial as each item was completed. Everything was right there, perfectly spelled out with no ambiguity. Luke had designed those checklists, and Jenna loved them.

Her back was to the doorway, but she saw the shadow fall from behind her. She turned. There was Sweet Tea Guy, blocking the exit. His grin was as wide as ever, but its goofiness had been replaced by something else.

"There you are, sweet thing," he said softly. "Let's have a little alone time, you and me."

As come-ons went, this one was pretty bald. It was insulting that he could possibly believe that Jenna or any other woman would take him up on it.

Her heart pounded hard, not with fear but with anger—against him and every other man who'd ever tried to take what wasn't his.

Jenna grabbed the push broom. She was

ready to rumble. Sweet Tea Guy was messing with the wrong woman. He had no idea how thrilled she would be to take out her frustrations on someone who so thoroughly deserved it.

But before either of them could make a move, a calm voice spoke from the passageway.

"Sir, this is an employees-only area. We don't allow customers back here."

Jenna couldn't see who'd spoken, but she didn't have to. She would know that voice anywhere. It was rich in timbre, with a smooth, rolling cadence—the kind of voice used by advertisers to sell fine wines or luxury cars.

Sweet Tea Guy didn't even turn his head, just waved a dismissive hand. "It's all right, Tito," he said. "I know this girl. We're having us a little visit. Go on back behind your bar."

"No," Tito said. His voice was still calm, but the pitch had deepened, and he'd dropped the *sir*. "Come on, R.J. We're closed for business now. It's time for you to go home."

R.J. did turn then, shooting a scowl in Tito's direction. He was a big, tall man, probably a good fifty pounds heavier than Tito.

"I'll leave when I'm good and ready," he said. "Now go back to the bar and mind your own business."

"You'll leave now," said Tito.

R.J.'s hands curled into fists, and he lumbered off to the left, out of Jenna's field of vision. She heard the sound of a scuffle, followed by a yelp of surprise. She hurried through the doorway of the closet in time to see R.J. with his arm bent behind him, being frog-marched by the bartender down the passageway and around the corner.

"Hey!" R.J. barked. "What do you think you're doing?"

The break room door opened, and Halley's shocked face peeked out.

"Close the door!" Jenna shouted. "I told you to stay put and keep the door locked!"

Halley did not shut the door. She came out and crept close to Jenna, almost touching but not quite. Together, they followed Tito into the dining room.

"Get your hands off me!" said R.J. "Who do you think you are? Let go!"

He kept hurling abuse at Tito all the way across the dining room to the glass door, finishing up with how he was never going to spend another dime in Tito's Bar or Lalo's Kitchen again.

"Funny, I was just about to suggest that very thing myself," Tito said.

He tossed R.J. outside, shut the door behind him and turned the bolt.

R.J. stood on the sidewalk, rumpled and indignant, glaring at Tito through the glass. There was no trace of a grin now, goofy or otherwise. His face was red and twisted with rage.

Unfazed, Tito took out his phone and snapped R.J.'s picture, then tapped his screen a few times. "I'm adding R.J. to the *do not serve* group text," he said.

He didn't look the least bit rattled or shaken. He certainly didn't look as if he'd just bounced a much larger man out of a bar. He didn't even appear capable of doing such a thing, which was probably part of the reason why he was so successful at it. Customers at Tito's Bar were generally well-behaved, but whenever one of them did need to be removed from the premises, Tito was up to the task. People underestimated him at their peril.

R.J. straightened his shirt in an exaggerated way and walked off down the sidewalk, his steps weaving a bit from side to side.

Tito flipped the sign on the door to the Closed side and turned to face Jenna and Halley. “Sorry about all that,” he said, picking up the abandoned beer stein and carrying it behind the bar. “R.J.’s always been a little on the obnoxious side, but tonight’s the first time I’ve seen him cross the line. You all right?”

“I’m fine,” said Jenna, but her voice shook a little, and a wave of weakness washed over her. She was still clutching the push broom. She leaned it against the back of a booth, steadied herself and said, “You didn’t have to do that, you know. I could have handled it.”

The words sounded ungracious in her own ears, but Tito didn’t seem to mind. He glanced at her over the bar top as he poured out the last of R.J.’s drink and said, “Okay.”

Then he picked up the dedicated cell phone used for streaming music and started tapping. The strains of indie pop that had been coming through the speakers instantly ceased.

Tito looked at Jenna and smiled. “It’s closing time," he said. "And you know what that means."

Jenna knew, all right. The best part of the night was about to begin.

## *CHAPTER TWO*

FROM ACROSS THE ROOM, Tito saw Jenna's lips curve into a smile. There was a kind of sweetness to her face, with its high rounded cheekbones and delicately arched brows, that made her look like a fairy princess. Even her voice was girlishly sweet. But Tito knew better. Jenna was tough as nails, full of sass and snark, with a passion for classic rock and eighties heavy metal bands.

Her green eyes sparkled with mischief. "I'll go get my till," she said. "Don't start without me."

While she hurried back through the pass-through to Lalo's Kitchen, Halley took down a barstool, plonked herself onto it, rested her arms and chin on the bar top and let out a sigh. Over the past few months, Halley had developed a wide repertoire of expressive sighs. This one conveyed exasperation with obnoxious customers and relief that the three of them finally had the place to themselves—feelings that Tito wholeheartedly shared.

He opened his cash register and removed his till. Then he reached under the counter and pulled out a zippered bag, a legal pad and his reading glasses. He set them all on top of the till, along with the music-streaming cellphone, and carried them to the table where R.J. had been sitting.

Jenna came back carrying her own till, set it catty-corner to Tito's and took a seat on the bench across from him. She frowned at Halley when she saw her sitting at the bar. She seemed oddly sensitive at times to the impropriety of keeping a child in close proximity to a bar for hours on end—and yet Lalo's Kitchen had been the first and only place where she'd applied for work after moving to Limestone Springs. Tito knew, because he'd been there the day she'd first showed up, in a Toyota Highlander stuffed to the gills with all the worldly goods they could carry away from wherever it was they'd come from. She hadn't even found a place to stay before coming to Lalo's to get a job.

"I'm just *sitting* here," Halley said before Jenna could say anything. "It's not like I'm having a drink. Tito would lose his liquor license if he served me alcohol."

"Yeah, I'm pretty sure I'd lose my *life* before the Texas Alcoholic Beverage Commission even got wind of it," said Tito. "Your mom would slay me on the spot."

"You've got that right," said Jenna. "Halley, go get the broom and start sweeping."

With another sigh, Halley got up from the barstool and trudged off.

Tito put on his gold-rimmed spectacles and wrapped the flexible wires around the backs of his ears. He'd found the specs in an antique store. They exactly suited his degree of farsightedness, and he thought they looked pretty sharp.

Peering over the tops of the lenses, he saw Jenna staring at him with a half smile on her face.

"What?" he said, a little defensively. Maybe his vintage specs didn't look so sharp after all. Maybe they looked nerdy and pretentious.

"Nothing," Jenna replied. "Whose turn is it to choose the first song?"

Tito handed her the streaming phone. “Yours.”

She took the phone, her fingers brushing his. She thought a moment and started tapping.

The opening bars came through the speakers. Tito listened. Keyboard intro, sort of a rough-edged organ sound, upbeat, brisk tempo. Key of D minor. A late seventies, classic rock sort of groove. Not one of the old standbys he heard regularly on retro playlists, and yet there was something familiar about it.

The guitar came in. He knew that riff. Jenna was watching him from across the table, with that half-angelic, half-mischievous grin, and moving to the beat. The words were right on the tip of his tongue…

He snapped his fingers. “‘Blue Collar Man,’” he said. “Styx.”

“Yesss!” She held up her hand for a high five. Tito raised his own hand, and Jenna smacked it so hard the palm stung.

After that they didn’t talk for a while. They were too busy counting money—and singing.

The first verse of the song started right

away, and Jenna sang along, loud and clear, nailing the lyrics and hitting every note perfectly. Tito let her take the verses alone—he wasn't 100 percent sure of the words—and came in to harmonize on the choruses.

They laid out all the bills, tallying how many they had of each denomination on their sheets of paper, and stacked their change in columns. Next door in Lalo's Kitchen, Halley was sweeping the floor with the big push broom.

A guitar solo started, giving Jenna a break from singing.

"Nice job," Tito told her. "You're giving Tommy Shaw a real run for his money on those lead vocals."

She chuckled. "Yeah, I like these tenor-range power ballads, because I can belt out the high notes with no trouble at all. It sounds like I'm crushing it, but really it's just that the song was written for a man to sing."

"That's only part of the reason," said Tito. "You've got a great voice, Jenna."

She darted a quick glance at him. "Thanks. So do you."

A brief, awkward silence fell. Then the

chorus started back up again, and they both went back to singing.

When the song ended, Tito glanced down at the screen on the streaming phone. It was his turn to choose a song—or he could let the streaming app's suggestion play through. That didn't count as a turn.

The app followed "Blue Collar Man" with "Jet Airliner" by the Steve Miller Band. Tito let it play. He sang lead on this one, with Jenna harmonizing on the choruses.

But when the grainy guitar intro of Pink Floyd's "Wish You Were Here" came on, he quickly picked up the phone and hit Pause.

Jenna frowned. "Why'd you stop it? That's a really good song."

"I know it is. But I—well, it's part of my depression playlist from my late teens and early twenties, and I can't listen to it now without being drawn into the way I felt back then."

He'd never spoken to Jenna about his depression before. Very few people outside of his immediate family even knew about it.

A silence fell. Then Jenna said, "I get that. Music can have powerful emotional associations. I've never been truly depressed, but there's stuff I can't listen to, as well. Pretty much anything from my senior year of high school puts me in a funk that lasts all day. I think that's one reason why I like classic rock so much. The music of my own youth is too…fraught."

"Yeah."

The mood had taken a somber turn all of a sudden. It would be nice if this led to more confiding on Jenna's part, but Tito knew it wouldn't, not with Halley right there with her push broom. Jenna was already looking as if she regretted sharing as much as she had. Tito wanted to bring back her smile—and he knew exactly how to do it.

He started tapping on the streaming phone.

"Let's shake things up a bit," he said. "Same decade, different sound."

The song was "Stayin' Alive" by the Bee Gees. Tito stood up and began to dance to the electric guitar intro, hips swinging and fingers snapping to the opening bars. Over in Lalo's Kitchen, Halley, still sweeping, did a double take.

The intro quickly gave way to the first verse. Tito jumped onto his bench and sang along with Barry in falsetto, then busted into the point move, à la John Travolta. By the time he reached the *ah, ha, ha* part, Halley was laughing so hard she had to hold on to a table for support.

It was fun to make her laugh. She was such a serious kid most of the time. Jenna, meanwhile, had stopped counting money and was watching and listening with her mouth hanging open.

"What's wrong with this kid of yours?" Tito asked Jenna over Halley's shrieks of hilarity. "What's she laughing about? Doesn't she have any culture?"

Jenna slowly shook her head. "I don't think she's ever even been exposed to disco before."

"Then it's high time she learned about it. This is some good stuff."

"Well then, don't stop now!" said Jenna. "Keep singing. And definitely keep dancing."

He did, with unabashed exuberance, to the accompaniment of Halley's gales of laughter and Jenna's dazed stare, until the lyrics faded out at the end of the song.

"Wow," said Jenna. "That was…wow."

Tito stepped down from the bench, dusted

it off, straightened his vest and took his seat again. "Didn't know I was a disco king, did you?" he asked Jenna.

"No," she replied. "No, I did not. Now, give me that phone."

Tito made as if to grab the phone for himself, but Jenna seized it first and hit Pause before the streaming app could start playing another disco song.

"Oh my gosh," Halley gasped from the next room. "What *was* that?"

"Only number ninety-nine of *Rolling Stone*'s '500 Greatest Songs of All Time,'" Tito called out. "'Staying Alive,' by the Bee Gees."

"Disco," said Halley. "I've heard of that. Is that what you listened to when you were a teenager?"

He made an indignant sound. "How old do you think I am? Disco came and went before I was even born."

"And for that," said Jenna, "we should all be deeply thankful."

"Hey," said Tito. "Don't hate on disco. It gets maligned today, but there's a lot to admire in it. Did you even listen to those lyrics? They're about survival, about fighting back against all the stuff that's trying to drag you down."

Jenna was already tapping away on the streaming phone. "That may be, but we're going to listen to Led Zeppelin now."

"But it's Halley's turn to pick a song," said Tito.

Halley waved her arm weakly and shook her head. "Oh, no. You two carry on. I wouldn't want to mess up your awesome retro vibe."

Not surprisingly, Jenna finished counting her money before Tito did. She zipped it into its bag along with the tally sheet and put it in the office for the night. By the time he'd stowed his own money bag in his own office, she'd started mopping the floor on the restaurant side, and Halley had almost finished sweeping in the bar. The restrooms had already been cleaned by part-timers late in their evening shifts.

Tito stood a moment watching Jenna clean the floor while singing another seventies power ballad. She was so enthusiastic about it, expending energy like there was no tomorrow, like a new hire trying to make a good impression, instead of a newly made manager who'd been working here for over a year.

His own bucket stood ready and waiting. Jenna must have wheeled it out and filled it with cleaning solution for him. He went to work.

Whenever Tito and Jenna shared a closing shift, they joined forces, taking care of their floors at the same time, helping each other with their deep cleaning tasks—and singing, always singing. They sounded good together, their vocal timbres blending perfectly. They traded off singing lead and seemed to have almost a sixth sense of what the other was about to do. It energized the closing, making the work fun.

"The chalkboard's messed up," Halley called out from the restaurant side. "And it smells like beer."

"Oh, yeah, I forgot about that," said Jenna. "Luke asked me to ask you if you wanted to try your hand at redoing it."

"Me? Really?"

"Sure. You're a good artist. You've seen Veronica do it before, and you know where she keeps the chalks and things."

Halley took the assignment very seriously,

shutting herself in the break room with orders that she was not to be disturbed. That left Jenna and Tito alone.

Jenna had a head start on mopping, so she finished her side first and came over to the bar to help Tito finish his floor.

"Man, I am worn out," she said. "Look at me. I'm all sweaty."

Tito didn't have to be told to look at her. Her face glistened, and damp tendrils of hair, darkened to a deep gold, curled around her forehead. She had the most beautiful skin, richly tanned and flawlessly clear.

"Singing while we clean probably takes things up a notch," he said. "I don't know if it counts as cardio, but I'm pretty sure we're expanding our lung capacity."

"I believe it. I never get this worn out closing with anyone else."

"You don't sing when you close with other people?" Tito asked, trying to sound casual. He'd wondered this before but hadn't want to ask, thinking it might come off as possessive or needy.

"Oh, you know, just under my breath. It's different when you're with someone who really knows how to harmonize."

He smiled at her as the two of them started rolling their buckets toward the back area of the bar. "It's all that Bach part-writing I had to do in music theory."

"Is that so? I thought you might have formal training."

"Yeah, I minored in music at the University of North Texas, and had a solid band and choir foundation in high school before that. How about you?"

"Just high school band and choir. What instrument did you play?"

"Oboe."

She flashed a grin. "Ha! That's exactly what I would have guessed. You're a classic oboe type."

Tito wasn't sure if this was a compliment. "Anxious and introverted?" he asked. "Temperamental? Neurotic?"

"I was going to say thoughtful and intelligent. It's a hard instrument."

They'd reached the floor drain. Tito held out his hand in an "after you" gesture, and Jenna emptied her dirty mop water and started rinsing her bucket and mop with water from the big spray nozzle.

"So what did you play?" Tito asked. "Wait,

don't tell me." He thought about it as he emptied his own mop bucket. Not flute, or clarinet, or any other woodwind. Possibly percussion, but she gave off more of a brass instrument vibe.

"Trumpet," he said at last.

She laughed. "Guilty as charged. Bold and brash, arrogant and loud."

"I was going to say confident, adventurous and extroverted."

As he rinsed and wrung out his mop, Tito silently filed away his newest bits of knowledge about Jenna. She tended to let information slip in the context of music—which bands she'd seen in concert, when she'd seen them, how old she'd been at the time. If he'd wanted, Tito could have Googled past concert schedules and figured out where she'd really come from, or at least narrowed it down. But he'd resisted the temptation. She'd told everyone that she and Halley were from Tennessee, and she must have a good reason for wanting people to believe it.

But it wasn't true.

At least, Tito was 95 percent certain it wasn't true. He'd been observing Jenna for a year and a half now, and she had a tell.

Tito's uncle—Original Tito to longtime patrons old enough to remember the bar's namesake—had been a master at reading people, and he'd passed his skills along to his nephew. From an early age, Young Tito had learned how to tell when someone felt comfortable around him, or fearful or angry, or was lying to him. And for the past nine years, ever since he'd inherited the bar from his uncle, he'd had ample opportunity to put his people-reading skills to work.

A lot of those nonverbal cues were highly individualized, having to do with a deviation from a baseline. Gaze aversion, for instance, wasn't a sure sign of lying. It might mean the person was momentarily distracted, or simply wasn't comfortable with sustained eye contact. In Jenna's case, direct eye contact was the norm. But when she told a lie, her gaze wavered, then turned down and away, and a brief, split-second flash of guilt appeared on her face.

She'd never lied about anything work-related, or given Tito any reason to think she was untrustworthy. But thc official story she'd told about her and Halley's lives prior to coming to Limestone Springs had been an invention.

Without actively trying to discover the truth about them, Tito had managed to piece together a few things. He was pretty sure Jenna used to live someplace with mountains, but within easy driving distance of the ocean. She had at least one sister but didn't seem to like talking about her. Her references to her sister had been few and brief and confined to childhood. She spoke of her mother in the present tense and her father in the past tense.

She'd never said a word about Halley's father, which was suggestive in itself. There'd been no wedding band on her hand on the day of her arrival in Limestone Springs, and no imprint or tan line suggesting that she'd recently removed one.

*I can't give you any references*, she'd told Luke when she'd applied for a job. *But I'm a hard worker, I'm motivated and smart, and if you hire me, you will not regret it.*

She'd looked him straight in the eye when she'd said that, and subsequent events had proven it true. But after Luke had hired her, and asked for her ID, things had gotten a little dicey. Tito had been around for that, too. She'd handed over a temporary Texas driver's permit and told Luke she'd lost her old license. Then her gaze had wavered and dropped, and a microexpression of guilt had flashed over her face, vanishing almost before Tito had registered it.

Instantly his mind had buzzed with questions and potentialities. Coupled with the lack of work references, the murkiness over the driver's license had seemed significant. Maybe she'd had a new one made after moving from out of state, and hadn't wanted to show the old one. Maybe it had been under a different name. Maybe she didn't want anyone to know where she'd actually come from.

But he'd kept his guesses to himself. And Luke, unsuspicious by nature and struggling to fill the scheduling gaps created by the two servers who'd quit without notice that week, had taken Jenna at her word. Within weeks she'd become his most trusted employee.

So. What was Jenna running from? That was the question that kept Tito awake night after night. Best guess was an abusive ex. She couldn't be in witness protection, or she'd have had a job lined up before moving and a driver's license that wasn't printed on paper.

He wished she would confide in him. He was accustomed to being confided in. But clearly she wasn't ready, and he wouldn't push. He was a patient man. He could wait.

## *CHAPTER THREE*

THEY PUT AWAY their buckets and mops. Jenna took her hair down from its big plastic clip, shook it loose and twisted it up again, performing the whole action with an unconscious grace that made something catch in Tito's throat.

She didn't seem to notice. "What's your deep cleaning task for tonight?" she asked.

"Um..." Tito forced his attention, and his gaze, away from Jenna. "Display wall," he said. "You?"

"Deep fryer."

"Okay. Let's do mine first, since the deep fryer is a dirtier job."

They went behind the bar. Tito climbed the sliding ladder and started handing down liquor bottles to Jenna from the top shelf. Once all the shelves were empty, he'd clean the mirrored wall behind them while she wiped down the bottles.

Before Jenna had come along, Tito had always taken care of this job alone. There weren't many people he trusted to handle the costly bottles or to put them back in their proper positions. You couldn't just stick the bottles up there any which way. You had to think about how often a particular bottle was used, its shape and size, even its color. The arrangement should be practical and convenient, as well as aesthetically pleasing.

He started, as he always did, with the Galliano, whose ridiculously long, narrow shape required him to keep it high on the top shelf.

"What is it with these weird bottles, anyway?" Jenna asked as she carefully took it from him. "Look at this thing. It's like a baseball bat—difficult to store and clumsy to pour from. How does the manufacturer not realize that?"

"It's a marketing ploy," said Tito. "Every manufacturer wants its product's packaging to be distinctive and memorable."

"Oh, it's memorable, all right," Jenna said. "I remember how irksome it is, and I don't like using it."

"Yeah, they definitely went way too far with that one. And don't even get me started on the 1800 Tequila bottle. A trapezoid? Really? That was the shape they decided to go with? And what's the deal with that wide lid?"

"And the Goldschläger! That chunky rounded base takes up way too much space, and the long neck is so awkward to pour from."

They continued making fun of eccentrically shaped bottles as they worked their way down the display case. Tito was spraying cleaner on the mirrored wall when he heard Jenna chuckling. He looked down and saw her holding a bottle of Kraken spiced rum.

"What's so funny?" he asked.

She held it up. "Who does this remind you of?"

He studied the sturdy bottle with its two rounded side handles. It didn't look like anyone he knew.

"Imagine it with a worried expression on its face," Jenna said.

Tito snapped his fingers. "Haha! It's Lalo! Because he's always standing around with his hands on his hips!"

Jenna flashed a brilliant grin. "Exactly! I knew you'd get it."

A comfortable warmth spread through Tito's chest. There was no one he had more fun with than Jenna. Their senses of humor just meshed.

Her gaze swept the other bottles for a moment. Then she seized the Green Chartreuse.

"This one is Luke," she said.

Tito looked at the green liqueur in its clear container. "It is," he agreed. "It's got the same calm, woodsy vibe."

"And Luke's always going hiking and camping," Jenna said.

They went on assigning booze bottles to employees on both sides of the pass-through. Some of the matches were simple and readily apparent. Eric, a redheaded bartender, was the red-lidded Luxardo Maraschino. Another bartender, Garrett, who liked wearing bolo ties, was the Avión Extra Añejo Reserva 44, because of the leather cord and pendant around the bottle's neck. Clint, with his broad linebacker's build, was the big square bottle of Disaronno Amaretto.

Others were less cut and dried.

"This one is Veronica," Jenna said, holding up the Crème de Violette. "I can't say why, exactly. It just looks like her."

"Yeah, it does," said Tito.

He picked up the Cointreau, a clear liqueur in an orange bottle, and said, "This one is Halley. Partly because of the coloring, and partly because of the flavor. Slightly sweet, and slightly tart."

"You've got that right," Jenna said dryly. "Let's see. Which one are you?"

She scanned the remaining liquors, pausing for a moment before a bottle of Tito's Handmade Vodka, a craft vodka made in Austin by some enterprising distiller with no connection to Tito Mendoza, or his uncle.

"Hmm," Jenna said. "This would be the obvious choice for you. But it doesn't really look or feel like you."

She went back to searching. Tito watched, anticipation building in him. It seemed deeply important which liquor bottle Jenna Hamlin thought looked and felt like him.

"Ah," she said at last. "Here we go."

She picked up a bottle of Johnnie Walker Black Label and held it up in triumph.

"This is you. Slender, high-class and formal. And the gold matches those cool vintage spectacles of yours."

Tito's heart gave a quick throb that was

half pleasure, half pain. There was something in her smile that he'd never seen there before, something more than the friendly regard of a respected coworker. The overhead pendant light shone on her hair, picking out strands of gold as bright as the trim and lettering on the bottle's slanted black label.

"Wow," Tito said. "Thanks."

Then he reached past Jenna and picked up the bottle of Tito's Handmade Vodka.

"And this," he said, "is you."

He didn't offer any explanation. In his mind, the resemblance spoke for itself. The classic shape of the bottle, the textured, cream-colored label with its black print and accents of metallic pink, the glittering pinkish coppery lid—somehow they were all Jenna, in spite of the fact that it was Tito's own name emblazoned in big italic letters. Jenna loved those pink lids with fanatical, unreasoning zeal. Tito had been saving them for her for well over a year now. She said she was going to make something with them someday, some sort of craft project, but she didn't yet know what. For now, she just liked having them.

Her smile deepened. "That's the one I was hoping for," she said.

*It doesn't mean anything*, Tito told himself. *We're just playing around.* But that wasn't the way it felt.

They put the bottles back on the shelves in pristine order, laughing and joking and singing, then moved on to the deep fryer. They ended the evening sitting on the floor, side by side, sharing a carton of fried okra, which they ate by hand, like popcorn. Sometimes they reached into the carton at the same time and their fingers bumped. The hearty aroma of peanut oil mingled with the sharp scent of cleaning solution, along with a faint hit of mango from Jenna's shampoo.

They talked and talked and talked—about books, music and sad or funny things that had happened to them as kids. Tito never talked as freely or deeply with anyone else as he did with Jenna. Most of the time he had to keep himself in check, to make sure he didn't bore the other person by going off on some wild tangent. But Jenna liked wild tangents. Sitting beside her with their legs stretched out on the nonskid floor mat, Tito felt as if the two of them were inside a bubble, safe from the rest of the world, beyond the reach of the passage of time.

The bubble burst when Halley came and found them.

"There you are," she said. "I finished the chalkboard. Come see what you think of it. I've been looking at it so long, I can't even tell anymore."

If she thought there was anything strange about the sight of Tito and her mother sitting hip to hip on the floor sharing finger food, she didn't say so. Jenna quickly got to her feet, as if she'd been caught doing something not quite respectable, but then held down a hand to Tito. He didn't need help up, but he took her hand anyway.

The chalkboard looked fantastic, with multiple fonts in a variety of sizes, and intricate scrollwork set off with flowers and leaves.

"Wow," said Jenna. "You really went all out. No wonder it took you so long."

"I had to start over a few times," Halley said. "I watched a couple of tutorials on YouTube. I wanted to get it right. I didn't want it to look like something some kid slapped together."

"Well, you succeeded. It looks amazing."

"As good as when Veronica does it?"

"Oh, yes. Definitely."

Halley gave Tito a questioning look.

"I agree," he said. "This is professional-quality chalkboard art right here."

Halley's cheeks turned pink, and she smiled.

Tito took the trash out to the dumpster. When he came back inside, Halley and Jenna had gathered their things to go home. But Halley, freshly energized from her triumph with the chalkboard, didn't seem all that eager to leave.

"How's Bunter?" she asked Tito, clearly stalling for time.

"Sleek and pompous as always," Tito replied.

Jenna looked confused. "Who are you talking about?"

"Tito's cat," Halley said. "You've seen him before, up in his windowsill, looking down at the town, judging everyone."

"Oh, okay," said Jenna. "Yeah, I've seen him. I just didn't realize he'd been named after Lord Peter Wimsey's valet."

"Who's Lord Peter Wimsey?" asked Halley.

"A sleuth in a British detective series from the early twentieth century," Jenna told her. "His manservant helps him solve mysteries. Lord Peter is the second son of a duke, so he's got plenty of money and leisure for his amateur detective hobby without having to work for a living, and without the bother of being a duke himself."

"Oh, he inherits the title eventually," said Tito. "His nephew and older brother both die, and the dukedom passes to Peter."

"Does it really?" asked Jenna. "How does he cope with that?"

It was a golden opportunity, Tito thought, almost too good to be true. Did he dare to take it?

"Finish the series and find out," he said. "I've got a complete set upstairs."

Halley turned an eager face to Jenna. "Can we, please? I want to see Tito's loft again."

Jenna hesitated. Tito held his breath, trying to look as if it didn't matter, but all the while thinking, *please, please*.

"Okay," Jenna said at last. "But just for a few minutes. We don't want to keep Tito up too late, or Bunter, either."

Tito felt silently exultant, leading the two of them up the long staircase with its beadboard siding and worn wooden steps. Old-fashioned sconces, mounted high overhead, lit the way.

They'd only been there once before, a few months back when Halley had started running a fever shortly after the start of Jenna's shift. The restaurant had been shorthanded that day, so Tito had offered to let Halley crash at his second-floor apartment above the bar. Halley had spent the day lying on Tito's sofa, reading books from his shelves, drinking juice from his fridge and petting his cat. The whole thing seemed to have become a treasured memory of hers.

He unlocked the door, opened it wide and stepped back for Jenna and Halley to enter first.

He watched as Jenna checked the place out. She probably hadn't paid much attention when she'd been there before; she'd been focused on taking care of Halley, getting her set up on the sofa with blankets and cushions. Now, he saw the apartment and its furnishings through her eyes—the efficient but well-proportioned living area with its crown molding and wainscoting, the moss green sofa and single wing chair, the wall of built-in bookshelves running all the way up to the ten-foot ceiling. To the left, Tito's bedroom door stood open, showing a tall dresser, a Windsor chair and a neatly made bed. Tito always made his bed. It was one of those keystone habits that kept him in a good headspace.

"Bunter!" said Halley, running over to him.

The black-and-white tuxedo cat lay stretched out in his usual spot on the windowsill overlooking the street. He turned on hearing his name and graciously accepted Halley's attention.

"Boy, talk about people who look like their pets," said Jenna, following Halley to the windowsill. "I half expect him to start wiping things down with a soft white cloth and offer me a drink."

"We don't look *that* much alike," said Tito. "Bunter is much fatter than I am."

"You have the same facial expression, though. And the same fashion sense." She stroked the cat under the chin. "Where'd he come from, anyway?"

“I found him in an actual dumpster, the one out back, not long after I took over the bar. I was taking out the trash at the end of the night and there he was, a little bag of bones scrounging for his dinner. I took him upstairs and gave him a bath and a can of tuna. He settled right in. I called him Bunter because he was so dignified, and because he looked like a little valet in his black-and-white fur.”

“Poor kitty,” said Jenna. “He must have been so scared before you found him. I wonder how he came to be there. I wish he could tell you the rest of his story.”

Tito didn’t answer. He wished the same thing about her.

“Look at this view,” said Halley. “Isn’t it great? You can see all the way to our house.”

“Can you really?” Jenna asked, kneeling down beside her. “Huh, you’re right.”

Tito crouched behind them both. “Which one is it?”

Jenna pointed. “See that metal roof, right in between the big oak tree and the row of crepe myrtles? That’s it. That’s our house.”

“I didn’t know that,” said Tito. But he knew it now, and he also knew that he’d never look through this window again without seeking out that metal roof.

Tito's knee brushed the small of Jenna's back, and his gaze slowly shifted to the back of Jenna's head. Crouching so close to her, he could smell that mango shampoo of hers again. A golden tendril had escaped from the gathered mass of her hair, hanging in a loose spiral down the nape of her neck.

"You ought to see this view in the wintertime," said Halley. "It was February when I was here before, and trees on the square were all lit up."

"That must be beautiful," said Jenna without turning around. "I always thought it would be cool to live in a loft."

All in an instant, Tito imagined knocking a hole through the wall on the right, into the space above Lalo's Kitchen, more than doubling his square footage, and giving him enough space to add a bedroom, another bathroom, maybe a home office. He'd thought about it, back when Tony and Alex Reyes of Reyes Boys Construction were renovating the bar and converting the old lawyer's office into a restaurant, but there'd been no need when it was just him living here.

But what if it wasn't just him? What if he had a wife and child? Could he turn the place into a comfortable home for a family?

Jenna turned suddenly, as if she'd sensed his thought, or felt his stare. She looked over her shoulder at him with those clear green eyes, her cheek making a perfect curve against the darkened window. He wanted to cup his hand against that curve, run his thumb lightly over her lips, lower his face to hers and…

She cleared her throat. "Let's find those books," she said. "Then Halley and I can get out of your hair."

Her voice sounded unnaturally bright and chipper.

"Right," said Tito. "Sure."

He stood and walked over to the bookcase, glad for the opportunity to turn his back to her, and hoping she couldn't see how weak and rubbery his legs had gotten all of a sudden.

"Here they are," he said, holding out a hand to a shelf. "The complete set—including all the short stories, and the unfinished novel that was completed by another author after Dorothy Sayers died, and the additional novels that were added to the series by that same author."

"Wow," said Jenna. "I had no idea there were so many. This is exciting. I have a lot of reading ahead of me."

She darted a quick glance at him. "You know, I actually had quite a crush on Lord Peter Wimsey for a while."

"Did you?" Tito asked. "That shows excellent taste."

"I guess it does. If only my judgment was always that good."

"So how far have you read?" Tito asked.

Jenna scanned the titles. "Let's see. I know I read *Strong Poison*, and the one set in Scotland, and the one where Harriet goes to that resort on a holiday and finds a dead body on the beach. I kind of jumped around in the series."

"You read them out of order?" Tito said in mock horror.

She gave him that sweetly mischievous grin. "Yeah, I'm kind of a rebel that way."

Tito reached for a volume. "Have you read *Busman's Honeymoon*? That's the one where Peter buys Harriet a house for a wedding present. They go there for their honeymoon, find a corpse in the cellar and have to solve the murder."

She made an indignant sound. "Peter and Harriet get married? Uh, spoiler alert!"

Tito chuckled. "Oops! Sorry."

"Oh, well. I'm glad to know they end up together. I wasn't sure they ever would. Harriet's pretty gun-shy after her awful ex."

"Yeah, she is. But Peter waits her out, and in the end she takes him."

In the silence that followed, the words seemed to take on great weight and significance. Jenna looked away. Was she embarrassed for him, thinking he'd made a bookish and clumsy attempt at a come-on? Or was she thinking that she, like Harriet, might come to love a very different sort of man from the one who'd hurt her? She'd once had a crush on Lord Peter Wimsey, after all. That meant she wasn't entirely averse to brainy men of average height with a history of mood disorder.

"How about if I just lend you the whole series?" said Tito. "Then you can start at the beginning and read everything in its proper order."

"Okay. Thanks. It'll be nice to have my

bedtime reading taken care of that far into the future."

Tito started pulling the books from the shelf. "You like to read in bed?"

"Every night, until my eyelids are too heavy to stay open."

"Even on nights when you work closing shifts? It must be pretty late when you finally turn out the light."

"That's the point. When I shut my eyes, I want to go right to sleep. I don't like to lie there and *think*."

"I get that," Tito said.

Jenna took a few steps back and scanned his shelves. "Wow, you have a lot of philosophy books."

"Yeah, I got my bachelor's in philosophy."

She chuckled. "A philosophy major and a music minor! It's like you were planning to be a bar owner from the start."

He carried the stack of books to his small dining table and took a plastic grocery bag out of the pantry. "Yeah, looking back, there is something inevitable about the whole thing, though I couldn't see it at the time."

Jenna was still looking at his bookcase, her head tilted to the side to read the titles on the spines. "You've got a big mystery section, too. A lot of Golden Age detective stuff. Nero Wolfe, Hercule Poirot..."

Tito set the books inside the bag. "I enjoy a good mystery," he said.

Suddenly Jenna was looking straight at him with those clear green eyes. "Yeah, well, you're something of a mystery yourself."

"Me?" Tito asked. "What's so mysterious about me?"

She walked over and took a seat at his dining table. "Well, for starters, how about the way you bounce obnoxious drunks out of the bar? I've seen you in action, and not just tonight. It's always the same. One minute the guy's making a jackass of himself, and the next minute he's out on the sidewalk, wondering what just happened. No fuss, no broken glassware, no scene. How'd you learn to do that?"

Tito glanced over at Halley. She looked contented enough, sitting on his sofa with Bunter, who was pacing back and forth over her lap, arching his back with delight and rubbing his face against her hand.

He sat down across from Jenna. "You've heard of my uncle, right?"

"Original Tito, yes. The bar's first owner."

"Exactly. I was always close to him. He was my mother's brother, and I take after her side of the family. Uncle Tito was a neat guy. Very intelligent and well-read. Funny, in a subtle way, but with something sad behind it all. He was married once, briefly, but his wife left him only two months into the marriage. She went away and never came back."

"Wow," said Jenna. "Dramatic."

"Yes. She was the love of his life. He never remarried or had any sort of romantic involvement again. He'd always been something of a loner, but now he turned into a hermit. He was in his bar pretty much all the time, or else upstairs in his apartment—this apartment."

"That's so sad."

"Yeah, it is. I didn't really see it at the time, though. It was just how things were. He was always good to me, and friendly to customers. It was only later, after he died, that I realized how lonely he was, and that he was probably clinically depressed."

He looked down, pretending sudden interest in the salt and pepper shakers, spinning first one and then the other ninety degrees, clockwise, over and over. "One day at school—I guess it was around fifth grade—this group of boys was giving me a hard time about something or other, which wasn't an unusual occurrence for me. But then one of them said that Uncle Tito had killed his wife and buried her body in the alley behind the bar. So I lit into them."

He could feel her watching him. "How did it go?"

"Not great. I got a couple of good punches in, but there were four of them and one of me, and boxing was not part of my skill set. This was back during the days of zero tolerance policies for fighting in school. I actually got suspended. My mom was taking my grandmother to the doctor that day, so my dad had to come pick me up. I had two black eyes and a busted lip, and my shirt was bloody and torn down the front. He asked me what had happened, and..."

He darted a quick glance at her. "Well, you've seen my dad. I think it's safe to say he hasn't lost many fights in his life. I was kind of embarrassed to tell him what happened, but I had to, so I did. He just looked at me with this stunned expression on his face.

Then he grinned, and said, *Well, if you're gonna get into fights to defend the honor of your family, I better show you how so you don't get your butt kicked next time.* He took me to Bart's Gym, and Bart taught me everything he thought I needed to know—which turned out to be quite a lot, because Bart has a pretty broad knowledge base in martial arts. I didn't just learn how to fight, I learned how to stop fights from starting—how to block punches, and do wristlocks and armlocks and holds and things. All of which comes in handy when you work in a bar."

He dared to look at her for real then. She was staring right back at him, and smiling. She seemed lit up with admiration and respect.

"Good for your dad," she said. "And good for you, sticking up for your uncle before you knew how to fight. That took a lot of courage."

"Thank you," said Tito.

Jenna's expression turned serious. "I don't know if I've ever told you this, but... I appreciate the way you and Luke look out for your employees, and back us up when customers get obnoxious. A lot of places would expect us—especially the female employees—to just take it, and go along with it, and not risk offending the almighty customer. But not you. So thanks."

Something warm and happy bloomed deep in Tito's chest. "Oh, well, you're very welcome," he said. "Honestly, I never even thought of that as something deserving of gratitude."

"I know," Jenna said. "That's the best part."

A silence fell, long enough to get awkward. Then Jenna said, "So that's how you learned to fight. But how did you come to own the bar? Did you inherit it from your uncle?"

"Yes. He died about nine years ago, and it turned out he'd left the bar entirely to me. I was doing postgrad work in North Texas at the time, and kind of at a loss for what I was going to do once I finished. There's not a lot of demand in the workplace for doctors of philosophy as such. I could always teach, of course, but the thought of being part of a collegiate system and dealing with actual undergraduates, not to mention the whole stupid tenure system, was not something that made me happy. But I wasn't exactly excited to come back to my hometown and work at the bar, either. I took a semester off from school to take stock and see where the bar stood financially. My plan was to hire good management and set myself up to be an absentee owner."

He ran a finger along a groove in the tabletop. "Once I got here, I saw that the place was overdue for some repairs. I hired the Reyes brothers for that. One thing led to another, and before I knew it, we were doing a full-scale renovation. Then the building next door went on the market, and I thought, why not expand? My uncle had left me a fair amount of cash, and the business was in good enough shape for a loan, so I went ahead with it. My cousin Lalo had grown up working in family restaurants, and he'd always wanted a place of his own, so he came in as front man and majority owner on the restaurant. Meanwhile, I was working full time at the bar. I couldn't find anyone I trusted to do as good a job managing the place as I'd do myself, and by that time I'd realized that I actually liked the work a lot. And I definitely wasn't looking forward to returning to school. So I stayed on."

He turned in his seat and pointed to a ragged photo stuck to his fridge. "This is my uncle. It's not a great picture of him, but it's still the best we have of him as an adult. My mom took it one day when he was standing at the bar. She had to act fast before he could run off. He didn't like having his picture taken."

"Ooh, can I see?" Jenna asked.

"Sure," Tito said. He pulled the photo free of its magnet and handed it across the table.

Jenna studied the image of the heavyset man dressed in black and white, with straight dark hair and a neatly trimmed Vandyke beard.

"You look like him a little," she said finally. "He's heavier than you are, and his facial hair is different, but I can see the resemblance in the eyes and the mouth."

She lightly laid a fingertip on the picture, and Tito tingled as if it were his face that she'd touched.

"Have you ever tried a Vandyke?" she asked.

"Briefly. It made my face look too thin. I've tried all sorts of facial hair over the years before deciding that the full beard is my best look."

Jenna looked up at him. "Oh, I don't know. I kind of liked that little Clark Gable mustache you used to have. That was a good look too."

Tito frowned. "How did you know about that mustache?"

"You had it, didn't you?"

"Yes, but that was years ago, way before you came to Limestone Springs."

"Well, you must have given it a second run, because I know I've seen it."

"No. I'm positive I've had a full beard continuously for over five years."

Something in her expression shifted. "Oh. Well then, I guess I must have seen it on social media or something."

For a moment Tito was honestly perplexed. Jenna didn't have any social media accounts—none, zip, nada.

Then her gaze wavered, and she looked down and away.

The whole thing lasted only for a second before she met his eyes again, but Tito saw it and knew what it meant. Jenna was lying.

Now he was more confused than ever. It

was one thing for her to lie about her origins, if she had something to hide. It was another thing entirely to lie about when and where she'd seen a mustache that Tito had had for two weeks, almost six years earlier.

What could it mean? Had he and Jenna actually met back then? He searched his memory. The mustache period had been a chaotic time, because it coincided with a late-summer storm that had done a lot of damage in Limestone Springs. Maybe Jenna had passed through town during that time? But if so, he'd have remembered her. He was sure of that. He had a good memory for faces, and hers was one he wouldn't forget.

Jenna stood abruptly and picked up the plastic bag. "Well, thanks for the books. Come on, Halley. It's time to go."

Tito stood too. "I'll walk you to your car."

"You don't have to do that," said Jenna.

She was clearly eager to get away from him now, but he walked her and Halley downstairs and out to the car anyway.

The battered Toyota SUV was parked in the lot behind the back patio. Honeysuckle and trumpet vines cascaded over the fence, filling the warm air with their sweet scent.

After a hard winter and a wet spring, a brutal Texas summer had settled in with a vengeance.

"Good night," Jenna said as she climbed into the driver's seat. "Thanks again for the books."

"You're welcome," said Tito. "See you tomorrow."

She gave him a brief smile. "Actually, no. Tomorrow's my day off."

"Oh," he said. Her days off always felt a little blank to him.

She shut the door and drove away. He watched her headlights disappear down the dark street.

## *CHAPTER FOUR*

THE TROUBLE WITH LIES, Jenna thought as she scraped bacon residue from the cast-iron griddle, was that they weren't true. No matter how carefully you constructed your lie, no matter how plausible it sounded in your head, you couldn't turn it into actual fact. That problem was compounded when you had to build a whole network of lies. The longer you fiddled with it, the more you realized just how flimsy it was, and how easily the whole thing could be knocked down by anyone curious enough to go digging and smart enough to put two and two together.

Truth, on the other hand, was unbreakable. It existed on its own with no need for convincing details or timelines carefully worked out for consistency. It didn't care if you believed it or denied it or laughed at it. The truth simply *was*.

After a year and a half of lies, Jenna had a

new appreciation for the beauty and strength of truth.

She ran hot water over the griddle with the spray nozzle, then wiped the surface dry with a paper towel. She'd bought the griddle at a thrift store in Limestone Springs, along with most of her kitchenware, a set of dishes, two table lamps and a decent collection of paperback detective novels. It would have been foolish to pack her own medium-quality household goods into a rented moving trailer for transport from Virginia, so she'd sold what she could, donated the rest, and packed her and Halley's necessities into a Chevy Trailblazer, which she'd traded in for a Toyota Highlander about a third of the way through Tennessee.

*Remember this place*, Jenna had told Halley over dinner that evening at a Cuban café. *From now on, if anyone asks you where we're from, you tell them we're from Crossville, Tennessee. Practice saying it so you'll be ready. It's true in a way, because we've stayed here overnight.*

And Halley had looked at her from across the table with those big trusting blue eyes, and said okay. And early the next morning, they'd gotten into the Highlander and driven to Texas.

Jenna had chosen their new home based entirely on internet research. She'd decided early on that she wanted to live in a small town in Texas. Her dad had spent some time in Texas as a young man and always spoke fondly of it, and a small town seemed like a good place for a fresh start. She'd liked the look of Limestone Springs, with its pretty downtown area, thriving economy and strong community spirit. But what had really clinched the deal was the old news video about how the residents had come together to help each other in the aftermath of a severe summer hailstorm. Part of the video had been filmed inside Lalo's Kitchen and Tito's Bar, where volunteer firefighters had gathered to rest and regroup, and people whose homes had been damaged had taken shelter. Tito had been there, serving food and drink with an encouraging smile, wearing crisp black and white, and sporting a debonair Clark Gable mustache.

She felt her cheeks grow warm as she wiped the counters. Why, *why* had she mentioned that mustache last night? And once she *had* mentioned it, why hadn't she simply told him truthfully that she'd seen it on that video, instead of telling him that half-baked lie about social media? It was reasonable enough for her to have watched the video at some point. But she hadn't thought fast enough for that. She'd panicked. And she never would have been in that position to begin with if she hadn't felt the need to weigh in on Tito's past facial hair, as if it were any business of hers. The way he'd looked at her after, with that shrewd, intelligent gaze—for one sickening moment she'd thought he was about to call her out on her lies, and unravel her whole fictitious backstory with a single tug.

And if he had, what then? Would she have stonewalled him? Or told him everything? She honestly didn't know.

The funny thing was, Tito was her best friend in Limestone Springs, or anywhere, and he didn't even know it. And if she was being truthful with herself, there was something inside her that wanted him to be more than her best friend—a lot more. But how could she possibly give in to that feeling when her past was so complicated? Yes, theoretically, she could tell him the truth. It wasn't as if she were a spy, or in WITSEC, or had a bounty on her head. Tito wouldn't look down on Halley for being a Latimore from Franklin County. He didn't even know the Latimores. And he certainly wouldn't get in touch with the Latimore clan and tell them where Jenna had taken Chase's daughter.

It might be nice, actually, having another person in on the secret—especially if that other person was Tito, with his clear, logical mind and warm heart.

But once she started, where would she stop? Where would it end? Would she and Tito tell Tito's parents? His brothers? His multitude of cousins? Once the story was let loose, there was no putting it back in the bag, and no predicting how far it would spread. Jenna wouldn't be able to keep track of it anymore. And how could she expect Halley to keep quiet if *she* couldn't be bothered to keep the secret herself?

No. The whole reason they'd left Virginia in the first place was to put the past behind them and make a fresh start. In order for that to work, their fake backstory had to stay airtight.

She'd have to be more careful from now on. No more going up to Tito's apartment. No more songfests. No more intentionally scheduling herself to close at Lalo's on the nights when she knew he'd be closing at the bar. No more letting down her guard. She couldn't afford to give her heart away to Tito. She couldn't afford to give away anything to anybody.

That wasn't easy in a small, friendly town where everyone knew everyone's business. She understood that now. The very things that had attracted her to Limestone Springs also made it hard to keep her secret. Even Tito. Especially Tito. He saw too much with those deep dark eyes of his.

She rinsed and wrung out her sponge, put it away and started the dishwasher. Its low, steady hum gave her a reassuring sense of things being under control.

In the small living room, Halley sat curled up in the armchair, reading a book and twirling her hair exactly the way Kara used to. Jenna longed to curl up with her own book and a fresh cup of coffee. She'd started the first of Tito's Lord Peter Wimsey books last night, and it was even better than she remembered—smart and funny, like Tito himself. But she still had utilities to pay, another load of laundry to start and next week's work schedule to finalize. And it was already after nine. Lord Peter would have to wait.

She'd always loved detective fiction, but since she and Halley had made their getaway, she'd started to see the stories with fresh eyes—how the killer planned the crime and covered his tracks, and how the detective deconstructed the deceit.

She'd read once that everyone who commits a murder makes twenty-five mistakes, and that anyone who remembers five of them is a genius. She hadn't killed anyone, but she'd erased two past lives, hers and Halley's and she was bound to have made some mistakes along the way.

"Why are you staring at me?" Halley asked.

Her blue eyes were peering at Jenna over the top of her book. Not open and trusting anymore like in Tennessee, but closed off, almost hostile.

"Sorry," said Jenna. "Just zoning out. Remember we have FaceTime with Gigi this morning."

Halley turned back to her book. "I know. Ten o'clock."

Jenna moved a load of darks from the washer to the dryer and started a load of lights. The washer and dryer added their voices to the soothing chorus of major appliances. She quickly sorted the pile of mail and paid her bills.

The small rental house needed a good dusting, but it was tidy. Jenna and Halley didn't have enough possessions to clutter it up, and they weren't home often enough to make a mess. Jenna liked things to be neat and clean, but today the place looked stark and utilitarian in her eyes. She thought of Tito's apartment, with its old woodwork and high ceilings, its bookcase wall and comfy sofa, the big front window with the black-and-white cat resting on the sill, looking out over the town. Tito's personality seemed to have infused every cubic foot of the space.

Remembering that her roof had been visible from Tito's front window, she stole over to her own back window and looked toward downtown. Through the limbs of a neighbor's pecan tree, she could just make out a patch of stonework that she was pretty sure belonged to the top floor of the building that housed the bar, but she couldn't quite see the window. Was Tito down in the bar, getting ready to open at noon? Or upstairs, enjoying a last cup of coffee and a good book? Or standing in the window, staring at her roof?

She checked the time. Two minutes before the hour. She opened her laptop and put the call through.

In the year and a half since leaving Virginia, she'd never once been late with a scheduled FaceTime session with her mom back home. She'd taken herself and Halley halfway across the country, thereby depriving her mother of her older daughter and only granddaughter. She'd also been the means, however unintentionally, of depriving her mother of her younger daughter forever. Being punctual for FaceTime truly was the least Jenna could do.

The face on the screen was thin and worn, with harsh, sharp cheekbones, and eye sockets dark with shadow. Tufts of untidy fair hair stood out in all directions like fluff on a baby chick. Caroline Travers had once been a beautiful woman who'd taken pride in her appearance and made the most of it with pretty clothes and immaculate grooming. Growing up, Jenna had rarely seen her mother without perfectly coiffed hair and full makeup. This woman was a tired old lady, and a stranger.

But her face lit up at the sight of Halley and Jenna, showing a glimmer of past glory.

"Well, hello, Kayla! Hello, Kirsten! How are you? It's so good to see you!"

Jenna tried to ignore a twinge of annoyance. Was it really that difficult to use the new names she'd taken so much trouble to secure for them? Yes, she and Halley were alone in the house, but what if they hadn't been? What if, one day, they *had* to video chat with Caroline when someone else was around?

"Hi, Gigi," said Halley. "How're you?"

Caroline waved off her own well-being with a casual hand. "Fine, fine. What a pretty shirt you have on, Kirsten!"

Halley looked down at her shirt. "Thanks, Gigi."

Jenna's mother leaned forward with an almost hungry expression. "Now tell me everything you've been up to," she said.

Everything Halley had been up to did not amount to much, but Halley gamely made the most of it, telling her grandmother about funny things that had happened at the restaurant, and what she'd been studying in her schoolwork, and the books she'd been reading. Caroline hung on every word, smiling, nodding, eager for more, her eyes fixed on Halley's face. Was she searching for traces of Kara? There was plenty of Kara to be seen there, along with a hefty dose of Chase.

*Chase.* The very thought of him soured Jenna's stomach. For the millionth time, she wondered how it was possible that she'd ever been enough of a fool to fall in love with him. All her life, she'd been told to stay away from the Latimores, that they were nothing but trouble and always had been. The whole clan was tainted by deeply entrenched generational problems going back at least two centuries. They'd started making moonshine not long after the American Revolution, and to date, their collective rap sheets included breaking and entering, possession with intent to distribute, assault, public intoxication, DUI, armed robbery and murder. If ever there'd been a Latimore in Franklin County who'd died of natural causes, it had happened too far back for anyone to remember.

And then there was Chase. Tragically handsome, sensitive and intelligent. A victim of circumstance, scarred by his awful upbringing, trapped by a reputation he hadn't earned. Jenna—or Kayla, as she'd been called then—was the only one who could see the truth about him, and her love could redeem him. Or so she'd told herself. Eight tumultuous months of covert trysts and heated parental arguments later, she'd realized she'd been wrong and everyone else had been right. Chase really was no good.

It was their first real argument that had opened her eyes. She barely remembered what had started it; some trivial thing or other that Chase had blown way out of proportion, no doubt. What mattered was Chase's reaction. He hadn't hit her, exactly, but he'd taken her roughly by the shoulders and shoved her down onto the pavement, hard, right there in the Dairy Queen parking lot.

She'd watched him stalk off, then gotten shakily to her feet and called her dad and asked him to pick her up. He'd come immediately. She hadn't told him Chase had hurt her—she'd been scared for his own sake of what he'd do to Chase if he knew—and, to her relief, he hadn't pressed for details. It had been enough for him to hear her say that she was through with Chase. So she'd hidden the scraped palms and swollen wrist, and toughed out the pain of a bruised tailbone. A few months later she'd gone off to college, feeling as if she'd woken up from a bizarre fever dream, and congratulating herself on putting the whole ugly episode behind her—only to come home for Thanksgiving and find that her horrible abusive ex was now dating her little sister.

Never in her wildest dreams would she have imagined such a thing. Kara was the obedient daughter, the one who did as she was told without talking back. But somehow Chase had managed to take all that unquestioning compliance and sweet affection and transfer it to himself.

And for that, Jenna had only herself to blame. Throughout her own relationship with Chase, Kara had been her confidant. She'd listened to Jenna's rants about how misunderstood he was—listened and sympathized. She'd gone along to the seedy parties where Jenna and Chase used to meet. Was it really surprising that with Jenna out of the picture, Chase had sunk his claws into Kara?

Kara never had a great moment of realization about Chase the way Jenna had, at least not permanently, and she'd endured worse violence at his hands than Jenna ever had. It made Jenna feel sick to remember her sister's bruises, and the bruised spirit that couldn't or wouldn't break free. Kara had held on to Chase with a tenacity that Jenna had never suspected her quiet, sweet sister possessed. Oh, she'd left him a few times, after Halley was born, when the maternal instinct to protect her child had competed with her loyalty to her man. But she'd always gone back.

Had Kara had any idea how stoned Chase was that terrible day when she'd gotten into the passenger seat of his Alfa Romeo to pick up Halley with him? Had she honestly thought he was competent to drive? Jenna had never had a chance to ask. She couldn't ask Kara anything anymore.

Halley's inflated recitation of her own all-too-sparse activities trailed to an end. An awkward pause fell.

"What else?" Caroline asked.

*Give the kid a break*, Jenna thought.

But before she could cut in on the conversation and help carry the load, Halley came up with another piece of news. "Gillian's started working at the equine center," she told her grandmother.

"That's nice," said Caroline. "Gillian's your friend that you met at Lalo's, right?" she added—unnecessarily, Jenna thought, since Halley didn't have any other friends to confuse Gillian with.

"Uh-huh," said Halley. "Her dad came to Lalo's a few weeks ago to watch a game, and she and I played Giant Jenga together."

The girls had seen each other once or twice a week since their first meeting, and only at Lalo's. Gillian's dad, Kevin, was a regular customer, and always brought his daughter with him. Kevin looked a bit young to have a daughter Gillian's age, but Gillian's mother didn't seem to be in the picture, and he appeared to be doing the best he could. There was something befuddled about Kevin, with his rumpled T-shirts and unruly hair standing up all over his head, and a perpetually mystified expression on his face, as if he'd woken up one day to find himself inhabiting his own life without any idea how it had come about. Jenna knew he and Gillian lived in an old farmhouse surrounded by lots of rusty tractors and things. But he was always courteous to the staff at the restaurant and bar, tipped well and never drank past his limit or made himself obnoxious.

Not that any of that mattered, because Halley wasn't going to Gillian's house. Sleepovers, trips to the movies and unsupervised sessions of "hanging out" were out of the question for Halley.

Jenna listened in silence to Halley's recital of Gillian's equestrian adventures, feeling simultaneously guilty and fearful. Guilty because Halley's own life was so limited that she had to live vicariously through book characters and her one and only friend. Fearful because even that one friendship made Halley vulnerable. Halley was smart and savvy, as well as naturally introverted. She thought before she spoke. But she was only twelve years old. Would she manage to keep her lies straight when talking with Gillian? Or would she slip up one day and reveal something that would somehow start a chain reaction that would pull down the whole house of cards that made up her and Jenna's false identities? Maybe Halley had slipped up already, and Jenna didn't know it yet.

Something inside Jenna's chest started to clench. She took a deep breath and forced herself to think of all the chores she had to do once the call ended. She wished she could do them now, and get them checked off, and bury her doubts under the illusion that she had everything under control.

"That equine center," said Caroline. "Isn't that the same place where you went for the barn raising?"

Oh, that barn raising. Jenna shuddered at the memory. It had been a big community-wide affair, with dozens of volunteers showing up to reassemble a salvaged hundred-year-old barn at the equine center. Tito and Lalo had donated beer and food, and Jenna had worked the event for half a day. It should have been fun—and for most of the people there, it had been—but all Jenna could think of the whole time was how many people were there, and how easy it would be for Chase to show up and take Halley. Which was ridiculous, because Chase was in prison, and how would he even know about the barn raising, anyway? It was infuriating, how he was always in Jenna's head, ruining everything.

"Yeah, that's the one," said Halley. "The owner's name is Susana. She's really nice. Gillian was already taking lessons from her before the barn raising. Now she and Susana have worked out a deal where Gillian gets the use of a horse in exchange for feeding him and all the other horses twice a day. She grooms him and takes care of him and gets to ride him whenever she wants. He still boards with Susana, but it's almost like he's her own horse."

"That sounds like a good deal," said her grandmother.

"Yeah, it is. And now Susana's having a horse camp this summer and I want to go."

Jenna's head whipped around. *What* did Halley just say?

Caroline clapped her hands together, and suddenly she didn't look sad and worn anymore. She looked like the mother Jenna remembered.

"Horse camp!" she said. "How exciting! What all do they do there? How long is it? Do you stay overnight?"

"Oh, no, it's just a day camp. Five days, Monday through Friday. You show up early in the morning and eat breakfast there. You learn about grooming and feeding, and how to take care of tack, and Susana gives you horseback riding lessons, and you muck out some stalls and go for a trail ride, and have lunch. That's the first four days. Then on the last day, there's an exhibition for the parents to see everything you've learned. Doesn't that sound like fun?"

"It sounds marvelous! Is Gillian going?"

"Yes. I want to go soooo bad."

She said it without a hint of guile in her voice, and without glancing Jenna's way. Jenna felt her mouth drop open. Why, that little schemer.

"Well, you should!" Caroline said firmly.

Things were escalating fast. It was time for Jenna to take back control of the situation.

"Halley," she said, "go to your room, please. It's my turn to talk to Gigi now."

Halley got up without a word of protest and without seeming troubled by Jenna's stern tone. "Bye, Gigi," she said, waving sweetly. "I love you."

"I love you too, precious."

Jenna waited until Halley's bedroom door shut, then turned to face the screen.

"What?" said her mother. Her smile had been replaced by a wary expression.

"What do you mean, *what*?" said Jenna. "You know *what*. Why did you do that? Why did you give in to her that way? She was obviously trying to get you on her side to force me to say yes."

Her mother lifted her chin. "And why shouldn't you say yes? Why shouldn't that child go to horse camp if she wants to?"

Jenna sputtered. She didn't even know where to begin.

"If it's a cost issue, I'll pay for it," said her mom.

"You know perfectly well that this isn't about money. It's about Halley's safety. I can't let her spend six hours away from me for five days. Why do you think I home-school her?"

Caroline sighed. "Honey, you've already changed both your names and moved fourteen hundred miles away from home. How much more will it take before you're satisfied?"

The words stung. "I didn't do all that for my own amusement," she said tartly. "I did it for Halley."

She glanced down the hall to make sure Halley's door was closed before going on. "It isn't just about safety, you know. Do you have any idea what it was like for her, after the accident? Having everyone know her as the daughter of the man who got behind the wheel stoned and killed all those people in that wreck? It was bad enough just being connected to that clan. As long as she stayed in Franklin County, she was always going to be a Latimore from Rocky Mount. Even as a ten-year-old she was already suffering from that in school. I didn't want a black cloud following her for the rest of her life. It's bad enough she has to live with the memories."

"I know all that," said Caroline. "But enough is enough, Jenna. She's twelve years old, almost a teenager, and you never let her out of your sight. Sooner or later, she's going to have to be away from you. You can't protect her all her life."

"I can protect her now. She's still a child, and I'm her legal guardian. Protecting her is my responsibility."

Her mother leaned toward the webcam. "But protection isn't all she needs! She needs interests, friendships, activities. She needs to spend time in places other than home and that bar. Week after week, it's the same. I ask her what she's been up to, and all she can come up with is a reading list, some lesson summaries and snatches of secondhand conversations. Does that child do *anything* for fun besides reading?"

"Of course she does! She also listens to music a lot, and sometimes she draws."

Jenna knew how inadequate that sounded even as she said the words. Caroline gave her a look.

"She needs more than that, and you know it. She needs something outdoors and physical—like horse camp."

"It won't stop with horse camp. Next she'll want lessons, then a horse-for-hire arrangement like Gillian's got. Then she'll want to learn barrel racing, and next thing you know, the whole thing will have taken over our lives, practically. Horseback riding is a very engrossing sport."

"All the better! If she's into horses, maybe that'll keep her too busy for...other things."

She didn't have to specify. Other things meant bad boys with flashy sports cars and drug habits.

"But horseback riding has its own set of dangers," Jenna said. "Did I tell you about the legal notice Susana has posted at the entrance to her facility? It's this whole inherent risk thing about how you can't hold the owners liable if you get hurt or killed, because horses are obviously huge, dangerous creatures, and everyone knows it."

"There's inherent risk in *life*, dear!" her mother said, her voice rising. Then, more quietly, "Look, I know you have regrets. I do too. But not all sins are sins of commission. The older I get, the more I understand that. Lost opportunities can be as costly as mistakes. They can turn into resentment and bitterness."

Jenna thought about the new thread of defiance in Halley's attitude. She was getting old enough to evaluate Jenna as a person and find her lacking.

"Let Kirsten go to horse camp," said Caroline. "If you clamp down too hard, you'll lose her. You of all people should know that."

Jenna bristled. "What's that supposed to mean?"

"You know exactly what it means. Part of what attracted you to you-know-who in the first place was that he was forbidden."

Jenna almost smiled then. Her mother couldn't or wouldn't remember to call Halley by her new name, but she always referred to Chase as you-know-who—as if speaking his name aloud would conjure him, or something.

"So what are you saying?" Jenna asked. "That if you and Dad had told me to go ahead and date Chase, he would have lost his mystique, and everything would have turned out fine?"

Her mother flinched at the sound of the name. "No, of course I'm not saying that. But maybe if we'd been better about trusting you to use your own judgment about other things… I don't know. Maybe it would have made a difference."

It was easy to get sucked into the "what-if" game. Every day, Jenna found herself playing out a thousand scenarios of things she could have said or done differently with Kara, and wondering if any of them could have saved her. She knew her parents had done the same thing. Had they been too protective? Not protective enough? What had been the exact combination of things they'd done wrong that had caused their daughter to go down that terrible path?

That game could break you. It had broken Jenna's father. Aortic aneurysm might have been his official cause of death, but Jenna knew he'd died of a broken heart.

She sighed. "I'll think about it," she said.

"Good," said her mother, with a smug smile that seemed to say the matter had already been decided.

## *CHAPTER FIVE*

WHEN JENNA WAS five years old, she wanted to be a princess—and so did Kara, who'd always followed wherever Jenna led. Caroline had reveled in being the mother of two girly girls and encouraged the enthusiasm by providing gorgeous dresses, tiaras, necklaces and sparkly shoes. In those days, there'd even been a real-life princess for a role model, Princess Diana—or, as Caroline had insisted on calling her, Diana, Princess of Wales. Even as little girls, Jenna and Kara had been avid followers of the beautiful blonde princess, starstruck by her grace and glamour, the fancy events and adoring crowds. Her death had left them sad and confused. Princess stories weren't supposed to end that way. A princess might fall into a long enchanted sleep, or take a bite of a poisoned apple that made her *look* dead, but she didn't stay that way. The prince always made her wake up again.

It wasn't until years afterward that Jenna had learned the rest of Diana's story, or at least the parts that had been made public—the desperately unhappy marriage, the constant torment from the paparazzi, the ongoing struggles with mental health. In the end, she'd gotten into a car driven by a man she'd trusted to know what he was doing, and he'd crashed that car into the side of a Paris tunnel, with the speedometer frozen at 121 mph.

A lot of rage had been directed at the paparazzi, who'd stood around taking pictures of the wreck instead of calling for help, and at the driver, whose blood alcohol had come in at three times the legal limit in France. But what could you expect? They were all out for what they could get.

You couldn't count on other people to look out for you and yours. That was on you. You couldn't abdicate responsibility for your own well-being. Some people called that preemptive victim-blaming. Jenna called it healthy self-preservation.

Not surprisingly, that mindset had had a profound effect on her personal life. All of her post-Chase romantic relationships had ended before they'd properly begun. She'd gone on a lot of first dates, and a few second and third dates, always taking her own car to meet the guy and driving herself home afterward, because somewhere along the line, she'd developed a full-blown phobia about being driven by other people. She couldn't actually remember the last time she'd let anyone drive her anywhere.

She'd been told more than once that she had trust issues. Well, of course she did. What was wrong with that? What *was* trust, anyway, but valuing someone else's judgment on at least an equal footing with your own, and surrendering control to that person? She didn't have that with anyone, and she didn't want to. And if that meant no romance for her, well then, so be it. That was the price she paid for security. She'd come to terms with it long ago.

So why was she slowly and laboriously wiping down a table that was already clean, pretending she wasn't keeping a peripheral eye on the conversation Tito was having at the bar with a very pretty woman?

The woman was tall and slender, and professionally dressed in a black pencil skirt, red blouse and black blazer. What was her name? Rosanna? Anastasia? Something multisyllabic and ultrafeminine like that. Jenna had never interacted with her much because she usually sat on the bar side, drinking blackberry mead and chatting with Tito, smiling her wistful smile and looking up at him with her big, sad, beautiful eyes.

Suddenly Tito braced his hands on the bar top, leaned toward the woman and delivered what looked like a pretty serious speech. Jenna couldn't see the woman's face from this angle, but judging from her posture and the set of her head, she was paying close attention.

He finished speaking and gave her an imploring look. She responded with a tiny nod. Tito's chest rose and fell in a sigh, and his lips curved into a gentle smile.

Okay, well, that could mean a lot of things. They could be having an intense conversation about philosophy or theology or…

Tito laid his hand over the woman's hand and gave it a squeeze.

A cold weight settled in Jenna's stomach. She'd never seen him do that before. That warm affection, that flow of heartfelt words—it looked as if Tito had himself a girl.

Well, why shouldn't he? He was a good man with a lot to offer—sensitive, intelligent...handsome. And it wasn't as if Jenna had any claim on him herself. There was no reason for her to feel this way, as if she'd been punched in the solar plexus. No reason at all.

Her own hand had slowed to a stop on the tabletop, still gripping the damp rag. Mechanically, she resumed wiping.

*This is good*, she told herself, and tried to believe it. If the sight of Tito with another woman was capable of stirring this much emotional turmoil in her, then it was just as well that he'd been officially taken off the market. Now Jenna wouldn't be tempted.

She walked back behind the counter, rinsed her cleaning rag at the sink and wrung it out. For the past ten days, ever since her slipup about his mustache, she'd been frankly avoiding Tito. She'd purposely scheduled herself not to close with him all of last week and done her best to keep away from him during hours of operation. It felt like a kind of penance. And while it had kept her out of his presence, it certainly hadn't kept him off her mind. If anything, she'd thought about him more than ever. She kept remembering that last Friday night, when they'd cleaned the display case together, and assigned all the different liquor bottles to people, and sat on the floor together eating fried okra by hand out of a shared carton, their fingers bumping occasionally.

Without those late-night songfests and cleaning sessions to look forward to, all the flavor had gone out of life. The thread of attraction that she'd sensed between them had been pleasant, and she'd savored it, even while she'd known she couldn't act on it.

And apparently Tito's half of it had been all in her mind. He didn't feel anything for her. The long talks, the warm smiles, the private jokes—they didn't mean anything special. He was just taking an interest, being kind. Being Tito.

All of which was for the best. Nothing remained now but for her to act natural, and congratulate him on his romantic success, as a good friend would. And the sooner she got it over with, the better. Her avoidance of him was childish and cowardly. Time to rip off that Band-Aid.

The lunch rush was clearing out. She took

the tickets to two tables and collected payment from three more. When she next turned her gaze toward the pass-through, she saw something that hit her like an ice pick through the heart.

Tito had come out from behind the bar and taken the blackberry mead woman in his arms.

This wasn't one of those quick, light hugs. This was warm, sincere, intimate.

Jenna actually gasped aloud. Then she spun around and walked blindly toward the back of the building, passing the counter and the kitchen, and finally taking refuge in the restroom.

It was empty. Jenna leaned her back against the door and took several steadying breaths. When her heart rate had returned to something approaching normal, she walked over to the mirror and looked herself in the eye.

She had her hair clipped high on her head, but some tendrils had come loose and were curling around her neck. Her shirt had a grease stain on the front that she hadn't noticed until now. She thought of the blackberry mead woman's impeccable clothes and smooth, sleek hair.

Enough! She had to get a grip. She couldn't keep letting her emotions run away with her like this. She and Tito could never be more than friends. She had to act like she was okay with that until it was true.

She took her hair down, ran her fingers through it and twisted it into a high, tight roll.

"You've got this," she told her reflection. Then she walked out of the restroom and down the hallway.

Out of habit, she scanned the dining room for Halley, but Halley wasn't there. Jenna had a brief moment of panic before remembering that Halley was safe and sound at horse camp—at least, Jenna had dropped her off at horse camp that morning. Whether she was safe and sound remained to be seen. All sorts of things could go wrong with a dozen or so high-spirited children and several huge, hoofed animals—even supposing that Chase stayed in prison where he belonged and didn't bust out and take Halley.

Jenna shut her eyes. Had she done the right thing in letting Halley go to horse camp? Her mother had made a pretty convincing case for giving Halley some freedom now to keep her from rebelling later. But was this the right time, and the right kind of freedom to give? Sometimes she felt as if she were driving on a slick road, trying to keep between the lines, but always in danger of swerving or overcorrecting.

She opened her eyes and let out a sigh. This was going to be a long day.

TITO WATCHED ANNALISA walk out of the bar. Her head was held high and her shoulders were squared, but he knew she felt anything but composed right now. Through the building's glass front he saw her draw herself up before briskly walking away down the sidewalk.

"Pretty girl."

He jumped a little and turned. Jenna had somehow managed to slip behind him with a small bin of the bar's pint glasses. With customers constantly passing back and forth between Lalo's Kitchen and Tito's Bar, sometimes an imbalance of plates, glassware and utensils built up on one side or the other, and the items had to be returned.

Jenna crouched and started transferring the glasses from her bin to the crate on the shelf under the counter. "Sorry," she said. "Didn't mean to startle you."

"That's all right," he said. "I guess I was deep in thought."

It was the first time in days that she'd spoken to him on her own initiative. Ever since the night she and Halley had come up to his apartment after closing, Jenna had been keeping her distance. Now here she was, in his space, on an errand she could easily have delegated to a part-timer.

She had her hair clipped high in a businesslike twist. As she carefully worked the crate back into its space, his gaze lingered on the nape of her neck. It looked strangely vulnerable without the usual escaped tendrils of dark gold hair curving around it.

Suddenly Jenna was on her feet again, facing him, looking him right in the eye. "What's her name?" she asked.

Tito blinked. "What's whose name?"

Jenna jerked her head toward the door. "You know who. That pretty girl who just left."

"Oh, you mean Annalisa?" Tito asked. "Annalisa Cavazos."

"That's right. I remember now. She works somewhere downtown, doesn't she?"

"Yes, at the law office down the block. She's a paralegal."

Jenna nodded. "Well, she's very pretty."

It seemed as if that had already been said, but Tito merely replied, "Yes. Yes, she certainly is."

A brief, awkward pause fell. Something about this whole conversation felt off. What was Jenna doing? Why was she suddenly making forced small talk, after a week of avoiding him? And why was she giving him that knowing, expectant look?

At last she said, "So?"

"So what?" asked Tito.

Impatient sigh. "So are you together?"

A quick shout of laughter escaped him. "*Together?* Annalisa and I? Oh, no, no. She's in love with my brother Javi."

"Ohh," said Jenna, drawing the word out. "Oh, I see. So…are *they* together?"

"Nope. Never have been."

"Well then, what—" Jenna stopped herself. "Sorry, I shouldn't pry."

"It isn't exactly a secret," Tito said. "Annalisa has had a thing for Javi since we were all kids. It's never been reciprocated. And she's finally coming to the conclusion that it's time for her to move on."

"Maybe she'll move on with you."

He gave her a sidewise look. "You seem awfully determined to pair me up with her. Why the sudden interest in my love life?"

Incredibly, Jenna blushed. "I'm just looking out for you, that's all. You're a good guy. Annalisa's a beautiful woman, and she seemed awfully intent on whatever it was that you were saying to her."

"Well, yeah. That's because I was talking about Javi."

Jenna gave him a deep, searching look, and he felt his own face heat up. What was happening here? Was it possible that Jenna was jealous?

He was familiar enough with the emotion of jealousy, but he couldn't recall ever being on the receiving end. Usually he was the one with that burning sensation deep in his chest, watching helplessly as the girl he wanted paid attention to some other guy. Did Jenna actually feel that way about him?

Not for the first time, he wished he could see inside her head.

"People confide in you a lot, don't they?" she asked.

"They do," he said. "Occupational hazard. It's natural to tell your troubles to the guy behind the bar."

"I don't think so," she replied. "I mean, yeah, that's true as far as it goes, but it's more than that with you. You're a good listener—compassionate and empathetic, and smart, and…trustworthy. I'll bet you were the kind of guy who was very popular with girls in high school."

Tito considered this. "If by popular you mean they told me all about the problems they were having with their boyfriends or the guys they liked, and listened to my advice, and told me how caring and emotionally intelligent I was, and how they ought to date guys like me, and then went right back to the jerks they'd been with before, or took up with other jerks, then yes, I was the most popular guy in school."

Jenna leaned her hip against the backbar as if settling in for a long chat. "That sounds kind of harsh and cynical for you."

"Yeah, I guess it does. I don't actually believe that every guy in the world besides myself is a jerk, but there've been times in my life when it felt that way."

"What about your brother Javi?"

"Oh, he isn't a jerk. He's actually a pretty good guy, just stubborn and clueless."

"Which one is Javi, anyway?" Jenna asked.

"You've never met him. He went west a few years back to work in the oil fields. He's kind of the angry rebel of the Mendoza boys. You know how it is with sibling relationships. We all have these roles, relative to each other, and we all know which one is which, even if we never talk about it. Johnny's the one most like Dad, Eddie's the handsome one, Enrique's the biggest and strongest, Javi's the rebel. It's confining and reductive, but we never fully outgrow it."

Jenna pondered this. "You really think Eddie's the handsome one?"

Tito chuckled. "You've seen him, right?"

"Well, yeah. He's good-looking, if you like that type."

"Tall and muscular, with classic features and perfect hair? That type?"

She waved this off. "It's all a matter of taste. So…which one are you?"

"Isn't it obvious? I'm the runt."

She gave him a playful smile. "I'd have thought you'd be the smart one."

Tito shrugged. "Tomato, tomahto."

"Oh, come on. That's a false equivalence and you know it. Who's being reductive now?"

"I am. That's my whole point."

She tilted her head to the side. "Yeah, I guess that's true."

The return of their old friendly ease felt good. He'd missed this. There was no one he enjoyed talking with more than Jenna. No matter what the subject, no matter how offbeat or abstruse, she could keep up, and more than keep up. She challenged him, stimulated him, kept him on his toes.

"How about you?" he asked. "You have a sister, right? What are your sibling roles?"

He was taking a big chance, prying into that deeply guarded background of hers, but her open curiosity about his love life had made him bold.

Jenna's face seemed to turn in on itself, a thoughtful crease forming between the finely arched brows.

"I'm the tough one," she said at last. "Kara was the sweet one."

There was a sad finality in her tone, which, coupled with her use of past tense, was highly suggestive. Kara was either dead, or irrevocably alienated from Jenna. No wonder Jenna didn't like talking about her.

But she'd answered the question, and spoken her sister's name to Tito for the first time ever. Surely she had to trust him a little, to do that much.

He'd pushed enough for one day. Time for a change of subject.

After a respectful silence, he asked, "How are you enjoying the Lord Peter Wimsey books?"

Jenna's face brightened. "Very much. I finished *Clouds of Witness* last night, and I have *Unnatural Death* on my bedside table, ready to go. And I noticed Halley thumbing through *Whose Body?* the other day, so maybe she'll start reading them too. The diction's pretty advanced for a twelve-year-old, but she's a smart kid, and she can always reread when she's older and catch all the things she missed the first time around. That's what I always did."

"Yeah, me too," said Tito. He scanned the

dining room next door. "Speaking of Halley, where is she? I haven't seen her today. Is she in the break room?"

"Halley's at horse camp," Jenna said. Her tone was grim, as if she'd said Halley was in juvenile detention.

"Oh, the one at Susana Vrba's place?"

"That's the one."

"You don't seem very happy about it," Tito said.

"I'm not. But she really wanted to go, and I can't protect her all her life. Or so I've been told."

He was pretty sure it wasn't the dangers of horseback riding that Jenna was worried about, or at least not primarily. She just didn't like having Halley away from her. Most parents of twelve-year-olds would be accustomed to having their kids spend significant chunks of time away from them, but that had never been the case for Jenna and Halley. Tito had never asked Jenna why, and she'd never volunteered information. He knew she wasn't a fussy, fearful person. She wouldn't be as cautious as she was without good reason.

He wished he could reassure her that everything would be okay, but that was impossible when he didn't know the particulars of the situation. He wished he could take her in his arms and tell her he'd protect her and Halley from harm, no matter what it was that threatened them, but that was impossible too.

Instead, he said, "Well, if it makes you feel any better, Roque Fidalgo's helping Susana with that camp, and he knows how to handle himself. I've sparred with him at the gym."

She studied him a moment. He was treading on new ground here, recognizing Jenna's security concerns, tacitly acknowledging the elephant in the room.

"Good to know," she said at last.

"So how long does the camp run?" Tito asked.

"Monday through Friday. Gillian's there, too. I dropped off Halley and Gillian at Susana's place at seven this morning, and Kevin will pick them both up and bring Halley here after they're finished for the day."

"Ah," said Tito, enlightened. "Is that why you're working all morning shifts this week?"

He regretted the words as soon as they were out. They sounded needy, as if she owed him an explanation for not closing with him.

"Mmm-hmm," said Jenna.

Her gaze faltered, darting away from him just for a second before returning to his face.

It happened so quickly that he'd have missed it if he'd looked away himself for even a moment. But he'd seen, and he knew what it meant. Jenna had just lied to him. Which meant that it wasn't because of horse camp, or at least not entirely, that she'd scheduled herself to work shifts that would overlap his by only a few hours. It was like he'd thought before. She was avoiding him.

And unless he missed his guess, it wasn't because she didn't want to be with him. It was because she was afraid of getting too close to him.

She was here with him now, though. She'd sought him out in order to ferret out the details of his relationship with Annalisa. And she'd stuck around afterward just to talk. Which might mean that she'd decided he was worth the risk, or maybe that she couldn't help herself.

Possibilities whirled through his head.

*Stop overthinking again*, he told himself. *Give it a rest. Stop trying to figure her out.*

But he might as well tell himself to stop breathing.

The front door opened, and a tall, bearded man walked in. He was dressed casually, in jeans and a T-shirt, but his manner and bearing, from his upright posture to the shine on his boots, clearly marked him as a cop. In fact, he was a county constable, which around here covered a wide range of duties, from issuing subpoenas to making arrests.

"Hey, Kowalski," someone called from a table. "Did you catch all the bad guys?"

Kowalski didn't answer. He went straight to the bar and took a seat on his regular stool.

"Give me a shot of Jack Daniel's," he said.

Tito silently poured and set the glass down. Kowalski threw back the shot, asked for another and gazed blankly ahead with the thousand-yard stare common to freshly off-duty law enforcement and trauma nurses.

Tito poured again, still without speaking. He'd known Coby Kowalski for a long time.

If he wanted to talk, he'd talk. Until then, Tito would leave him in peace.

"Another," Coby said.

Tito and Jenna exchanged a glance. Coby usually stopped after one shot and moved on to beer. Three shots in quick succession was approaching dangerous territory. On the other hand, he wasn't actually intoxicated yet, so cutting him off would be premature. Tito didn't relish the idea of having to refuse service to a respected member of local law enforcement, but having a drunk cop on his hands wouldn't be so great either.

He filled the shot glass again. He'd play this thing by ear. If necessary, he'd send a discreet text to Rick Henderson, Coby's work partner, and hint that it would be a good idea for him to come to the bar.

Coby cupped his hand loosely around the glass, stared into its amber depths a moment and asked, "Why do battered women stay with their abusers?"

Tito wasn't sure how to answer. As a member of law enforcement, Coby certainly knew far more about the subject than Tito did—which meant that he wasn't seeking information. He just needed the release of talk.

Jenna's presence was an added complication. She could have quietly gone back to Lalo's and left Tito to it, but instead she picked up a cloth and started polishing glasses, clearly stalling. Why? Because she wanted to hear what Tito said? Or because she wanted to contribute an answer herself? Either way, he'd have to tread with extra care. He didn't know for a fact that Jenna was a survivor of abuse herself, but circumstances did seem to point that way.

He forced his attention back to the question. Why *did* battered women stay with their abusers?

Some people, Tito knew, would reply that a better question would be, *Why does society let abusers get away with their abuse?* But Coby wasn't society. He was one man. He was also a cop. If there was anything he could lawfully do about whatever particular situation he had in mind, he'd have done it by now.

"It's a complex issue," Tito said at last. "I think sometimes they're beaten down emotionally and mentally as well as physically. They don't believe it's possible for them to get away—or else they've been gaslit to the point where they think that nothing's really wrong or that the abuse is their fault. From what I've read, abusers tend to be skilled talkers and manipulators. They know how to direct a conversation and make people think what they want them to think."

Coby raised his head, and Tito saw the raw desperation in his eyes. "I wish I could—I wish there was a way to get them away, out of that environment. Once she was out from under his influence, she'd start thinking straight again, right?"

"I don't know," Tito said. He wished he had something better to offer, but false comfort was worse than nothing, even if Coby could believe it.

Then Jenna spoke up.

"Sometimes it's more than gaslighting," she said gently. "Sometimes abusers make threats about what they'll do if the abused person ever leaves—threats to hurt or kill that person, or other people, or animals. And the abused person knows that they aren't empty threats."

Coby looked at her. "Yeah, that's true. It's risky to leave. But it's risky to stay, too. If only she would press charges, at least there'd be something to *do*, something proactive. A way forward. It'd sure be better than waiting around to see what's going to happen next."

"Maybe she needs an exit strategy," Jenna said. "A plan that covers all foreseeable contingencies. That's where a third party can be especially helpful. You might be able to help her get everything in place before she leaves, if she's open to that."

"Yeah, I can do that," Coby said. "But she still has to follow the plan."

"That's right, she does. And you can't make her do that. No matter how much support you give, or how well you prepare, you can't make her press charges, and you can't make her leave."

Coby downed his third shot. He didn't order a fourth, and he didn't speak again.

In the silence that followed, thoughts and questions swirled through Tito's mind. Had Jenna spoken from personal experience? If so, how had she gotten away from her own abuser? Had *she* had an exit strategy? Had someone helped her? What threats had her abuser made that had caused her to run away with her daughter and start over someplace new? What had he done to make them so afraid?

He wished he could do more than wonder. He wanted to help protect them both, make them feel secure. But he couldn't do that unless Jenna let him in.

Through the glass front of the building, he saw a battered Dodge pickup pull into a parking space and shudder to a stop. There was a blonde head in the back seat, bent close to a reddish head. Two young girls having a whispered conference together.

He nudged Jenna. "Isn't that Kevin's truck?"

Jenna sucked in a quick breath, then let it out in a relieved sigh. "Yes, it is," she said. "Halley's back."

She flashed him a quick, bright smile and hurried back to Lalo's Kitchen.

Tito watched as Halley got out of the pickup, waved goodbye to Kevin and Gillian and came through the door, flushed and windblown, with a tired, happy smile. She took a seat at the counter and started chattering away to Jenna. Tito couldn't hear the words, but it looked as if her first day at horse camp had been a good one.

He was glad Jenna had let her go. The kid

needed to spend time somewhere other than inside these walls. What good was survival if you didn't truly live?

## *CHAPTER SIX*

JENNA HAD THE driving dream again that night, the one where she was sitting in the passenger seat of an out-of-control car, trying and failing to take hold of the steering wheel. It was a recurring anxiety dream for her; she had it at least once a week. But this time the car was hitched to a horse—plunging, rearing, dragging the car into oncoming traffic, with an infant Halley screaming in her car seat.

All that being the case, her unease on the second day of horse camp was worse than on the first day. Throughout the morning, her thoughts were clouded by dread—and not just of Chase showing up and taking Halley away. All sorts of things could go wrong at horse camp. Halley could get trampled by a horse, or thrown from one, or kicked in the head. Once you started being afraid, there was no end to it.

Jenna left her phone sounds turned on and checked for incoming texts or calls every few minutes or so, ping or no ping. She caught a lot of resentful glances from Veronica, with whom she'd had to take a hard line regarding phone usage during work hours. Jenna knew she was being unprofessional and hypocritical, undermining her credibility as a manager, but she couldn't make herself care.

The breakfast crowd cleared out, and preparation for the lunch rush began. Nothing terrible had happened yet, but Jenna's sense of dread only grew. She couldn't shake the feeling that a bomb was about to drop.

When the fateful text finally came, it had nothing to do with equine catastrophe. It wasn't from Halley or Susana at all. It was from her mom.

Chase is out of prison.

Jenna stood with her phone in her hand, staring down at the screen. She couldn't move, couldn't think. Now that the horrible thing had happened, it didn't seem real.

What do you mean? she typed back.

I mean he's out of prison, came the reply. They released him.

*Wake up, wake up*, Jenna told herself. She shut her eyes tight, willing herself back into her nice cozy bed at home, with sunlight streaming through the curtains, and the whole day ahead of her, and Chase safely incarcerated.

She opened her eyes. She was still in Lalo's Kitchen, and the terrible words on her phone screen were still there.

How do you know? she asked, grasping after facts in a last attempt to make the thing not real.

Myra told me, her mom answered. She saw it on the Internet. All the Latimores went to meet him at the penitentiary when he got out. They were posting pictures on Instagram.

Jenna felt a sudden plunging sensation, as if the floor had just dropped deep into the earth. Myra was her mother's oldest friend. Jenna didn't like her very much. She was opinionated, officious and overbearing, constantly interfering in things that were none of her business. But she wasn't one to go off half-cocked. Jenna had never known her to get her facts wrong.

How is that possible? Jenna typed. He barely served the minimum sentence! How can he be out so soon?

I don't know, her mother replied. Good behavior? Overcrowding? All I know is, he killed my daughter and now he's a free man.

Jenna raised her head, dimly aware that Veronica was standing in front of her, saying something. Jenna could see her lips moving, but the words were just sounds with no meaning. She didn't know how long Veronica had been there or what she was saying. None of it mattered. Nothing mattered except Halley. Jenna had to find her, *now*, and keep her safe.

Jenna turned her back on Veronica, hurried behind the counter and reached into the space where she kept her purse. It wasn't there. She groped blindly for a while, her heart rate speeding up, before stumbling off toward the break room.

The brick-lined hallway had never looked so long. It was like something out of a nightmare. Her legs felt heavy and slow, as if they had weights strapped to them, and she could almost feel Halley's arms wrapped tight around her neck like when she was little, and hear her voice begging Jenna not to let Kara take her away.

She found her purse on the break room counter. She fumbled inside for her keys, found them, and promptly dropped them on the floor. A whimper escaped her throat, a frightened animal sound. She bent to pick up the keys and whacked her head on the counter, so hard that she saw stars.

Tears of pain stung her eyes. Something hurt deep inside her chest, as if there were some vicious wild creature inside her rib cage, clawing and scrabbling to get out. She was breathing way too fast and couldn't stop. She had lost control of her own body.

What was happening? Was she having a heart attack? Was she actually about to die, here on the break room floor?

She didn't know how long she sat there, alone and hyperventilating. But suddenly, there was Tito, holding her face between his hands, staring her straight in the eye.

"Jenna, listen to me. I want you to focus on your breathing. In through the nose, out through the mouth. In through the nose, out through the mouth."

He was kneeling on the floor in front of her. His hands were warm against her cheeks.

"Breathe," he said. "In through the nose, out through the mouth. Do it with me."

She tried. It took a long time, but gradually her breaths grew longer and steadier.

"That's good," said Tito. "Now hold it a few seconds before you let it out. Do it with me."

She was gripping his arms now. They were lean and strong; she could feel the muscle and sinew through his shirtsleeves. The two of them were breathing together, their faces inches apart, as if Jenna was in labor and Tito was her birthing coach. She kept her gaze locked on his, and he stared right back at her, his eye contact anchoring her in reality.

She was breathing almost normally now, and the pain and constriction in her chest had eased up. Tito smiled and gently rubbed his thumbs under her eyes, wiping away her tears.

Unless Jenna missed her guess, she'd just had a full-blown panic attack—and Tito had known exactly what to do about it. Of course he had.

"Better?" he asked.

She nodded. "I have to go get Halley," she managed to say.

"Why? Is she hurt? Sick?"

Jenna shook her head. The panic, which had subsided to a feeble flutter in her stomach, started to rise again.

"I have to get her," she said. Her voice sounded childishly high.

"Okay," said Tito. "But not by yourself. I'll drive you."

Fresh tears welled up in Jenna's eyes. "Thank you," she whispered.

She followed Tito out the back door, through the patio and into the parking lot.

Tito's daily driver was a 1969 Cadillac Eldorado in metallic red, a restomod with up-to-date air-conditioning and power steering and the like, but retaining its original dashboard and upholstery in pristine condition. Jenna already knew this. She'd walked past the car in the parking lot just about every day for the past year and a half, and Tito had told her all about the restoration work his father had done on it. But this was her first time inside the vehicle.

The engine started with a low rumble.

"Horse camp?" Tito asked as he pulled out of the parking lot.

"Yes," she said.

They drove in silence for a while. Then, all in a rush, Jenna said, "Halley's father is out of prison."

She hadn't consciously decided to tell him that. The words had come out on their own.

"And you're afraid he'll come after you and Halley," Tito said.

"Not me. Just Halley."

He gave her a questioning look. "I mean, he's not thrilled with me," she said. "He's bound to be mad that I took her away. But she's the one he's interested in. If he got hold of her, he wouldn't bother with me."

"Okay. Where was he incarcerated?"

"Green Rock Correctional Center. It's in Southern Virginia."

"And when did he get out?"

She stared blankly at him a moment. "I—I don't know. My mom texted and said he was released, but she didn't say when."

She felt like an idiot. The exact timing of

Chase's release was pretty critical information, but she'd lost her head the minute she'd learned that he was free.

She thought of Myra, that wellspring of information. She wasn't at all surprised that the Latimores had chosen to use Instagram to commemorate their felon relative's release from prison, but it did seem odd that Myra followed them on social media. Myra had never had any use for any of that clan. Maybe she just checked up on them once in a while without actually following them, to keep tabs on what they were up to. That sounded like something Myra would do. Nosy, but useful. How often did she check in? Daily? Weekly?

"Text your mom and ask her," Tito said.

Jenna reached for her phone, but it wasn't in her pocket.

A wave of nausea washed over her. "I don't have my phone," she said. "I must have left it at work."

She brought her fists down hard on the dashboard. "How could I have been so *stupid*? Letting my phone out of my sight is unforgivably careless."

Her mom was probably blowing up her

phone with texts right now, wondering why Jenna wasn't responding.

"Whoa! Whoa!" said Tito. "Let's dial it back a bit here. I don't think anyone at Lalo's is going to take your phone and do anything nefarious with it."

"It's the principle of the thing. Don't you see? I can't afford to let down my guard. If I do, if I'm careless even one time, then it opens a whole floodgate, and where's it going to end?"

Her voice was rising to a hysterical pitch.

Tito laid a hand on her arm and said calmly, "Well, there's nothing we can do about your phone right now. So the next question is, does Halley's father know where you are?"

That was the pertinent question, all right. Jenna forced herself to focus on it.

"I hope not," Jenna said. "I took all the precautions I possibly could. When I changed our names, I didn't have to go through the usual public disclosure thing where the new names are printed in the newspaper. Sometimes you're allowed to do it on the sly. It's up to the discretion of the judge, and he was an old friend of my father's."

"That's good," Tito said encouragingly. "What else did you do to cover your tracks?"

"Well, I erased myself from social media. That took some doing. Halley was too young to have her own accounts, of course, but I wasn't. I deleted all my accounts and untagged myself from other people's photos. I didn't want someone in Limestone Springs coming across an old tagged photo of me under a different name."

Tito nodded. "That makes sense. Social media must make it hard to establish a new identity."

"It sure does," Jenna said with a sigh. "And it's hard enough anyway. It's possible to get a new social security number, but that happens at a federal level. And if you do it, then you lose everything that's tied to your old number—credit report, bank accounts, job history, college degrees. You don't get set up with a whole new turnkey identity, with a job and a place to live and all that, unless you're in some high-level witness protection type of deal, which we're not. Or unless you have the money to pay for it through private channels, which I didn't. I had to do the best I could on my own."

"So the social security number you gave Luke when you applied at Lalo's was your original social security number?"

"Yes."

"But you didn't give him any references or job history to go along with it."

She glanced over at him, surprised that he remembered this. "Well, no. I had a fake backstory in place, and it didn't include me working or living in…the place I came from. Still, it would be easy enough for anyone who had my social—like Luke or Lalo, or you—to look up my work and school history and piece things together. I just had to hope none of you would do it."

"Sounds exhausting," Tito said.

"It is," said Jenna.

Downtown Limestone Springs lay behind them now. The land opened up into big residential lots, then into ranches and farms. Jenna suddenly realized she had her right foot pressed against an imaginary accelerator. The speedometer's needle showed that Tito was driving above the speed limit, but not by a lot. She supposed that was smart—getting pulled over would delay them even more—but she had to fight the urge to tell him to floor it.

He handed her his phone. “Look up Chase and see if you can find out when he was released,” he said. “That ought to be a matter of public record.”

She recoiled at the thought of entering Chase’s name into Tito’s phone, as if it would pollute the new life with the old. But it was a little late for that now. She steeled herself, typed his name and the prison’s name, hit Enter—

And there was Chase’s mug shot glaring up at her from the screen.

A fresh wave of nausea rose in her throat. It had been a long time since she’d seen even a digital image of that face. The bright blue eyes were squeezed half shut by swollen purplish bruises, but they still managed to glare defiantly at her. The dark blond hair stood up in disarray as if he’d just tumbled out of bed, and his cheeks and forehead showed dozens of tiny cuts made by slivers of shattered glass in the accident that had killed Jenna’s sister. Chase had blown through a red light, and his flashy little Alfa Romeo had been T-boned on the passenger side by an extended-cab pickup. He'd suffered only minor injuries. Kara had never stood a chance.

Jenna swallowed hard and started scrolling.

"Here it is," she said. "He was released yesterday."

"Okay," said Tito. "Well, it sounds to me as if you took every precaution available to you to get yourself and Halley away from him. Given all that, how likely do you think it is that he'll find you at all, much less the day after he was released?"

She didn't answer right away. "I don't know," she said at last. "But Chase is smart. Not book smart, but people smart. I can't afford to take anything for granted where he's concerned."

"All right," Tito said.

They didn't speak again for the rest of the drive. Tito turned on to a country road lined with pecan trees that made a dense green arch overhead. At the end of the road was a driveway that wound past a plain barndominium-style house to a covered arena.

The Cadillac pulled into the driveway and parked near the house—close enough for Jenna to see what was happening in the arena, but not close enough for them to draw attention to themselves.

Halley was in the arena, a helmet over her blond hair, riding a brown horse with a black mane and tail and legs—a bay, according to Jenna's memory of horse books she'd read as a child. Susana was in the arena too, calling out instructions. Other campers stood gathered around outside the fence.

Jenna didn't know much about horsemanship, but she could see how confident and relaxed Halley was. The expression on her face was almost beatific.

"She looks good, doesn't she?" Jenna asked.

"She does," said Tito. "You want to watch a while? Let her finish her ride?"

"I guess there's no harm in that," Jenna said.

He shut off the engine, and a restful silence settled over them both. Jenna scanned the crowd of kids standing at the fence. She recognized Gillian right away, but she didn't know any of the others. It was about 80 percent girls, all young teens or preteens.

If Halley had a normal life, she might be

friends with some of those kids. They might see movies and go shopping together, maybe have sleepovers and do each other's hair. But Halley didn't even do those things with Gillian, her one friend of her own age in Limestone Springs. Prior to horse camp, she'd only ever seen Gillian at Lalo's when Gillian's dad happened to bring her there. Even for an introverted kid like Halley, it wasn't much of a social life.

Jenna took a deep breath and let it out. "Okay," she said. "I guess I don't have to take Halley out of camp this very instant. It's possible that I overreacted just a bit. Chase probably isn't hiding behind a clump of cactus waiting to grab her and run. She'd be pretty embarrassed if I made her quit in front of the other kids, and it would be a hard thing to explain to Susana. So I'll just let Halley finish her day and then sleep on it."

"I think that's wise," Tito said.

Jenna turned to face him, admiring the clear-cut lines of his profile against the deep green of the trees outside the window.

"I see what you did here," she said.

Tito glanced at her. "What do you mean?"

"You know what I mean. The way you reasoned through this whole situation with me, asking all the right questions so I'd figure things out on my own. You didn't tell me what to do. You just helped me see it for myself. You're so devious, with your quiet, soothing presence and your irrefutable logic."

The corner of his mouth edged up ever so slightly, but he kept a straight face and said, "I don't know what you're talking about."

She punched him on the shoulder, and he turned to her, smiling broadly now. "You knew what you had to do. You just needed a little help getting there."

"Well, thanks," said Jenna. "You're a good friend, Tito."

They were facing each other now across the bench seat. The tension melted away from Jenna's body, leaving a deep sense of security and peace. She always felt safe with Tito.

He had the most wonderful hair, dark and glossy, fine and thick. It fell over his forehead from a widow's peak, barely skimming his eyebrows. His crisply pressed, snowy white shirt gave off a clean scent of laundry detergent and light starch. Did he iron his shirts and slacks for the week, up in his bachelor apartment above the bar? If so, what did he wear while he did the ironing? Did he even own a pair of jeans? Workout clothes? A bathrobe?

"You don't seem very fazed by the fact that I'm living under an assumed name," she said.

"Oh, I'm not. I've known for a while that you were on the run from something or someone."

She sat up straight. "You have?"

"Sure."

"You never said anything about it."

He shrugged. "Well, no. I figured if you wanted to keep it a secret, that was your business."

"How did you know I wasn't dangerous? A criminal fleeing justice?"

His gaze softened. "You didn't strike me as an unsavory character, and my intuitions tend to be correct."

He was watching her closely, his expression grave. His eyes were a rich warm caramel brown beneath expressive black brows. His face was comfortingly familiar—that long thin nose, that lean jaw beneath the neatly trimmed beard.

His right arm rested along the back of the Cadillac's bench seat, his hand almost touching her shoulder. He had beautiful hands, long and slender and sensitive.

His fingers stretched out a fraction of an inch toward her, then folded back in on themselves. She saw his chest rise and fall in a quick breath. In that moment she knew beyond a doubt that what he felt for her went beyond friendship and being a good guy. He wanted to kiss her, but he wasn't going to, because she was so vulnerable right now and he was too much of a gentleman to take advantage.

But if she were to kiss *him*, he would respond.

The ball was in her court. She had the power to make it happen. Right here and now, she could lay her hand against his cheek and close the distance between them with one swift movement. What would it feel like to kiss him? She wanted to know.

His face was deadly serious now. He moved infinitesimally closer to her. It was going to happen. She was finally going to kiss Tito, right here in the front seat of his classic Cadillac.

Realization washed over her in a cold wave. She was in Tito's *car*. She had gotten into a car with a man and let him drive her—willingly, without a second thought. She had surrendered control—like some sort of princess, letting a man take care of her.

Some change of emotion must have shown in her face, because Tito drew back, his own expression suddenly startled and mortified. Jenna faced forward again and stared at the dashboard. The interior of the car felt cramped and airless. Her heart fluttered in her chest like a trapped bird.

Even as the panic rose, she knew she was making a false equivalence. Tito wasn't the drunk French driver who'd smashed the Mercedes-Benz into the side of the Parisian tunnel, killing himself and Diana and Dodi Fayed. He wasn't Chase, who'd been stoned out of his mind when he'd taken the wheel of his Alfa Romeo to pick up Halley, with Kara in the passenger seat. Tito was a hundred times the man Chase was. She'd known him a year and a half and had never seen him lose control. He was a good man, a trustworthy man. She ached to confide in him, to steal into his arms and let the whole story come pouring out in sweet release.

But then what? Then he would know, and she could never take back the words.

She raised her head, sending her gaze back to the arena, and Halley. Without looking at Tito, she said, "Well, thanks for the ride. I guess we'd better head back."

The words sounded cold and hateful in her own ears, but she didn't have any better ones to offer. The sooner she and Tito both got out of this car and back to work, the better. For a moment neither of them moved or spoke. Then, in a voice that held no trace of confusion or hurt, Tito said, "All right," and backed the Caddy out of Susana's driveway.

Jenna concentrated on her breathing—in through the nose, out through the mouth. When her heart rate had returned to something approaching normal, she forced herself to face some facts. She'd gotten into Tito's car without a moment's hesitation. She'd forgotten to feel afraid—and she couldn't afford to do that again. She'd made it this far by not trusting anyone but herself. She wasn't about to change that now.

"I want you to do me a favor," she said.

Out of the corner of her eye she saw Tito turn and look at her. "Sure," he said. "Anything."

"Please don't talk to Halley about any of this. I don't mean just the fact that we drove out here to pick her up, but, you know...all of it. The whole thing with Chase. And please don't do any internet research on him, or on Halley and me. I know it wouldn't be hard to find the whole story, but I'd appreciate it if you'd leave it alone."

"All right," said Tito, and Jenna knew he meant it. Of course he wouldn't press Halley for information about the abusive ex-con father she'd had to run away from. And he wouldn't press Jenna either, if she didn't want him to. He would be discreet. He would respect her boundaries. He'd go on being the friend and coworker that she needed, and not push for more, because that was the kind of man he was.

A barrier had come down today. Jenna had suffered a hull breach, and things wouldn't be quite the same. She had to preserve the distance she had left, keep a buffer of privacy around herself and Halley. That was the only way to keep them safe.

## *CHAPTER SEVEN*

ALL THROUGH THE ride home that afternoon, Halley chattered away, telling Jenna everything she'd learned in horse camp that day. It was rare for her to be so talkative, so… bubbly. She was such a serious kid, very mature for her age. She'd had to grow up fast.

"Susana says I have a good natural seat," Halley said. "She could hardly believe I'd never had lessons before. She's thinking about opening a class to teach barrel racing. Gillian and I could do that together."

She didn't ask if she could, and Jenna was glad. There was no need to thrash the matter out right now. The barrel-racing class might never happen, or Halley might lose interest in horses altogether.

She waited until Halley had talked herself out and subsided into a contented silence. It was a shame to ruin the mood by saying what had to be said now, but it couldn't be helped. Halley had to know.

Jenna steeled herself, then said, "I have some news."

Halley's head spun around to face her. "Tito asked you out," she guessed, her voice breathless with excitement.

"What? No," said Jenna.

"You asked Tito out," Halley said.

"No! Of course not. Why would you even think that?"

Halley rolled her eyes. "Oh, come on. You two obviously like each other. All those closing-time songfests, the way you look at each other and talk for hours on end. I don't understand why you don't just *go* for it already. The two of you would be great together."

Jenna gripped the steering wheel and stared straight ahead. "Tito," she said firmly, "is a good friend and a respected coworker, and nothing more."

Even as she kept her eyes on the road, she could feel the disbelieving look Halley was giving her from the passenger seat. Halley wasn't fooled.

"*Anyway,*" said Jenna, "that isn't the news. The news is that your father is out of prison."

Silence. Jenna stole a glance at her niece. Halley was still swiveled around toward her, but her face had gone blank.

"How?" Halley asked. "I thought he was sentenced to four years."

"He was. But sometimes people get off early for good behavior."

"*Good behavior?*" Halley repeated. "Him?"

"I know," said Jenna. "It doesn't sound like him. But there were probably enough Latimores in prison with him, and enough Latimore shot-callers on the outside, to give him plenty of protection. That would make it possible for him to keep his head down and his nose clean if that was what he wanted to do. And he did want that…because he wants you. And now that he's free—"

"Wait," said Halley. "You're not going to pull me out of horse camp, are you?"

"Well—" Jenna began.

"Oh, please, please let me finish horse camp! I'll be so careful."

Jenna sighed. "Halley, you know your father wants you back. He's angry that I took you away, and that I didn't bring you to visit him in prison. All the other Latimores made sure I knew it, and they're all angry too. As far as he's concerned, he's your father and you belong with him. And he doesn't care if he has to break the law to get you back, as long as he doesn't get caught."

"But he couldn't take me from horse camp! There's such a crowd there. How could he grab me in front of all those people?"

"I admit it doesn't seem like a smart thing to do, but he's crazy enough for anything. He's bold and reckless and smart. We can't afford to take any chances where he's concerned."

Halley turned to face forward again. "It's not fair," she said, her voice thick with tears. "A thousand miles away and he's still ruining my life."

"I know," said Jenna. "I'm sorry."

After a brief silence, Halley tried again. "Please let me finish horse camp, Mother. There are only a few days left, and my dad can't have figured out where we are the second he got out of prison. I'll be super, super careful. Just let me finish camp and I won't ask for anything else."

Jenna didn't answer right away. She could

feel herself weakening. Halley didn't often ask for things for herself, and she'd already lost so much that a child ought to have. Was it really necessary for Jenna to take this one thing away from her?

Finally Jenna spoke. "I want you to stay with the group at all times. Stay close to Susana and Roque. Don't ever, *ever* wander off. Got it?"

"Got it," said Halley brightly. "Thank you, Mother."

She reached into her bag and took out a book. Within seconds she was lost to the world, deep in her story, twirling her pale gold hair the way Kara used to. Jenna saw so much of Kara in Halley—in the shape of her face, the tilt of her nose, the aching vulnerability that made Jenna want to shield her from all the wickedness in the world. But only half of her DNA had come from Kara. The other half was all Chase.

Was Jenna doing the right thing in letting Halley finish horse camp? She wished she could be sure. She wanted to keep Halley safe, and also raise her to be an emotionally healthy adult, in spite of all the trauma she'd experienced at a young age. Was Jenna succeeding? She hoped so, and some days she thought so. Other days, she honestly had no idea.

More and more often, as Halley got older, Jenna found herself completely and utterly perplexed. This single parenting gig was *tough.* She and Halley spent so much time alone together, and sometimes Jenna longed for another perspective. A third person could break up the rut and open the way to meaningful communication—especially a third person with a clear, logical mind and a wise, compassionate heart.

Jenna shook her head hard, impatient with herself. It was a sign of weakness, thinking the solution was a man, wanting to rely on him for stability and strength. Halley was her responsibility, not Tito's, and she'd managed just fine so far. She'd figure it out. She had to.

SELECTING THE RIGHT music was a crucial part of the running of a successful restaurant or bar. You wanted all the songs to fit the overall vibe of the place while also providing a good mix of tempo, energy and valence. You had to take into account the age and background of your customers and provide plenty of material that was familiar to them, but you didn't want to draw too heavily on any one genre or era, because if a customer recognized every song, the music became a distraction rather than a pleasant background.

It was a lot to consider, and Tito did consider it, laboring over his playlists, striving for the proper balance, and changing the lists regularly so they didn't get stale. But right now, with only himself to please, he'd chosen an old personal favorite, a blend of folk rock classics from the sixties and seventies—Jim Croce, Simon & Garfunkel, Carole King. It was an introspective, contemplative playlist. Even the relatively cheerful songs were tinged with melancholy, which perfectly suited the stormy weather outside, as well as Tito's present mood.

If Jenna were here, she'd be mixing it up with Lynyrd Skynyrd or Aerosmith. But this was early Sunday morning. Both Tito's Bar and Lalo's Kitchen were closed until noon. Tito was all alone.

Empty of customers, the two connected spaces felt vast and cavernous. But a phantom Jenna haunted Tito's mind, appearing whichever way he turned—carrying a food-laden tray high above her head, singing classic rock at the top of her lungs while wiping down countertops, frowning in concentration over her laptop as she placed orders from suppliers.

Most of all, he saw her sitting in the front seat of his Cadillac, mascara smeared, eyes red and puffy from crying, looking young and lost and achingly beautiful.

He'd replayed the scene again and again for the past five days. With his arm lying across the back of the seat, his fingers inches from her shoulder, it would have been so easy to take her in his arms. It would have been a perfectly natural move on the part of a good friend. But it would have meant something more to him than comfort and sympathy. And it would have been unconscionably pushy and presumptuous, taking advantage of her at a vulnerable moment to gratify his own desires, even if he'd had reason to think the advance would be a welcome one.

So he'd kept himself still. But then their eyes had met, and Jenna's gaze had sharpened, and darted down, unbelievably, to his lips. And just for a moment, he'd been joyously certain that the attraction wasn't all on his side, and that she was seriously thinking about kissing him.

Apparently he'd been wrong. The next instant she'd drawn back with a look of what might have been revulsion on her face, and said that they should head back.

Which might mean simply that she was fighting her feelings for him. He could understand that. She'd been hurt, physically and emotionally, by a man she'd presumably loved at one time. She'd worked hard to get away from him and start a new life with her child. She couldn't afford to take another chance on romance. All her energy had to be focused on keeping herself and Halley safe.

Or it might mean that Tito had horribly misinterpreted the whole thing, and Jenna had never wanted to kiss him at all. He was usually good at reading signals, but in this case his feelings might be clouding his judgment, making him see what he wanted to see.

After all, she hadn't even meant to confide in him in the first place. The story had come spilling out of her after her panic attack, leading him to imagine an intimacy that wasn't there—unless, of course, she really was just gun-shy, in which case he needed to be patient.

Now here he was, caught in an endless loop of overthinking and second-guessing deep inside his head, exactly where he did not want to be.

A year and a half ago, Tito had been reconciled to being alone. He'd learned to take satisfaction in other parts of his life. But then Jenna had shown up and upset the delicate equilibrium.

His phone let out a ding. Tito picked it up from the counter, irrationally hoping to see a text from Jenna—a stupid thing to hope for, since the two of them had never texted about anything not work-related, but that was no reason they couldn't start. Their easy in-person banter could translate into a playful back-and-forth, a pleasantly stimulating continuo to tide him over through nonwork hours. It might even turn into more than that. Some people let their guard down while texting in a way that they didn't or couldn't in person.

He had a text, all right, but it wasn't from Jenna. It was from his cousin Lalo.

Lalo's long, convoluted, overly detailed, anxiety-filled message was a poor substitute for a flirtatious interchange with Jenna. He was a pretty good guy overall, conscientious and highly ethical, both excellent qualities in a business partner. But he worried too much, and tended to get in his own way.

Right now he was worrying over some policy of Luke's, and wondering whether he ought to step in and override it. Well, at least he was asking Tito's opinion rather than going behind Luke's back and undermining his authority. That was a step in the right direction.

Tito leaned his hip against the bar top and began to type.

Don't do it. Luke is the manager. Let him manage. He's better at it than you are. That's why you put him in charge. Remember what happened the last time you tried to micromanage him?

I remember, came the reply. I just thought I might sort of nudge him in a different direction. But if you think he's doing the right thing, then I'll stay out of it.

I do think so, answered Tito. Stop worrying.

Even as he hit Send, he knew that was useless advice. Lalo would never stop worrying.

Tito glanced at the Kraken bottle, the one Jenna had said looked like Lalo, and chuckled. The rounded handles really were a dead ringer for Lalo's fussy, hands-on-hips posture.

Memories of that night, when he and Jenna had cleaned the display shelves together and assigned the different bottles to various employees, washed over him. They'd had such a good time.

*Stop it*, he told himself.

He exited from the Messages app, double-clicked the Home button and started clearing his tabs, swiping them up and away. Swipe, swipe, swipe—

His finger froze above an image of a man's face, bruised and swollen, facing the camera head-on. It looked like a mug shot.

Tito didn't recognize the guy. He tapped the tab to bring it up to full screen.

It *was* a mug shot. And it belonged to one Chase Latimore, lately of Green Rock Correctional Center, in Chatham, Virginia.

A chill ran down Tito's spine. This had to be Jenna's ex. Jenna had used Tito's phone to look up details on his release, and the information was still here.

A pair of bright blue eyes glared at him from the screen. The unflinching gaze, the proud angle of the head, the defiant jut of the jaw—whatever Chase had done to get himself incarcerated, he didn't look sorry for it. The bruising around the eyes, a nasty abrasion on the forehead and a sprinkling of tiny cuts all over the face made Tito wonder. Had Jenna fought back? Or had Chase received these injuries in some incident, like a bar fight, completely unrelated to the offense that had landed him in jail? What exactly *had* landed him in jail? What had he done to Jenna, or to Halley, or to both of them, that had earned him a prison term lasting at least as long as Jenna and Halley had been in Limestone Springs? It had to be a felony offense.

A few minutes of internet research could tell Tito everything—not just Chase's crime, but Jenna's and Halley's old names, and where they came from.

His fingers itched to start tapping. Surely there wasn't any harm in finding out any of these things. But he'd given Jenna his word that he wouldn't go digging for information.

Well, he knew Chase's name, anyway, and what he looked like. That would come in handy if Chase ever did show up in Limestone Springs.

He double-clicked the Home button again and swiped Chase's mug shot away. Then he put his phone in a shallow drawer, picked up a bottle of glass cleaner and a lint-free cloth, and turned his attention to the back bar.

Next to the display case with its mirrored back, another, longer mirror, encased in an ornate Victorian frame, ran most of the width of the wall, reflecting the room in its entirety. Tito had gotten it at auction when doing the renovation years earlier. It was a handsome piece. The dark, carved wood gave off an old-fashioned ambience, and the mirror expanded the visual space while allowing Tito to keep an eye on things when his back was turned—to see who needed a refill, who needed to be cut off, who needed to be bounced.

He climbed the ladder and started cleaning at the top. The mirror was starting to develop some black spots, especially around the edges, evidence of its age, but Tito didn't mind. He liked the effect.

A brisk tapping made him turn around. A woman stood outside the door, silhouetted against the moody gray rain-washed street, peering through the glass with one hand shading her eyes and clutching a big shapeless tote bag.

Tito crossed the floor, unlocked the door and opened it just a crack.

"We're closed," he said in his sternest tone.

She gave him a bright smile. "I know the owner."

Chuckling, he opened the door wide, and she came in and gave him a hug, her bag flopping against him.

"Hey, Mom," he said.

"Hey, baby," said his mother.

Rose Mendoza was small and feisty, with a halo of thick dark curls. Tito alone of his brothers had inherited her slender frame instead of the bull-like build of his father. She set her bag on a long table, in the underside of one of the upturned benches resting there.

"So what have you got in your bag of tricks today?" he asked. All his life, his mother had been hauling around capacious, brightly colored tote bags filled with exercise gear, library books to be returned, packages to mail, stuff to donate to the thrift store, stuff she'd bought at the thrift store while making donations, and food to deliver to people who'd just had a new baby or were recovering from illnesses. This one was patterned with big flowers, and judging from its heft and shape, it was stuffed full.

"Oh, just a few odds and ends. A care package for Javi. This cute little clock I found at the thrift store. Some barbacoa to take to Ellen Rogers—she just had cataract surgery."

As she spoke, she removed the things from the bag and set them in a row on a narrow sliver of tabletop between the two benches.

"No barbacoa for me?" Tito asked, pulling a sad-eyed face.

His mother smiled, then reached into the

bag again and drew out another food container.

"This one's for you, baby. Oh, and check out this shirt I got you from the thrift store."

"Nice," he said, taking the shirt from her. It was a button-down, deep blue, with a woven stripe—his size, his style, his cut—and looked brand-new. Rose Mendoza was an expert bargain hunter, her skills honed by decades of bringing up five boys on a small income.

She beamed at him. "Good! You can wear it to the party."

Ah, yes—the Fourth of July party. There was always a party coming up in the Mendoza family. Birthdays, holidays—any excuse to invite all the relatives and half the town over to their tiny house and cook enough food to feed an army.

She was watching him closely. "You're coming, right?"

"Sure, wouldn't miss it," he said with a cheerfulness he didn't feel. He didn't especially want to go but figured he'd better. He'd skipped out on this year's Cinco de Mayo bash and hadn't yet heard the end of it.

"Good! We're going to have a great time. Lots of people you know will be there."

Rose started naming them, focusing on single women around Tito's own age. He recognized quite a few names of female friends from high school who'd confided in him about their wretched relationships once upon a time.

"That's a lot of people, all right," he said. "I'm guessing you'll want some beer kegs for the party?"

"Yes. And some of those what-do-you-call-thems, those jugs that you put the mead in. Grumblers?"

"Growlers," he said. "Come on over to the bar top and we'll get it taken care of."

He took down a barstool for her to sit on, turned down the volume on the music and got her order placed.

"Let me bring some food from Lalo's for the party," he said. "My treat."

She waved her hand. "No, no. Don't worry about that. I can handle the cooking."

"I know you *can*. But it's a lot of food for a lot of people. I don't like to think of you slaving over a hot stove in the middle of the summer in that shoebox of a kitchen."

"My mother's kitchen was smaller than mine, and that didn't stop her."

"I know it didn't. But you work too hard, Mom. You're always taking care of people. I'm worried you're going to wear yourself out."

She gave him a look. "You're a fine one to talk. When's the last time you had a day off?"

"We're closed Sundays mornings until noon. You know that."

She laughed. "Baby, this *is* Sunday! And here you are, working! Do you ever rest at all?"

"Sure I do. I read, watch movies…"

"By yourself."

"No, not by myself," he said, thinking of Bunter.

"Your cat doesn't count. You spend too much time alone, baby."

"I'm with people all day, Mom. I need time alone to recharge."

She gave him a thorough once-over, sizing him up, searching for signs of neglect and strain, as she did every time she saw him.

"You're too thin," she said at last.

"Thanks," he said. "That's nice to hear."

"You know what I mean. Are you eating?"

"Yes, and working out. I've just got your metabolism, remember? I burn it all off. Don't worry about me. I'm fine."

"Are you? Okay, so you go to work, and you go home, which is right upstairs from work, and you go to the gym, which is practically next door to the other two. And I guess you go across the street to H-E-B once in a while to pick up groceries. Do you go anywhere else? Do you ever leave this one-block circuit of yours?"

"I'm not seeing anyone," Tito said, answering the question behind the question. Then, before she could ask, he went on, "My diet is excellent, I never drink more than two alcohol units a day, I'm staying hydrated, I get between seven and eight hours of sleep a night, and my mood is stable."

He tried to look and sound happy and healthy, but he knew she wasn't satisfied, because if he *wasn't* doing any of those things, if he was sliding toward a depressive episode, he would say the same thing.

The recurring bouts of depression that had started in his early teens had been incomprehensible to his father. *What have you got to be depressed about?* Juan had asked—not in a mean way, just honestly baffled. And Tito hadn't had a good answer. He had a loving family, a roof over his head, clothes on his back and plenty of food to eat. He was better off than most of the population of the world. What *did* he have to be depressed about? He didn't know, but the added layer of guilt, and the implication that he should simply count his blessings and snap out of it, didn't help.

Rose had understood a little better, because she'd been through it all before with her brother. Like Young Tito, Original Tito had suffered from several depressive episodes in his teens and early twenties. After that, his depression had appeared to clear up. In reality, as they'd realized after his death, he'd simply gotten better at hiding it.

Uncle Tito had always had a strict policy of not drinking on duty, but the autopsy had told a different story. The coroner's ruling had been congestive heart failure, with advanced cirrhosis of the liver. Uncle Tito had spent most of his waking hours at the bar, which meant he'd either been drinking at work on the sly in defiance of his own policy, or seriously hitting the booze after hours.

Going through her brother's belongings after the funeral, Rose had found old pictures of his ex-wife in the top drawer of his desk, evidence of the one unreasoning passion that he'd never gotten over.

"You're listening to James Taylor," she said now. It sounded like an accusation. Tito knew she was thinking of all the times she'd seen him lying on his bed, staring up at the ceiling while "Fire and Rain" played out of his iPod.

"I'm fine, Mom," said Tito. "Really."

She scrutinized him for another long moment. "If you start to get down, you tell me, okay?"

"Okay," said Tito, trying to look as if he meant it.

She repacked her tote bag and kissed him goodbye. "Fourth of July. Don't forget."

"I won't."

The bar seemed quiet after his mother had gone. He went back to work, cleaning the whole surface of the mirror and dusting the ornate scrollwork on the frame, using cotton swabs to get into the grooves. He wondered what Jenna was doing right now. He wished she was here to tease him about his hippy-dippy music. He wished he had an excuse to text her, or even to call her. In general he preferred texting to talking on the phone, but he liked the sound of Jenna's voice—sweet and girlish, lilting and musical.

But he didn't have an excuse, and he couldn't push her. He had to give her plenty of space. Be patient. Earn her trust.

He caught sight of his own face in the bar mirror. Earn her trust? And then what? What exactly did he think was going to happen here? That she would actually want to be with him?

His reflection stared back at him. In his crisp white shirt and black vest, with his neatly trimmed beard, he looked like a character in an old black-and-white film—a minor character, who existed only as a means to get the hero to talk. Once the hero left the bar, the bartender might as well not exist.

Jim Croce started singing about unrequited love. A cold heavy weight settled in Tito's stomach. He walked over to the music-playing phone, paused the playlist and exited the streaming app. He'd had enough music for one day.

The silence bore down on him. It had substance and mass.

He opened Audible and started scrolling through his library of audiobooks, desperately searching for something that would engage his intellect rather than his emotions. He scrolled desperately through his library. Plenty of abstruse stuff here, history and philosophy, but none of it caught his interest. He settled at last on a Wooster and Jeeves audiobook. Humor, that was what he needed.

He had to stop the downward spiral before it started.

## *CHAPTER EIGHT*

"TITO? YEAH, he's kind of cute, if you like that shy, nerdy, awkward type. But he's too much of a beta for my taste. I'm only attracted to alpha males."

The woman who had just said this astonishing thing had her chin resting on her hand and her eyes narrowed in a shrewd, evaluating expression. She swirled her celery stick through her Bloody Mary in a bored sort of way before languidly lifting it out of the glass and biting into it with a loud crunch.

Jenna, who'd just brought the cocktails to the Bloody Mary woman and her dining companions and was now clearing dishes from a nearby booth, barely contained the urge to let out a derisive snort—not at the crunch, but at the ridiculous words.

There were three of them at the table—the Bloody Mary woman, Annalisa Cavazos and Eliana Mahan, Luke's wife. Bloody Mary had already sunk pretty low in Jenna's estimation because of all the substitutions she'd made in the salad she'd ordered—pumpkin seeds instead of slivered almonds, butternut squash instead of roasted corn, feta instead of mozzarella, extra bell peppers, no guac. Jenna could understand the occasional request to hold the onions or put the dressing on the side, but Bloody Mary's alterations were enough to turn her order into an entirely different dish. If she had that little faith in the cook's judgment, what was she even doing here? Why not go home and fix her own lunch?

"I think Tito is very good-looking," said Annalisa, with a definite undertone of friendly loyalty warming her tone. "He's very intelligent, too, but he doesn't show off. He likes people and cares about them."

"That's what I'm talking about," said Bloody Mary. "He's a beta. He's too nice—and too nice is boring."

She picked up her coaster and started shredding it, the way people sometimes shredded cocktail napkins. Jenna hated it when customers did this. Cocktail napkins were disposable, single-use items, and cheap. But this was a sturdy cardboard coaster, printed with the logo for Lalo's Kitchen on one side and Tito's Bar on the other, and designed to be reusable. Apparently Bloody Mary was the sort of person who liked tearing things, and people, into tiny pieces.

Jenna thought of Tito standing up to the boys who'd insulted his uncle, taking them on in a fight he knew he couldn't win. He'd had ten times more grit in him than all of those little bullies put together, and still did.

She'd finished loading dirty dishes onto her tray. Now she took a seat in the booth and started fiddling with the gerbera daisies in the bud vase, keeping the table in her sight line. Bloody Mary was staring through the pass-through at Tito, who was standing behind the bar in that way he had, slim and upright in his crisp white shirt and black vest, his dark hair slanting across his wide forehead to skim his thick black brows, his gaze sweeping over his domain, alert to anything that needed his attention. Pride and affection for his bar shone in his face.

The truth was that Jenna had been looking at Tito a lot these days, and even when she wasn't watching him, she was deeply aware of his presence, as if there were an invisible thread linking them. Every time they made eye contact, she remembered how she had almost kissed him in the front seat of his Cadillac, and wondered if he was thinking about that, too.

She'd also been avoiding him. She'd let her guard down way too much that day at horse camp. She couldn't let herself get that close to him again. But that didn't stop her from wanting to.

Which made it all the worse to see some celery-munching woman checking him out from across the room, sizing him up like a cut of meat, and a substandard one at that. Who did Bloody Mary think she was? Who was she to pick and choose? The way she talked, you'd have thought Tito was hers for the taking, as if all she had to do was lift a finger and he'd come running. What if *he* didn't want *her*? Wasn't that at least a possibility?

Eliana took a sip of her mint julep. "I don't know what people mean when they talk about alphas and betas," she said. "I know those terms are used in the dog world, but they don't seem to make sense when applied to people. But I do know it's a mistake to assume that nice guys are weak."

*Yeah, you tell her, Eliana,* Jenna thought. She had been slow to warm up to Eliana, who was the sort of ridiculously beautiful, perfectly put together woman who tended to draw every male eye in the room. Her engagement to Luke had come as a shock to everyone who worked at Lalo's Kitchen. No one had thought it would last. And when Eliana had broken the engagement, Jenna had been outraged on Luke's behalf, and not just because the breakup had been part of the reason Luke had left his job and cleared out of town. But then he'd come back, and married Eliana after all, and anyone could see that Eliana adored him and that he was a very happy man.

Bloody Mary gave Eliana a condescending smile. "Well, of course you *would* say that. You married a beta yourself. Luke *looks* like a roughneck, but he's really a teddy bear. Don't get me wrong. Obviously Luke's a nice person and all that. But he's almost *too* nice and kind. I like a little arrogance in a man. I like a man who says exactly what he thinks and takes exactly what he wants with no apology."

Now Jenna was *really* angry. Bloody Mary would probably like Chase, with his swagger, his domineering air and showy good looks.

"I used to date guys like that," said Eliana. "Multimillionaires, investment bankers, CEOs. Real take-charge types. Then one day I was just done. I realized that being an overbearing, abrasive jerk was not strength. Luke is not just a nice guy. He's a good man, and the strongest man I know."

Then Eliana caught Jenna's eye and gave her a tiny conspiratorial smile as if to say, *You and me, we get it. We know.*

Well! Maybe Eliana was a lot more perceptive than Jenna had realized.

And suddenly Tito was right there at the table, smiling warmly at the three women.

"Hello, ladies," he said. "Enjoying your cocktails?"

A shiver passed through Jenna. That voice of his got her every time, even when he was only saying something like, *We need more soap in the men's room soap dispenser.* It was as rich as chocolate fondue.

"Excellent as always," said Eliana.

"Good," said Tito. He went on chatting with the women. Bloody Mary chatted right back, smiling up at him, being perfectly charming, as if she hadn't been picking him to pieces moments before. It made Jenna feel strangely protective of him.

She had to get away. She slid out of the booth and picked up her tray.

But before she could head back to the kitchen, Tito stepped in front of her, those dark eyes looking straight into hers.

"Can you help me in the bar this afternoon?" he asked. "Garrett called in sick, and I can't get ahold of Sam."

"Okay," Jenna said.

"I'm sorry to ask," said Tito, "but there's no one else to do it."

She often helped out at the bar when Tito was spread thin. Unlike most of the wait staff at Lalo's Kitchen, she was over twenty-one and had actual bartending experience, so she was the natural choice. It had never been an issue before. The fact that Tito was apologizing now meant that he'd noticed that she'd been avoiding him.

"It's no problem, really," she said.

But it was a problem. She couldn't keep

any sort of emotional distance from him if she was working with him. She just couldn't. She'd be drawn in the way she always was.

She took her tray of dirty dishes to the kitchen, then headed to the bar. Taking her place beside Tito, Jenna felt lighter than she had in days. Being close to Tito certainly had its dangers, but that didn't stop her from liking it.

DURING THE HOURS when Tito had Jenna working behind the bar with him that day, all of her reserve seemed to melt away. Maybe she thought it wasn't necessary anymore, that she'd made her point and Tito understood that she wasn't interested in him, and now they could go back to being friends. Or maybe it meant something completely different.

He wished he could be one of those stone-faced guys whose hearts were never touched—like his brother Javi. He didn't want to turn into his uncle, dying sad and alone, pining away after someone he could never have. He might be alone, but he didn't have to be sad about it. The key was to manage expectations. He couldn't let himself be tricked into thinking he was special to a woman when really he was just a placeholder, a shoulder to cry on—good enough for now.

More than anything, he hated being made a fool of—having that football pulled out from in front of him for the thousandth time, like Charlie Brown.

But he wasn't Javi. He was himself. He could swear up and down that he was going to be detached and rational, but at the end of the day, he was a romantic. And Jenna drew him more than any other woman he'd ever known. He knew he ought to keep his head level and not be drawn in, but he couldn't. It was too easy to fall into their old patterns of banter.

"I heard a new come-on line today," she told him after the afternoon rush had subsided. "Next door, during breakfast. This guy was squinting up at the menu board overhead like he couldn't read it. I asked him if he needed a paper menu, and he looked me straight in the eye and said, *I already know what's on the menu. Me-N-U.*"

Tito groaned and shook his head. "Oh, that's awful. What did you say?"

"Nothing. What *could* I say in response to such wit?"

Tito thought a moment, then reached under the bar top and took out the pen and spiral notebook he used for counting cash at the end of the night. "You need to start writing down all these clever come-on lines," he said. "We owe it to future generations to preserve these brilliant gems."

Jenna took the pen and clicked it. "Okay, but it's going to be a long list."

As it turned out, she didn't make an actual list. She used a separate scrap of paper for each come-on line, tearing the page in pieces as she went. Tito folded up the scraps and put them inside a small carved box below the display shelf. They quickly went through an entire sheet of paper. Jenna remembered half a dozen right off the top of her head, and Tito reminded her of several more that had been used on her and Veronica.

As she tore the last bit of paper out of the spiral and handed it to Tito, she asked, "That's all I can remember right now. Your turn."

"My turn for what?" Tito replied.

"For writing down all the come-on lines that have been used on you."

"Me? No. That's never been an issue for me."

"Oh, come on. I don't believe that for a minute. Customers must hit on you all the time."

He shook his head. "Sorry to disappoint, but no, they really don't."

"Of course they do. You're just missing the signals. It isn't possible that you've never had a customer come on to you. Look at you. You're good-looking, intelligent, sympathetic, a good listener. Women must eat that up."

Why was she saying this, and being so emphatic about it? Maybe it was her way of building his confidence, of letting him know that although *she* didn't find him attractive, plenty of other women probably did, so he should go find one and forget about her.

Well, he wasn't going to play along.

"No, they really don't, in the bar or in the world at large," he said. "My romantic relationships have been few and brief, usually with me in the role of rebound guy, or fall-back guy. The closest thing I've ever heard to a come-on line is, *Tito, will you please take me to homecoming to make my ex jealous?*"

Jenna stared at him. "Are you serious? Someone actually said that to you?"

"Someone actually did."

"And what did you say back? I hope you told her where she could get off."

Tito felt his ears turning red. "Um, I believe my exact words were, *What time should I pick you up?*"

Jenna's jaw dropped open. "No. You didn't! Did you? Did you seriously take this person to homecoming?"

"I seriously did. It worked, too. She and her ex got back together right there at the dance, and I went home alone."

Jenna swatted him on the arm. "Tito! That's terrible."

"I know. But what can I say? I'm a nice guy."

For some reason that made her frown. "Don't call yourself that. You're not just a nice guy. You're a good man. You're smart and attractive and a pillar of the community. Any right-thinking woman would agree."

As a list of merits went, this one didn't

reach any great emotional heights, but it was something. It dared him to take a chance.

"Well," Tito said, "if any right-thinking woman ever comes along, she's going to have to take a pretty direct approach. Something like, *Tito, you're an intelligent and respected business owner, a good conversationalist and not bad looking on the whole. And I'd very much like you to take me to dinner this weekend.*"

Jenna studied him a long moment. As her clear green eyes stared into his, his heart went from zero to sixty in three seconds flat. For one glorious, terrifying moment, he thought she was actually going to say those exact words back to him, right now.

But before she could say anything, the front door opened, and a big man with a shaved head and a handlebar mustache swaggered into the bar. "Rigoberto!" the familiar voice called out, in a loud roar like that of a friendly lion.

Jenna turned away, and Tito felt his heart sink down to his knees. The moment was lost.

"Hey, Dad," he said, forcing his voice to sound cheerful.

Juan Mendoza was dressed in his usual

work clothes—worn jeans, battered boots and a T-shirt. He was so big that his arms stood out from his sides.

Taking possession of his usual barstool, he looked at his son and said, "How you doing, *huerco*? Working hard or hardly working?"

Then he laughed—as if he'd never heard anything so funny, as if he hadn't been asking that same question every day since his son had come into possession of the bar, and asking it of his brother-in-law every day before that.

It was the sort of question that was impossible to answer, and Tito didn't even try. "A pint of Thirsty Goat?" he asked.

"You know it," said his dad.

Tito filled a pint glass with the amber red ale and set it before his father.

"Thank you, son," said Juan. Then he did an exaggerated double-take at Jenna, as if he'd just noticed her standing there, though Tito was sure he'd seen her from the start.

"Oh, so they got you working the bar today, huh?" he asked in mock surprise. "You keeping this boy of mine on his toes?"

"Nope," said Jenna. "I'm too busy keeping the customers in line."

Juan let out a loud appreciative laugh. "I believe it," he said. Jenna was a great favorite of his. Tito could hardly believe the ease of their banter. She sassed him, stood up to him, and he liked it. Tito had heard him say more than once that she was like the daughter he'd never had.

"How are you today, Juan?" Jenna asked.

Juan took a swallow of beer and braced his thick forearms on the bar top. "Oh, can't complain. Me and the boys have been doing some earth-moving work out in Schraeder Lake. We tore down some old fencing, got the brush all cleared and reconfigured the pastures. Now we're digging a big tank."

"What are these tanks I'm always hearing about?" asked Jenna. "Do Texans have giant aquariums in their pastures?"

Tito could see the wheels turning in his father's mind as Juan tried to come up with a mischievous answer. Before Juan could speak, Tito said, "They're stock tanks. Ponds for the stock to drink out of."

Juan scowled. "Oh, man. Why'd you tell her? I was all set to go with that aquarium thing. I could have worked up a whole story."

"Yeah, I'll bet you could," said Jenna. "So,

basically, you've been digging a big hole in the ground, huh?"

Juan made a scoffing sound. "There's a whole lot more to it than that. There's a real art to digging a stock tank. You want it to look nice as well as hold water. A real big one like this one we've been working on takes days to make. See, you use the excavated earth to build up the banks, and shape it in a way that harmonizes with the land."

"That does sound fun," said Jenna.

"Yeah, it is. We ought to finish this one tomorrow or the day after. If we ever get any rain again, it'll fill right up, and then the guy is going to stock it with fish, so it actually will be sort of like an aquarium after all, only you won't be able to see the fish because the water won't be clear enough."

He took another drink of beer and turned to his son. "How about you, *huerco*? What've you been up to lately?"

"Well, let's see," said Tito. What *had* he been up to lately? He'd recently started reading a new book about the history of Spain during the High Middle Ages. And the night before, he'd taken a pressure washer to the inside of the empty beer vats and run a chlorine solution down the pipes to keep mold from building up. He'd also disassembled the taps, run a cleaning solution through all the lines and poured boiling water down the drains to prevent mites from breeding in the beer residue. He'd been proud of the work he'd done. It was satisfying to get things sparkling clean and stay on top of the routine maintenance that would keep the bar running right and avoid problems.

But in view of his father's earthmoving, brush-clearing and stock-pond-digging, it all sounded fussy and trivial.

"Oh, you know," he said at last. "Same old, same old."

Juan frowned at him. "You're in a rut, Rigoberto. You need to shake things up. Try something new." Then he looked at Jenna. "Fourth of July's just three days away," he said with an expectant grin.

"That is certainly true," she replied. "You'll get no argument from me there."

He went on grinning. "So? Are you gonna ride the bull?"

She narrowed her eyes at him. "Is that anything like cow tipping? Because I wasn't born yesterday."

Juan let out another appreciative bellow of laughter. "No, no. I'm talking about the party."

Jenna clearly wasn't following. "What party?"

"What party?" Juan repeated. He turned to his son. "You haven't invited this girl to the party?"

"Uh," said Tito.

He didn't have time to get any further. Juan turned back to Jenna and jerked a thumb in Tito's direction. "Can you believe this guy? He doesn't like parties. Told us to stop throwing him birthday parties when he was still a little boy."

"I was fourteen," said Tito.

Juan ignored this. "*You* like parties, don't you?" he asked Jenna.

"Sure," she said. "I like parties fine."

"Good! Then we'll see you there, Fourth of July. And you can ride the bull."

"I still don't understand about this bull," Jenna said. "What bull are we talking about?"

Juan's eyes twinkled. "Big ole mean Brahma we keep in a pasture. Weighs twenty-five hundred pounds with wicked sharp horns *this big*." He spread his hands three feet apart.

"It's a mechanical bull," said Tito.

His dad let out an exaggerated sigh. "Ah, you're no fun, *huerco*."

"Oh, a *mechanical* bull," said Jenna. "Is that all? Sure, I'll ride."

Juan gave Tito a triumphant look. "There, you hear that? *She's* not scared."

"I'm not scared either," said Tito.

"If you're not scared, then how come you won't ride the bull?"

"Can't I just not want to?" Tito asked. "Why does it have to be about being scared?"

But a voice inside his head said he *was* scared—not of getting hurt, but of looking foolish in front of a crowd, of not measuring up to his father and brothers, of being less than.

"Oh, I know *you're* not scared," said Jenna. "Anyone who's as steely-eyed as you are with belligerent drunks isn't afraid of a little riding toy."

Juan glanced back and forth between Jenna and Tito. For a second Tito thought he was going to take issue with his mechanical bull being called a little riding toy, but instead he demanded, "What belligerent drunks? Who's steely-eyed?"

Jenna answered before Tito could open his mouth. "Your son is steely-eyed, and he chucks belligerent drunks right out of the bar before they know what's happening to them. A couple of weeks ago, this great big guy followed me into a supply closet. Tito put him in some sort of fancy hold, bounced him out of the bar and told him not to come back. He never even raised his voice or looked the least bit flustered. It was impressive. And it wasn't the first time I'd seen him do it, either."

Juan looked at his son with something like awe. Then his face slowly spread into a smile. "How about that? You know, Jenna, he was always scrappy, even when he was a kid. He's the only one of my boys that ever got suspended from school for fighting. He took on a whole gang of punks because they threw some shade on his uncle."

"I believe it," said Jenna.

"So it's all settled," said Juan. "Tito's taking you to the party, and you're both gonna ride the bull. You be sure to bring Halley, too. There'll be lots of other kids there."

He finished his beer and paid his bill,

leaving Tito a big tip. After the door shut behind him, Tito turned to Jenna.

"What just happened?" he asked.

Jenna gave him a guilty smile. "I think I just invited myself to your parents' party and volunteered you to ride a mechanical bull. Sorry. I guess I got a little carried away."

"No, no, that's fine. I meant the part where you stood up for me to my dad and told him what a tough guy I am. Where did that come from?"

Jenna shrugged. "I don't know. I guess I get tired of good guys like you being undervalued. I don't mean your dad doesn't value you," she added quickly.

"No, I get it," said Tito. "He teases. That's his way of showing affection. But, yeah, it does get a little old at times. So…thanks."

"You're welcome," said Jenna.

An awkward silence fell.

"So do you really want to go to the party?" Tito asked.

She thought a moment. "A party," she said. "At your parents' place. How big a guest list are we talking about? More people or fewer than at the barn raising at Susana Vrba's place?"

"Oh, definitely fewer. My parents don't have the space for that big a crowd, though they certainly make the most of the space they have."

"Well, we went to the barn raising," Jenna said. "And nothing terrible happened. But that was before."

Tito knew what she meant. Before Chase got out of prison.

He didn't dare speak. He wanted desperately for her to go, but she had to decide on her own.

Then she looked at him and smiled.

"I told your father I'd go, so I'm sort of honor bound now. And I know Halley would be thrilled by a chance to hang out with someone other than me. We'll go."

Happiness flooded through him, and he felt a goofy smile spread across his face. "Good," he said.

She picked up a damp cloth from the sink and started wiping down the bar top. "I used to love parties," she said. Then she glanced at him and said, "How about you?"

"Oh, I'm definitely going," he said. "I missed Cinco de Mayo. I can't miss Fourth of July too."

"No, that's not what I meant. I meant, is it true that you don't like parties? Did you really tell your parents to stop throwing parties for your birthday?"

"Oh, that. Yes, it's true, but it wasn't quite the way he said."

She rinsed the cloth and wrung it out. "So how was it?"

Tito picked up a pint glass and started polishing it. "Well, my family's always been big on parties. Between Christmas, New Year's, Cinco de Mayo, Fourth of July, Memorial Day, Labor Day and all the birthdays, there's some sort of celebration going on pretty much every month of the year. My birthday is in July, and so is my brother Eddie's, which made July kind of a busy month for us, party-wise. So we used to celebrate my and Eddie's birthday together, in one big bash, near the end of the month so it didn't get subsumed by the Fourth of July. I didn't mind so much when I was little, but the older I got, the less fun it was to share a party with my better looking, more popular brother. Girls of my age used to angle to get an invitation from me so they could come to the party and spend time with my brothers."

Jenna looked outraged. "That's terrible!"

"Yeah. It got to where I dreaded my birthday. So finally I told my parents that I'd rather skip my half of the party and have a small family celebration instead."

"You could have told them the truth," Jenna said. "Asked for your own party."

Tito shook his head. "It would have been a pretty humiliating thing to admit. Besides, I still wouldn't have known if people were coming because they liked me, or because they liked my brothers. No, it was easier to bow out of the whole thing, and tell my parents I didn't like parties."

He set down the gleaming pint glass and picked up another.

"That's really sad," said Jenna.

"It's all right. It was just the way things were. And it really was a huge relief not to have to share a birthday party with Eddie anymore."

He darted a quick glance at her. "I've never told anyone that before."

"Thank you for telling me," she said.

After another awkward pause, she said, "So what time is the Fourth of July party?"

"All day, but it's come and go. It's cooler

earlier in the day, but if you want to see the fireworks, you have to stay late."

"I don't mind the heat," said Jenna. "And I do like fireworks."

"Okay. Maybe arrive around four o'clock, then? There should still be plenty of food left at that point."

"Sounds good."

"All right," said Tito. "Should I pick you up?"

He tried to sound casual, as if it didn't matter, but it did. If she said she'd meet him there, then this wasn't a real date. If she said yes, then…well…maybe.

Jenna seemed to think it was a weighty question as well. She considered a moment, then said, "Sure. That would be great."

A fresh wave of elation washed over him, leaving him weak at the knees.

"Good," said Tito. "Great."

He opened the mini fridge and took out some fresh lemon wedges. He could feel Jenna watching him.

Then she said, "Hey, can I ask you a question?"

That sounded serious.

"All right," Tito said.

She looked gravely at him. "What does *huerco* mean?"

This was so unexpected that he laughed. "Oh! Well…there's not really a direct English translation. The way my father uses it, it means something like kid or brat, with an undertone of someone who's sad or dejected."

Jenna nodded. "I see. What about that other Spanish word he calls you—you know, the one with all the syllables? It's like rolo or rogo-something."

"Rigoberto?"

"That's it! Rigoberto. What does that mean?"

He laughed again. "That's my name! Rigoberto Mendoza."

Her eyes widened. "That's your *name*? You never told me that."

She sounded so indignant about it. "Uh, I'm sorry?" he said.

"You should be. When your given name is Rigoberto, that's the sort of thing you ought to tell people right from the start."

She was a fine one to talk. She had legally changed her own name, and he still didn't know what her original name had been. But that wasn't something he could tease her about, so he said only, "Well, now you know."

"So where does Tito come from?" she asked. "Is it your middle name?"

"No, no. My middle name is Luis. Tito is a diminutive for Rigoberto."

"How do you get Tito out of Rigoberto? That doesn't make any sense."

"It makes as much sense as Bobby being a nickname for Robert, or Billy for William."

"Good point. So I guess you were named after your uncle?"

"Not exactly. My uncle's name was Alberto. Tito is a diminutive of that, too."

"Really? That's wild."

"I know, right? Tito is actually a diminutive for a lot of different names—Humberto, Roberto, Norberto, Ernesto—basically anything that ends in '-to.'"

Before he knew it, they were deeply involved in a whole discussion of Spanish diminutives and naming conventions. Even more remarkably, Jenna seemed truly interested. Ordinarily Tito had to be careful when talking about some esoteric subject, and cut himself off before boring his listeners to the eye-glazing stage. But Jenna was as voracious for knowledge as he was. It was something he'd noticed about her early in their acquaintance. She just liked knowing things, whether or not she had an immediate use for them. He loved that about her.

By the time Sam showed up for his shift and Jenna went back to Lalo's, Tito's mind was a hopeless agitation of pleasure and suspense, and he still didn't know if the two of them had a date.

## *CHAPTER NINE*

JENNA TOOK AN anxious look in the mirror and cautiously admitted to herself that she was more than usually satisfied with her reflection. Her hair was gathered into an asymmetrical French braid that started at the left, slanted across the back and ended in a thick braid trailing over her right shoulder. Different shades of blonde wove in and out of the braid, from deep gold to streaks of an almost flaxen color. The style was a definite step up from her usual hair clip twist. She'd even put on some makeup—not just her usual quick coat of mascara, but a touch of lip color as well. In keeping with the Fourth of July, she was wearing a red top, blue cut-offs and white Keds. Casual, but pretty. That was the look she was going for. It wasn't as if this was an actual date, after all.

Halley stood behind her, shaping some loose wisps into open curls that framed

Jenna's face. Jenna could see her intent expression in the mirror.

"You look great," Halley said. "Tito will be blown away."

Jenna opened her mouth to retort that she wasn't trying to blow Tito away, then shut it, because she wasn't sure it was the truth.

"Thanks," she said instead. "You're a genius with hair."

"I know it," Halley said complacently. "I got in a lot of practice. My mom used to French braid my hair, and she showed me how on that Barbie hairstyling head toy that I used to have when I was little. I learned to do all sorts of hairstyles on that thing."

"I remember," said Jenna.

It was unusual for Halley to voluntarily talk about her mother, or anything from further back than a year and a half in the past. When she did, it was from a certain emotional distance, like a much older person reminiscing about a long-ago childhood. But Halley was a child still. It hadn't been that many years since she'd played with the Barbie hairstyling head, or her sparkly plastic ponies, or her treasured stuffed animals.

Jenna waited to see if Halley would go on

reminiscing, but she didn't, and Jenna knew better than to push her.

She picked up a bottle of rose-scented lotion and squirted some into her palm. "There is one thing I wanted to mention before we go," she said. "All our usual rules about identity security still apply. So don't be talking about where we came from or what our names used to be."

She could feel Halley staring at her in the dressing table mirror but kept her own gaze fixed on her hands as she rubbed the lotion into them.

"Of course I won't talk about that," said Halley. "When have I ever?"

"No, I know. But it is a party. There'll be a lot of friendly, curious people there. I just don't want you to get too relaxed and let your guard down."

Long pause. "Why would you even say that? Have you let *your* guard down?"

Jenna squirmed. She was not prepared to tell Halley about her panic attack on the second day of horse camp and the revelations she'd made to Tito in his car. "Not exactly. But Tito is pretty observant. I think he'd be quick to pick up on any inconsistencies."

"So Tito doesn't know?" Halley asked.

"He knows we came to Texas to get away from someone, but he doesn't know the details."

"Well, maybe you should tell him."

Jenna met Halley's gaze in the mirror. "I can't do that."

"Why not?"

"Because the whole point of a secret identity is that it's secret. I worked hard to make a fresh start for us. I can't just throw it all away and blab everything to the first attractive man who comes along."

"Tito isn't the first attractive man to come along. He's Tito."

She said it as if the thing were self-evident, with no further explanation needed. Tito was Tito. His trustworthiness was inherent.

Jenna looked down at the dressing table and started setting bottles and jars in order. "I know. Maybe one day we can tell him, but not yet."

"Okay," said Halley. "So what time will he actually get here? I know he said four, but does that mean he's picking us up at four, or picking us up in time to reach the party at four?"

"I don't know," said Jenna. "We weren't that formal about it. I mean, it's not like this is a *date*. His dad was the one who actually invited me to the party. Tito just volunteered to drive us."

She saw Halley's tolerant little smile in the mirror. Then Halley said with conviction, "He'll be here at ten 'til."

Jenna glanced at the crystal clock on the dressing table. It was already a quarter 'til. A flutter of anticipation rippled through her stomach.

There was nothing left to do but wait. Halley settled herself onto the armchair in the corner of Jenna's room with a book. Jenna stayed at the dressing table, playing with a stack of gold bangles Kara had given her for a teenage birthday, admiring the way the sunlight from the window played on their light, graceful shapes. It had been a long time since she'd worn them. She worked with her hands; she couldn't afford to have thin metal bands clanging around her wrists.

The soft rumble of an engine sounded from the street, and a flash of metallic red passed outside Jenna's bedroom window and pulled into the driveway. The crystal clock read 3:50 on the dot.

She whirled around on the small upholstered bench, dropping the bangles to the floor.

For the past three days she'd been telling herself not to get excited, that she and Tito were simply two friends going to a party together. But now that he was here, her body was betraying her with pounding heart, shallow breathing, shaking hands and weak knees—all of which felt an awful lot like panic. She wanted to run away, and at the same time she couldn't wait to open the door.

She knelt to pick up the bangles. She could feel Halley watching her from her corner.

"Do you want to let him in, or should I do it while you take a minute to calm down?" Halley asked.

Jenna set the bangles back on the dressing table. "I can answer the door," she said huffily.

She forced herself to walk slowly and calmly down the short hallway.

And there he was, Tito Mendoza, on her actual doorstep, in khaki shorts and a button-down shirt in a deep indigo blue that suited him perfectly. The sleeves were rolled up to just above the elbows, carefully casual, but precise. There seemed to be an extra gloss about him today. His dark hair shone like polished wood, and his eyes were brighter than usual. He looked familiar and strange and unbearably handsome.

His eyes did a quick appreciative sweep of her outfit and returned to her face. He gave her an eager smile and said, "Hey."

"Hey," she said.

A painful silence fell. Jenna rushed to fill it. "You look different," she said. "I've never seen you wearing a color before."

"You look different too," he said. "I've never seen your legs."

His smile went a little stiff. "I mean—because you usually wear pants," he said.

"Right," she said. "Yes, that's true. I do."

Wow. They were off to a great start. Was this really the good friend she'd talked with for hours on end on every subject under the sun? She felt her cheeks warming up. Great—now she was blushing.

"Um—come in," she said. "I've just got

to get something out of the fridge and we'll be ready to go."

As he came inside, she caught a whiff of scent—something woody, with notes of leather and bergamot. Tito was wearing cologne. She couldn't remember him ever doing that before.

"You didn't have to bring food," he said.

"I know, but we wanted to. Anyway, Halley's the one who made it."

He waited in the living room. When she came back with the cream cheese tart in her arms, she saw him standing at the back window, crouching a little, just as she had after she'd learned that her roof was visible from Tito's apartment.

"Can you see Bunter?" she asked.

He straightened and chuckled. "Not quite. That tree hides the second-story window. But I can see the building."

He raised his eyebrows at the sight of the stars and stripes tart, with its rows of halved strawberries making the stripes, and blueberries forming the field of blue in the corner, and bits of the cream cheese showing in between like stars.

"Wow," he said. "Halley made this?"

"She did," said Jenna.

Halley hadn't put in an appearance yet. Probably wanted to give Jenna and Tito some time alone. Jenna hoped she wasn't going to be too obvious about expecting the two of them to get together.

"Halley, come on!" she called. "It's time to go."

Halley walked into the living room, wearing a pasted-on smile, and said hi to Tito.

"Hello," he said. "I didn't know you were a pastry chef. Your dessert looks really good."

"Thanks," said Halley.

There was no trace of the usual friendly ease between the three of them. It felt as if they were all meeting for the first time.

"Well, let's go," said Jenna, trying to sound natural and relaxed.

The Eldorado was a coupe. Tito went around to the passenger side, opened the door and tilted the front seat forward. Halley settled into the back seat with the tart, and Tito pushed the seat back in place for Jenna.

This was the second time he'd driven her. He didn't know, had no way of knowing, how significant that was. In the years since her breakup with Chase, when she'd called her dad to pick her up from that Dairy Queen, she'd allowed another person to drive her exactly twice, and both times, that person had been Tito.

And she felt okay about it. Better than okay. She felt great. Even the new awkwardness between them was exciting, because it meant that despite her efforts to the contrary, they were more than friends.

It was a beautiful summer day in the Texas Hill Country. The lots in this older, established neighborhood all had mature trees, mostly oaks and elms and pecans, big enough to shade the lawns and create a lush, leafy canopy over the streets. Several houses were displaying flags, Texan and American, and there was plenty of red, white and blue bunting to be seen.

Jenna and Tito filled the short drive with stilted small talk, taking turns offering remarks about decorations and the weather, until Tito turned into a gravel driveway and said, "This is it."

The place was not what Jenna had expected. For starters, she'd imagined it a lot bigger. She'd figured that people who entertained as often as the Mendozas did must have plenty of space to do it in. Besides, hadn't she heard Juan saying that he'd rented an old horse trailer on the property to Roque Fidalgo, and let him pasture his horse there? This lot looked to be about half an acre—larger than in most modern subdivisions, but hardly big enough to pasture a horse. And she didn't see any horse trailer, just a hodgepodge of outbuildings and a house decidedly on the small side for a family as big as Tito's. A big covered workshop area sheltered Juan's earthmoving equipment, along with a flatbed trailer, a riding lawn mower and several vintage cars in various states of restoration.

The party was in full swing, with guests eating and drinking, laughing and talking. Music was playing from a speaker somewhere, loud enough to hear and enjoy without drowning out conversation. Jenna saw lots of people she recognized—Luke and Eliana, Susana and Roque, Coby Kowalski—and lots more who were strangers. A big tent stood proudly open, showing tables of food and beer kegs within. Tony Reyes, a regular at the restaurant and bar, was wearing a Texas flag apron and manning a grill. Small children played in the grass, and some older kids had a game of cornhole going on.

Tito parked in a shady spot under a pecan tree. “Welcome to Casa Mendoza,” he said.

As they were getting out of the car, Jenna saw one of Tito’s brothers watching them. It was Eddie, supposedly “the handsome one” of the Mendoza brothers, and the one with whom Tito used to have to share his birthday parties when they were kids. Jenna supposed he was pretty good-looking in a flashy, pretty boy sort of way, but his smile was a little too toothy for her. She’d seen him before at the restaurant and the bar, but hadn’t interacted with him beyond bringing him his food.

Tito’s mother came to greet them. Jenna had seen her at Lalo’s Kitchen as well. Rose was a pretty, vivacious woman, always on the go. Today she was wearing a sundress with stars on a blue field for the bodice and a red-and-white-striped skirt.

“Hi, baby!” she said, kissing Tito on the cheek.

Then she turned to Jenna and Halley. “Hello! So glad you two could make it.”

She certainly looked glad. There was an

unmistakably hopeful sparkle in her eyes as she glanced between Jenna and her son.

"We're happy to be here," said Jenna as Halley handed her the stars-and-stripes tart and scrambled out of the back seat.

Rose came near to see the tart. "Ooh, how beautiful! I haven't set the desserts out yet. I didn't want them to melt in the heat. Let's take this inside and put it in the fridge."

The house looked as small on the inside as it had on the outside, but comfortable and inviting, with cheerful cushions on the overstuffed sofa and chairs, and bright, colorful prints on the walls. Rose led the way to the tiny kitchen, where desserts covered every available inch of counter space. She opened the fridge door, and Jenna carefully balanced the tart on top of a banana pudding.

Halley had halted in the living room to check out the bookcase. She was standing with her head tilted to the side, reading the titles on the spines.

"They have *The Lord of the Rings*," she told Jenna.

Rose smiled. "Do you like *The Lord of the Rings*?" she asked Halley.

"I love it," said Halley. "It's the ultimate."

"I agree," said Rose. "I reread it about once a year. I first read *The Hobbit* to my boys when Tito was three, and the trilogy after that."

"Wow, that's pretty young," said Jenna.

Rose beamed with pride. "Yes. I wasn't sure if he'd be able to follow, but he did fine. Every evening, right after he got ready for bed, he'd climb onto the sofa and sit there waiting for me, all clean and cozy in his PJs."

Jenna darted a quick glance at Tito. He looked a little sheepish, but he was smiling.

"It was easy to follow the story with you as the reader," he told his mother. "You had a different voice for every character. I could just see it all in my mind."

The bookcase stood next to a hallway, which was crammed with family portraits. Jenna saw one of a young Juan in chaps, boots and a cowboy hat, grinning and holding up a prize belt buckle from a rodeo, right next to one of him in a Marine dress uniform, somber-faced and rigid.

"Quite a contrast," said Jenna, pointing.

Rose saw the direction of Jenna's gaze and chuckled. "Yes. Juan was always an adventurer. He rode bulls for years when the boys were small. He was pretty good, too. But then he got hurt—not too bad, but enough for me to put my foot down. So he quit riding bulls…and joined the Marines just in time to be sent to Iraq for Desert Storm, which wasn't exactly what I'd had in mind. But he made it back in one piece, and after a while he started his earthmoving business."

Jenna moved slowly down the hallway, eyes roving over the wealth of pictures, tracing resemblances. The older boys all had their father's powerful build, but Tito was made on a smaller scale. Lots of sports shots of them, band and choir pics of him.

He followed her, keeping a couple of paces behind. "I may have gone through a bit of an awkward phase," he said. "One that lasted five to ten years."

"Oh, I don't know," she said. "This one of you in your band shirt posing with the oboe is pretty lit."

He winced. "Ugh, that goofy grin," he said.

Jenna pointed to a photo of a young Tito standing beside his uncle at the bar. "You're not grinning in this one," she said. "You and your uncle have the exact same stony-faced expression. You can really see the resemblance here."

He drew near, leaning in to see, and Jenna caught another whiff of cologne. "Yeah, you can. I remember that day. I was helping him with the deep cleaning at the bar. Mom took that picture when she came to pick me up afterward."

The image quality wasn't great, but there was something about the picture that appealed to Jenna. The unsmiling faces gave it an old-timey vibe. She wondered how the picture would look in black-and-white.

The hallway gallery ended at an open doorway that showed a small bedroom.

"That was my room growing up," Tito said. "I shared with Eddie and Javi."

It must have been a tight fit. Jenna thought of her own childhood bedroom, with its canopy bed and dollhouse and frilly linens, and Kara's similarly girlish room across the hall. She felt a new respect for Tito's parents, raising five boys in a small space, and practicing hospitality as a matter of course.

Halley joined them in the hallway.

"Have you finished scanning the bookshelves?" Jenna asked her with a smile.

"Yes. Can I go find Gillian? I saw her as we were driving in."

"Okay," said Jenna. "Just remember…"

"I know," said Halley. "I will."

They all went outside. Halley headed toward the cornhole game and Rose went to greet some new arrivals.

"Are you hungry?" Tito asked Jenna. "There's plenty to eat—sausage, brisket, ribs, fajitas, burgers, hot dogs, chili. There might even be something resembling vegetable dishes in the tent."

"I'm not really hungry yet," said Jenna. "I want to look around."

"Can I get you a beer, then? I need to go check the kegs anyway."

"Sure. I'll take a 9-Pin Kolsch, if you have it."

"I do. I'll be back in a minute."

Jenna watched him walk away, slender but sturdy, with an air of contained strength in his step and in the set of his head.

He disappeared into the tent, and she turned her attention to the crowd. So many people milling about or standing in groups, talking, eating, drinking, laughing. Ordinarily the presence of such a mass of humanity would have made her nervous, but today it made her feel strangely lonesome. This really was a tight community. She thought of school friends from back home, people she'd assumed she'd be close to forever, and had now lost track of completely. Just as well, since every one of them knew what an idiot she'd been over Chase.

Someone laid a tentative hand on her arm. "Hi! You're Jenna, right?"

It was Annalisa, holding a soft drink in a red, white and blue coozie, and smiling her wistful smile. She wore a white sundress and had her hair piled high in a neat bun.

"I'm Annalisa Cavazos," she said. "It seems strange that we've never really met when I've seen you so many times, but Tito's told me so much about you that I feel as if I already know you."

"He's told me about you, too," said Jenna. "Great party, huh?"

"Oh, yes. The Mendozas are always throwing parties. I've lost count of how many birthdays and holidays I've celebrated with them."

"You've known them a long time?"

"All my life."

There was the wistful smile again. Jenna wondered just how long Annalisa had been in love with Tito's brother Javi.

"Didn't I hear something about Roque Fidalgo living here in an old horse trailer or something, and pasturing his horse here?" she asked.

"Oh, no," said Annalisa. "That wasn't here. That was on The Property."

Jenna could hear the capital letters in the way Annalisa pronounced the words.

"Oh," she said. "So where is The Property?"

"That's a long story," said Annalisa. "Maybe we should sit down."

They found a couple of chairs and settled in.

"The Property is on Highway 281, on the edge of town," Annalisa said. "It's in sort of a middle ground between the residential area and the farms and ranches. Most of the lots in that area are one to ten acres. The Property is a one-acre lot. It's got a big metal barn on it and an old slab foundation for a house that was never built."

"Oh, I know that place," said Jenna. "I've

driven by it lots of times. I had no idea it belonged to Tito's family."

"Yes, they've owned it for about twenty-five years. It's all that's left of an old ranch that was here before Limestone Springs was a town. The original owners sold off most of the land over the course of several decades, and the Mendozas bought the last of it. The plan was to build a nice big house with four bedrooms. The younger boys would still have to share, but Johnny, the oldest, would have his own room, and after he left home Enrique would get Johnny's old room, and Eddie would have his and Enrique's old room to himself, and once Eddie left home there'd be just Javi and Tito left, and bedrooms to spare. The boys were all pretty pumped about it. I remember seeing the blueprints of the house spread out on the kitchen table. It would have been nice, really nice."

"So what happened?"

Annalisa took a sip of her drink. "Well, at the time when Mr. Mendoza bought the property and started the house, he was planning to go into business with a friend of his."

"What kind of business?"

"Classic cars. Buying, selling, restoring, servicing."

"That sounds like a perfect fit for Mr. Mendoza," said Jenna. "Didn't he do all the work on Tito's Eldorado?"

"Yes," said Annalisa. "But he couldn't have chosen a worse business partner. Have you ever had any dealings with Carlos Reyes, or heard of him?"

"I don't think so. I know Alex and Tony Reyes from the restaurant and the bar."

"Carlos is their father. He's basically a very charming, very handsome con man. Half the people in town have been burned by him in one way or another. Mr. Mendoza fronted most of the money for the business, and of course he was the one who actually knew about classic cars. Carlos was supposed to be the front man and handle the business end of things. But before they even got started, Carlos cleaned out the business account and left Mr. Mendoza with nothing."

"Oh," said Jenna. "That's awful."

"Yeah. The family never really recovered financially, although they've done well enough in the years since. And they never gave up hope on The Property. Always said they'd finish the house one day just like they'd planned. But between one thing and another, it's never happened."

Jenna thought of friendly, boisterous Mr. Mendoza, with his loud laugh and constant jokes, and Mrs. Mendoza, always cheerful and busy. There was no hint of bitterness in either of them. She never would have guessed they'd suffered such a brutal disappointment.

She and Annalisa chatted awhile longer. She learned that Annalisa was at work on a book about the history of Seguin County, and that she'd already written another book some years earlier about ghost stories of the Texas Hill Country.

"I had no idea you were an author," said Jenna.

Annalisa smiled. "It's not as cool as it sounds. The publisher is a small press, and the books haven't had a wide distribution at all. But I love writing about this area and its history, and sharing that with people."

Tito came back with a 9-Pin Kolsch for Jenna and a Bock-N Röhl for himself. He drew up a chair and joined the conversation. He and Annalisa did most of the talking, reminiscing about people Jenna didn't know and events that she didn't remember. It was restful, listening to them, as the party playlist switched between Tejano music, old country, new country and classic rock. More and more, she loved this community where she'd chosen to make her home. She wanted to be a part of it, the way Tito and Annalisa were.

It had been a long time since she'd had a female friend to confide in. She missed that.

She finished her beer and got to her feet.

"I think it's about time I rode that bull," she said. "Where is it, anyway?"

"In the workshop," said Tito. "I'll take you there."

Annalisa said she was going to get something to eat, so Tito and Jenna went alone.

The mechanical bull looked something like half a barrel on a pole, covered with brown-and-white-spotted cowhide, with a horned head at one end and a rope tail at the other. Inflatable cushions covered the surrounding floor. Tito's brother Eddie was just tumbling off the back end of the bull when Jenna and Tito came in.

Mr. Mendoza sat at a control console. When he saw Jenna, his face lit up.

"Well, look who finally showed up to ride Brush Hog!" he said in his big booming voice. "Took you long enough. I thought you'd chickened out."

"Not a chance," said Jenna. "I'm not scared."

"All right, then! That's what I like to hear. You ready to go?"

"Not yet. I'm just going to observe for a few minutes."

He winked at her. "Smart girl."

Several men took turns on the bull, some of whom Jenna knew from Tito's Bar and Lalo's Kitchen. Tony Reyes was really good, and so was his brother-in-law, Marcos Ramirez. Now that Jenna knew about Tony's father cheating Mr. Mendoza of his money, it seemed strange for Tony to be here, but Mr. Mendoza didn't seem to hold the sins of the father against the son.

A teenage Mendoza grandson, one of Johnny's boys, did pretty well on the bull, too.

"We'll make a rodeo man of you yet," Juan said to the boy, ruffling his hair.

Then he turned to Jenna. "You ready yet?"

"Ready as I'll ever be," she said.

"Good! Someone show her what to do."

Eddie stepped forward right away, his toothy smile as bright as ever. The man was like a toothpaste ad.

"Are you right-handed or left-handed?" he asked.

"Right," said Jenna.

"Okay. Grab the strap with your left hand—underhanded, like this." He demonstrated with his own left hand, taking the opportunity to flex his biceps. "Then swing yourself onto the back. You'll want to use your right arm for balance. Use your thighs to grip the bull, but stay loose in your hips and spine. Just let the movement flow through you."

"Got it," said Jenna.

She gripped the strap and climbed on, then glanced at Tito. He still had his beer in his hand, and he was smiling. She grinned at him, lifted her arm and nodded at Juan.

The bull pitched forward with a jerk. Jenna leaned back, keeping her seat. Back and forth it went, up and down, while also rotating from side to side. It was a lot to keep track of, and impossible to predict. Better to not overthink it, and just take all the shifts and pitches and turns as they came.

She was in a groove now, and it felt great. Up and down, back and forth, all around. The bull sped up, and she stayed on. The room whirled around her in a kaleidoscope of floor and ceiling and walls. She couldn't see faces, but she caught an occasional glimpse of Tito's indigo shirt.

When she finally came off, she fell forward, rolling onto her back. The workshop's ceiling, really just the underside of a metal roof, spun overhead.

"Eight seconds!" said Juan.

A face appeared above her. She couldn't make out the features, but the flash of white teeth couldn't be mistaken.

"Are you all right?" Eddie asked.

"I'm fine," Jenna said.

He took her by the hand and helped her up. A wave of applause broke out. She let go of Eddie's hand and raised her arms high. The applause got louder.

She made her way back to Tito, her head still spinning, and stumbled on her last step. He took her arm, holding her steady.

"That was fantastic," he said. "You were smiling the whole time."

"It was fun," she said.

He was still holding her arm, his face glowing with pride and something else. It would be so easy to slide her hand into his right now.

"Rigoberto!" called Juan's voice. "Your turn. Come on, *huerco*. You're not getting out of this any longer. Get on that bull and let's see what you're made of."

Tito's smile went a bit stiff, but he handed his beer to Jenna and said, "Okay."

A chorus of *oohs* made it plain that no one had expected him to go through with it. Jenna watched him walk over to Brush Hog and get on. She felt an anxiety for him that she hadn't felt for herself. She wanted him to do well.

He gripped the strap with his left hand and swung onto the back, positioning himself as far forward as possible, with his feet in front. Without taking his eyes off the bull's head, he raised his right arm and nodded.

The bull started, slowly at first. Jenna watched as Tito seesawed with its movements, leaning back when the bull pitched forward, and leaning forward when the bull went back. So far, so good.

The bull sped up. Tito stayed on. Jenna couldn't see his face. His arm was almost whipping through the air now as the bull changed direction.

When he finally came off, he slid off the back and rolled onto his side. From his seat at the console, his father roared, "Fifteen seconds! Fifteen seconds!"

Jenna realized she'd been holding her breath. She let it out now. Tony and Marcos were looking at each other with raised eyebrows, clearly surprised and impressed.

Juan left his console, walked over to his son and hefted him to his feet, then gave him a big hug with several whacks on the back.

"Fifteen seconds!" he said again. "I can't believe this! That's better than any of your brothers ever did. You been holding out on me, Rigoberto! All these years, I never knew you had it in you!"

"You ought to go on the circuit!" called Tony.

Tito just grinned. He walked slowly back to Jenna, keeping his feet under him all the way.

"Nice job," Jenna said. "Looks like you're a natural."

He took his beer back. "Must be all that disco dancing," he said.

By sundown, Jenna had sampled more meat dishes and met more people than she could possibly hope to remember. She checked in on Halley every few minutes or so and always found her with Gillian, looking happier and more animated than Jenna had seen her in years. Sometimes there was a Mendoza grandson or two hanging around.

At twilight, the whole crowd gathered to hear Alex Reyes, Tony's brother, read the Declaration of Independence—not just the Preamble, but the whole thing.

Alex was a historical reenactor; Jenna had often seen him at the restaurant in one of his old-fashioned outfits, on his way to or from an event. Usually he was dressed as a freedom fighter from the Texas Revolution, but today he had on eighteenth-century garb. He read well, in a clear, carrying voice. His wife, Lauren, hugely pregnant, listened with a smile, holding Peri, their three-year-old daughter, by the hand.

Jenna felt stirred with pride and gratitude by the beautiful and powerful words. Those brave men and women, daring to break free from a bully, and to start a new kind of life in a new home, and to make a better future for themselves and their children—she identified more strongly with them than she ever had before. No one could show them the way, because no one had ever done it before. They had to blaze their own trail. But they weren't alone. They had allies. They had each other.

She darted a quick glance at Tito. The sight of his stern, solemn profile sent a jolt through her heart, half pleasure, half pain.

"… And for the support of this Declaration," Alex said, "with a firm reliance on the protection of divine Providence, we mutually pledge to each other our Lives, our Fortunes and our sacred Honor."

The silence that followed seemed to have weight and substance. Then someone started singing the national anthem, and the rest joined in.

With its octave-and-a-half vocal range, "The Star-Spangled Banner" was a difficult song to sing well. But Jenna and Tito hit every note.

At the end of the song, people started cheering, and firecrackers went off.

Tito turned to Jenna with a smile. “We’re good together, aren’t we?” he asked.

She didn’t know if he meant their voices, or something else. But she answered, “Yes. Yes, we are.”

## *CHAPTER TEN*

It was nearly dark now, and Mr. Mendoza was busy setting up what looked like a huge fireworks display, with rockets supported on bricks, and enough space between the different types of fireworks for him to be able to move quickly from one to another. Tito left to check the kegs again, and Jenna went into the tent to get some dessert.

The tent was lavishly decorated with red, white and blue streamers, and rosettes made from ribbons, crepe paper and old newspapers whose edges had been cut with pinking shears. The dessert table held a proud display of trifles, cakes, cookies and pies, mostly with some sort of red, white and blue thing going. Halley's stars-and-stripes tart had already been cut into, and several pieces were missing.

Jenna had just picked up a dessert plate

when a man stepped in front of her, and she saw a familiar toothpaste-ad smile.

He pointed both index fingers at her. “It’s Jenna, right?”

“That’s right,” she said. “And you’re Eddie.”

He held his hands up. “Guilty as charged.”

Jenna started filling her plate with cookies. She wasn’t particularly eager to prolong the conversation. Ever since learning about the joint birthday parties of his and Tito’s childhoods, she’d felt vaguely hostile toward Eddie, though the two of them had never interacted much. The handsome one, indeed. Didn’t people have eyes? He was all muscle and teeth. Tito was *much* better looking.

Eddie didn’t take the hint. “Have we met before today?” he asked. “You look very familiar to me.”

“I work at Lalo’s Kitchen,” she said.

He snapped his fingers. “That’s right! I knew I recognized you from somewhere.”

Jenna resisted an urge to roll her eyes. She’d served Eddie his burgers and fries probably a dozen times, but apparently, he’d never really noticed her until today, when she’d put extra effort into her appearance.

"Hey, good job on Brush Hog today," he said. "I was impressed."

The way he said it clearly communicated that for him to be impressed was a huge deal and that Jenna should be deeply flattered.

"Thanks," she said, keeping her tone courteous but cool. "But Tito's time was better than mine."

"Ha ha! Yeah, how about that? Beginner's luck, I guess."

She didn't answer. Tito's success was beginner's luck, but Jenna's was deserving of praise from the great Eddie Mendoza? Please.

A silence passed. Eddie seemed to be waiting for Jenna to fill it, but she didn't. She took a bite of cookie instead.

He gave her a thorough once-over, head to toe, and said, "I'll bet you're a dancer. That's why you did so well on the bull."

"Nope," said Jenna through her mouthful of cookie.

"Are you sure?"

"Pretty sure."

"Well, you look like a dancer. You're so graceful and slim."

This whole flirtatious undertone was…

not creepy exactly, but definitely inappropriate to use with a woman who'd come to a party with his brother. Maybe he couldn't help himself. Maybe this was just his default mode with women.

"Let's put it to the test," said Eddie. "We'll go out dancing together, this Saturday, you and me."

Jenna swallowed her bite of cookie. Had he really just asked her out? Was he really this obtuse?

"I don't think that would be a good idea," she said.

"Oh yeah?" he said playfully. "Why not?"

She stared at him a moment.

"You do realize I came here with your brother," she said.

His flirtatious grin morphed into a confused grin. "Who, Tito?"

Now she was *really* angry. "Yes, Tito," she said. "You remember him. Bearded guy. Runs a bar."

"Well, yeah, but—I mean, he just gave you a ride, right? It's not like the two of you are actually in a relationship or anything."

"How do you know? Did you ask him?"

The grin was rapidly melting away now. "Um, no."

"So you made a move on your brother's date, and you didn't even bother to verify first whether they were together?"

Eddie squirmed. "Well, I mean, that's just Tito. He has a lot of women friends, but they're just friends. It doesn't actually *mean* anything."

"Oh, it means something," said Jenna. "It means he's a sensitive, intelligent, compassionate man. He's protective and caring and funny. And I don't know how this has escaped your notice, but he's also extremely handsome. Why is it so out of the question that a woman could find him attractive?"

Eddie's smile was gone now. He raised his hands again, this time in a gesture of surrender, and started backing away. "Okay, okay! Sorry."

Jenna took a deep breath and let it out. Her heart was pounding, and her face felt hot. She had gone into full-on fight-or-flight mode, and now that it was over, the energy was draining from her body, leaving her knees weak.

Had she been overly harsh with Eddie? Maybe. But the guy radiated ego and wouldn't take no for an answer, and it made her mad to hear him underestimate his brother. The words had come spilling out beyond her control. It had felt good to say them. But now that they were out, she couldn't take them back.

THE BEER KEGS were fine, as Tito had figured they would be. He'd been intentionally giving Jenna her space today, fighting his instinct to cling to her like bindweed to a fence post. It was good to see her and Halley relaxing and interacting with people. He hadn't forgotten how tense Jenna had looked at that barn raising at Susana Vrba's place a few months back. If she could relax now in her new community, maybe she could start to put down roots.

He felt as if a weight had been lifted off his shoulders, one that he hadn't known he'd been carrying. His father had been after him for years to ride that mechanical bull, and now he'd done it. And the funny thing was, when he'd finally climbed on, it hadn't been to prove anything. It certainly hadn't been to impress Jenna. He hadn't expected to last more than a few seconds.

But he'd seen the way Jenna had gotten

onto the bull herself, how fearless she'd been, and suddenly he'd been fearless too. He had sung disco in front of this woman, and she still seemed to like him. He didn't have to stand on his dignity all the time. He could be himself. He could fall off the bull and it would be okay.

Only he hadn't fallen—at least, not until fifteen seconds in, a more than respectable time.

Maybe there were other chances he could take that would turn into triumphs.

He was just beginning to wonder whether enough time had passed for him to find Jenna again without seeming clingy, when Eddie walked up to him, with an expression on his face that Tito had never seen before.

Tito's first thought was that something terrible had happened. Had someone at the party gotten sick or hurt? Or had Javi had an accident out in the oil fields of West Texas? It had to be something bad for Eddie to look like that.

"What is it?" Tito asked. "What's wrong?"

"I, uh," said Eddie. He cleared his throat and went on, "I want to apologize. I had no idea you and Jenna were together. I never would have imagined—but that's no excuse. I should have verified."

Tito stared. He didn't know what to think, what to say, or what Eddie was talking about. His brother was apologizing to him, and looking thoroughly chastened. It was something that had never happened before.

"Anyway," said Eddie, "I'm sorry."

And he walked away.

Tito stood there a moment, then headed to the dessert table to find Jenna.

She was already coming out of the tent, moving so fast that they almost ran into each other. Her face was flushed, and she looked flustered.

"Hey," said Tito. "I just had a confusing conversation with my brother Eddie."

"Yeah," said Jenna, drawing the word out. "He, um, he asked me out."

"Oh," Tito replied. "And you said…?"

Her eyes flashed. "I said no!"

"Wow," Tito said. "I don't think he's ever been turned down before."

"Yeah, I got the impression it was a first for him. He had a lot of nerve, coming on to me when I'm clearly here with you."

She looked down at the ground. Her voice

was shaking. It matched the shaking inside his own chest.

Tito wished he could watch a replay of the whole episode and hear exactly what Jenna had said to his brother. Had she really told him that she and Tito were…well, together? Eddie seemed to think she had. Was it possible that she'd said it just to get rid of Eddie? No. That wasn't her way. She wouldn't make up a fake boyfriend to get a guy to leave her alone. She had absolutely no problem telling a man to his face that she wasn't interested.

He steeled himself. "Look, Jenna, you have to know by now that I think you're pretty fantastic. And sometimes…sometimes I think maybe there could be something between us. But then I think maybe I'm just fooling myself, seeing what I want to see. Or maybe you do like me but you don't want to act on it because of the whole thing with Chase. And I can't take the uncertainty anymore. So just tell me."

The silence felt unbearably long, though in reality it was probably only a few seconds. Slowly her gaze returned to his.

Then, unbelievably, her hand reached for his.

It was a slight touch, their fingertips

barely brushing, but it sent a shock through his entire body.

"Tito," she said, "you're the smartest man I know, and the kindest. You make me laugh and you make me think. I love being with you. I can't take my eyes off you. And I'd very much like you to kiss me right now."

He felt as if he were falling—or was it soaring? But at the same time, he knew he had both feet firmly on the ground. This wasn't a fragile girl, weepy over a breakup with some guy she wasn't over, and looking for something to make her feel better in the short term. This was Jenna, who knew who she was and said what she meant. And she'd just said that she wanted him to kiss her.

He laced his fingers through hers and felt her clasp tighten against his. Then he took a step closer and lowered his lips to hers.

EVERY SENSATION STOOD out in exquisite clarity. The roughness of Tito's beard against Jenna's chin. The whisper-touch of that straight fall of dark hair, brushing against her forehead. She laid a hand against his chest and felt his heart beating fast and strong through his shirt.

Then, at the exact same moment, moved by the same impulse, they put their arms around each other. He was holding her tight now. She could feel how much he wanted this, and it was all mixed up with her own want. She'd been fighting this feeling for so long, and now she'd finally given in, and it was glorious.

Lights burst in brilliant, colorful patterns from beyond her closed eyelids. She heard popping sounds and muted booms and cheers. Part of her was still aware that they were at a party, and making a very public display of affection, but the fireworks and celebratory voices all felt like part of their kiss.

Their lips parted. She opened her eyes and saw Tito's face, so bright with joy that she thought her own heart might burst.

She rested her head against his shoulder and watched the fireworks light the sky.

## *CHAPTER ELEVEN*

FOR THE REST of the evening they stayed close to each other, holding hands, and occasionally stealing behind buildings or shrubs to kiss. Tito felt like a teenager, except that his own teenage years were never this good. People kept smiling at them—Annalisa, Luke, Eliana. Tony Reyes gave him a huge grin and clapped him hard on the shoulder. Rose looked as if she was about to cry with joy, and Juan gave him a wink and a thumbs-up. Halley wasn't quite so obvious about it, but every time she saw them, she grinned.

Around midnight, when the fireworks were all spent and the party showed signs of winding down, Jenna picked up the tart pan, empty now except for a few pastry crumbs, and thanked Tito's parents for the party. They both hugged her, and Halley too, and Rose kissed Tito on the cheek. So did Juan. It felt strange, taking leave of his parents not as his solitary self, but as part of a small group—not his own family, not yet, but it didn't seem that out of the question anymore.

He put on some music for the drive home. No one talked much, but the silence felt good, with Halley in the back seat and Jenna beside him, and Jenna's hand in his, in the middle of the bench seat.

The thing that used to be between them, that barrier by which they'd kept each other at a distance—that was gone. They were being their true selves now, with nothing hidden. Tito felt overwhelmed by the wonder of it all. Jenna knew him—his history of depression, his nerdy sense of humor—and still she'd chosen him. She wanted him—not his brother Eddie, and not the mean ex who'd broken her heart, but him, Tito Mendoza.

He tried to contain his joy, to manage expectations, to be reasonable. It wasn't as if she'd made a vow to him. They'd had one date—assuming this was a date, which by now he was pretty sure it was. Their romantic relationship, if that was what this was, was less than a day old. But the joy kept bursting through his caution, telling him that this time was for real.

When they reached the house, Halley hurried inside with the tart pan, saying all in a rush, "Thanks for the party, Tito. I'm really tired and I'm going to go to bed right away. G'night."

She rushed down the hallway into her room and shut the door.

"Did she just take the tart pan with her to her room?" Tito asked in a low voice.

Jenna was trying to suppress a laugh. "Yes. I guess she really wanted to leave us alone together."

"So...is it safe to assume that she approves?"

Jenna's eyes widened. "Approves? She's been actively gunning for us to get together. She likes you."

"Really?" Something warm and bright bloomed in Tito's chest, swelling his throat shut for a moment. "I'm glad to hear that," he managed to say.

She smiled at him. "Is it so surprising?"

"Well, yes, actually. She's got good reason to be wary where men are concerned, after everything she went through with her father. And aside from that, her approval is worth having. She's a smart kid, and she's *your* kid. I want her to like me."

Jenna's smile stiffened, then slipped away.

Then she said, "Come sit down with me. I need to tell you something."

"Okay," said Tito. He kept his voice level and calm, hiding his sudden unease. Why did Jenna look so grave? Had he said something wrong?

Once they were situated on the sofa, she took his hand in hers.

"I'm not Halley's mother," she said. "I'm her aunt. Her mother was my sister, Kara. After Kara died, I was appointed Halley's legal guardian."

"Oh," said Tito. "I must have misunderstood. I thought Chase was your ex."

Jenna squirmed. "Yes, well…he is. I dated him in high school, during my rebel phase. He was bad news even then, and I knew it. The whole town knew it. All my life, I'd been warned away from him and his entire family. But I thought I was in love, and I thought he loved me. Then…he hurt me. Not seriously, but enough to open my eyes. I broke it off right then and there and never looked back. I thought that was the end of it. But after I went off to college, he took up with my sister."

"Wow," Tito said. "That's a twist."

"Yeah. Physical violence was a deal-breaker for me, but it wasn't for Kara. It was a nightmare, seeing what he put her through, and being unable to convince her that she had to get away from him. Then she had Halley, and I thought surely she'd leave him now that she had a child to protect, but it didn't happen. I'd go through all the arguments, I'd tell her she had to get away from him for Halley's sake, I'd talk myself blue in the face. Sometimes, when things were really bad, she'd say yes, I was right, and that she was going to leave him, but then he'd do his charming repentant act, and back she'd go—over and over and over again."

He rubbed his thumb gently over the back of her hand. "That must have been horrible."

"It was. For our parents, too. I kept Halley with me as much as I could, to try to give her some semblance of a normal life in a healthy environment. At times it felt like she was more my child than Kara's. She even started calling me Mother, all on her own, when she was four years old."

Jenna blinked back tears and swallowed hard. Tito waited.

"Finally, when Halley was ten, Kara said she'd had enough, she was done, she was leaving Chase and not going back. Well, I was thrilled, of course. Kara and Halley moved in with me—I had a nice little three-bedroom house, with plenty of space for us all, and a room already set up for Halley where she used to stay whenever she visited me. I really thought Kara meant it that time. We all did."

She shook her head. "I should have stayed with her, twenty-four seven, to make sure she followed through. But I had a job, a really good job as a business analyst in a software company, making good money. I had a mortgage, responsibilities. I couldn't constantly supervise my sister. And one day while I was paying bills, Kara said she was going out to pick up a few things for her and Halley. I thought she meant shopping—and that's probably what she wanted me to think. But instead she went back to the house she'd shared with Chase and started packing clothes and toys, nothing important, nothing that couldn't be easily replaced."

She glanced at him. "You can probably guess what happened next. Chase came home while Kara was there. He said he was sorry, he loved her, he'd never hurt her again, the whole routine. And she fell for it, like she always did. And she called me to say that she was coming back to my place to pick up Halley and take her back home. And I said… I said, *Over my dead body is that child leaving this house.* And then Chase took the phone away from Kara and cussed me out, and told me that Halley was his child and I had no right to keep her from him, and that he and Kara were coming over right now to pick her up and I'd better not stand in his way. I could tell by the way he talked that he was high on meth. After he hung up, I prayed. I prayed for something, anything, to stop him. And…well…something did. Chase ran a red light, and his sports car got hit by a truck. Kara was killed instantly. Chase didn't even have to go to the emergency room."

Tito remembered Chase's mug shot on his phone—the black eyes, the scraped forehead, the tiny cuts scattered across the face. All consistent with a car accident.

"It wasn't your fault," Tito said. "You know that, don't you?"

Jenna shrugged. "Maybe not the actual accident. But I was the one who brought Chase into our lives to begin with. Kara was…she was different from me. Shy and soft and sweet. She never would have even spoken to Chase if I hadn't gone out with him first. I thought I was so cool, dating a bad boy. And Kara was my best friend. She helped me meet with him in secret, she listened to all the ridiculous arguments I came up with to justify his behavior. I guess it all sank in. And once Chase got his claws in her, he never let her go."

Tito shook his head. "You're taking too much on yourself, Jenna. You're making it sound like everything depended on you, like Kara had no choice in the matter. And that's not true. She was a grown woman and she made her own choices. Blaming yourself for her decisions is pretty egotistical."

She gave him a wry smile. "You want to hear something even more egotistical? I used to wonder whether Chase got involved with Kara just to get back at me for breaking up with him. If he did, then it was a pretty thorough form of vengeance. Except for one thing."

"Halley?"

Jenna nodded. "Halley was the only good thing to come out of that whole sorry situation. Everything I've done since then has been about keeping her safe. And that meant starting over somewhere far away. Chase's family is as bad as he is, and clannish, too. They were furious when I was made Halley's legal guardian, and they did not hesitate to tell me so. I had my tires slashed, my windows broken, death threats left in my mailbox. I had to get her away from them—and from everyone who knew them. Even as young as Halley was when we moved away, people were already treating her differently because she was a Latimore, like she was no good. Not just other kids, but teachers, too. That's in addition to all the kids who were Latimores themselves. It was hard."

Jenna's head bowed. Suddenly she looked achingly small and vulnerable. Tito put his arms around her, and she nestled against him, her head on his chest.

"Thank you for telling me," he said.

"I'm glad you know," she said. "I've wanted to tell you before, lots of times."

He pressed his lips against her hair. "Why didn't you?"

"It just seemed better to leave all that stuff in the past. Safer and…cleaner, somehow. I wanted us to have a truly clean slate. But maybe that's not possible."

"From what you told me before, it sounds like you did a good job covering your tracks. Maybe it's time to relax a little, and not live in fear all the time."

She was quiet a moment. Then she said softly, "Maybe it is."

"YOU NEED TO go on a real date," Halley told Jenna. "Just the two of you. Without me."

Jenna parked the car, shut off the ignition and turned to face Halley. "But where would *you* go?" she asked. "I can't go out and leave you on your own."

Halley thought. "Why can't I stay with Tito's parents? They're nice, and they want you and Tito to be together. And Mr. Mendoza is tough. If anyone tries to kidnap me, he'll be there to stop it."

"Kidnap you?" Jenna shuddered. "Why would you even say that?"

"Well, it's what you're worried about, isn't it? It's why you never let me go anywhere. Almost never," she amended, seeing Jenna open her mouth to object.

"Of course I'm worried about it," said Jenna. "I think about it all the time. I just don't like the flippant tone you just used."

"Okay. How's this tone?" Halley laid a hand on Jenna's arm, looked her solemnly in the eye and said gravely, "Mr. Mendoza is a tough man, Mother. If anyone tries to kidnap me, he will surely prevent them from succeeding."

Jenna laughed grudgingly. The idea was tempting. Juan and Rose were such warm, friendly people. They'd be wonderful grandparents, so young and active and full of fun.

But hold on. *Grandparents?* How had she gotten there? She and Tito had had their first kiss not twenty-four hours ago, and she was already planning their future life together?

It was way too soon to think that way. But Tito was so remarkable. Ordinary rules didn't seem to apply to him. Maybe, wonder of wonders, a dream was coming true that she hadn't even dared to dream.

"Besides," Halley went on in a normal tone, "Tito's been teaching me some self-defense moves."

"What? When? I didn't know that."

"It was a few days ago, while you were doing the ordering for the restaurant. He showed me how to break different kinds of holds and told me what to do if anyone ever tried to pick me up and put me in a car and how to get out of a locked trunk. Tito's pretty tough too, you know."

Jenna smiled. "Yes, I know."

"So what do you think?" Halley asked as they got out of the car.

"I think you should curb your enthusiasm," Jenna said. "Tito hasn't even asked me out yet for this just-the-two-of-us date."

They were halfway through the parking lot behind the restaurant when the back door opened and Tito stepped out, all straight and slim and bandboxy in his usual black and white. Jenna's heart leapt into her throat. He wasn't taking out the trash. He was walking toward her, purposefully.

"I'll go inside," Halley said, breaking into

a run before Jenna could reply. "Hi, Tito!" she said as she hurried past.

"Hi," he said, but Halley was already gone.

Jenna reached him at the edge of the patio, under the leafy canopy of the vines.

"Hey," she said. "What are you doing out here?"

"I wanted to catch you before you went inside," he replied. "I, uh, I was wondering if you wanted to go to dinner with me Saturday. We're both off that evening. I was thinking maybe we could go to the River Walk, since you haven't seen it. Halley can stay with my parents, if you're okay with that. I already asked them, and they said it's fine. I hope I didn't take too big a liberty there but—"

She kissed him. She could feel his surprised pleasure as his arms went around her, holding her to him.

When the kiss ended, he asked, "Is that a yes?"

His face was so open and eager. He really liked her. He knew her better than anyone in this town, but he was still nervous with her, uncertain. He didn't take her for granted. He wanted to make her happy.

"Yes," she said. She didn't want to let go of him—not now, not ever.

"Good," said Tito. "Then it's a date."

## *CHAPTER TWELVE*

IT DIDN'T TAKE Jenna long to realize that she had nothing to wear for her date with Tito. This wasn't a cookout in his parents' backyard. This was a dressy date—not black tie, but at least a step above her usual jeans-and-a-nice-shirt work attire.

She stole a look at Tito across the pass-through. He looked so polished in his pressed black trousers, snowy white shirt and crisp black vest. He'd even looked polished at the Fourth of July party, and he'd been wearing shorts. And she wanted to look polished, too. She couldn't just mail this in.

She'd owned dressy clothes, once upon a time, but she'd gotten rid of them all when she and Halley had moved to Texas and never replaced them, because she had nowhere fancy to go, and no space to spare for transporting and storing things she didn't need.

Well, she needed them now. And a day

and a half was not a lot of time to update her wardrobe.

"Hey, Jenna! Your lunch is ready."

Abel, the cook, had set her cup of creamy yellow tomato soup on a platter alongside a grilled cheese sandwich.

"Thanks," she said, and took the soup and sandwich to the break room. The lunch rush hadn't started yet, but it would soon, so now was the time for her to eat.

She set her food on the table, took her phone out of her back pocket, looked at it, set it down, picked it up again and finally began to type.

What's the closest place around here to go clothes shopping?

She hesitated a moment longer before hitting Send. She and Annalisa had exchanged phone numbers last night, and Annalisa was the closest thing to a woman friend that Jenna had in Limestone Springs.

Annalisa's reply came quickly. Why are you asking? Do you have a date???

Jenna smiled. Yes. And I have nothing to wear. And you know how dressy T always is. I want to look nice.

She started on her soup while watching the dancing dots.

What time do you get off work? Annalisa asked.

Eight, Jenna told her. Tomorrow I'm off at 3. And he's picking me up at 4:30.

Hmmm, came the answer. That's pretty tight. That's not enough time to reach New Braunfels, much less San Antonio, and do any meaningful shopping. I would lend you something, but I'm taller than you are, and we're very different style-wise. But let me ask around.

Jenna typed fast. Please don't bother. I don't want it to be a whole thing.

It's no bother, Annalisa responded. You don't want to wear tired old work clothes on a nice date, do you? I'll ask Eliana. She knows everyone.

Jenna wasn't sure how she felt about "everyone" being informed about her date. A little nervous, definitely. But also kind of happy and proud. It was nice, getting drawn into this cozy community where everyone knew everyone's business.

Within minutes, Jenna was part of a group text with Annalisa, Eliana and Lauren Reyes.

Messages flew fast, mostly between the others. Jenna soon became too busy with the lunch rush to reply to or even read most of them, but the others seemed perfectly capable of carrying on without her input.

By the time the rush ended, Lauren had arranged to bring three dresses to the restaurant for Jenna to try on. She was the closest to Jenna's height, build and coloring.

She brought her little girl with her. Peri was a beautiful and charming child, with her flaxen curls and dimpled smile. Halley helped look after her while Jenna tried on dresses and looked at them in the restroom's full-length mirror.

"When is the baby due?" Jenna asked as Lauren helped her with the tricky buttons at the back of a gorgeous turquoise dress with a flared skirt.

"Three weeks. My dad will be here next week. He lives in Pennsylvania, but he's moving down here to be closer to the grandkids. He's talked about relocating for years, and now he's finally doing it, and I'm so glad. I'm an only child, and he and I have always been close."

Jenna's throat got tight at the thought of

her own widowed mother, fourteen hundred miles away. "I'm an only child too," she said. "At least—I am now."

Lauren's eyes met hers in the mirror. "It's a big responsibility, isn't it?" she asked.

"Yes, it is," Jenna said.

Then Lauren stepped back and gave Jenna a long look. "Okay, this color looks fabulous with your skin and hair," she said.

It did. Jenna imagined the look on Tito's face when he saw her in this dress. Anticipation rose up inside her like champagne bubbles.

"I think this is the one," she said.

"Great! I'll take a picture and put it on the group text. You and Eliana wear the same size shoe. She'll want to see your dress so she'll know what shoes to bring for you to try on."

"You're all going to an awful lot of trouble," said Jenna.

"It's no problem. We're happy to do it."

Soon after Lauren left, Eliana came by with several pairs of shoes and a cute handbag in creamy leather with silk flowers in turquoise and yellow and pink. Annalisa contributed the jewelry, and Eliana's sister-in-law, Nina, threw in a gold-and-pearl hair clip.

By 4:15 the following afternoon, Jenna was ready and waiting, her stomach fluttering with excitement. She hadn't felt this way in years. She smiled at herself in the mirror. Was that even her, with the sparkling eyes, the dangly earrings, the curled hair?

"You look great," Halley said. "Now go out and have a good time, and don't worry about me."

The Eldorado pulled up in her driveway promptly at 4:30, and Tito came to the front door, wearing a Madras shirt in royal blue, turquoise and yellow. Jenna was absurdly pleased that their colors matched.

"You look beautiful," Tito said. It didn't sound like a rote thing to say, not the way he said it, with shining eyes and a voice rich with feeling.

"Thank you," said Jenna. "It was a group effort. You look very handsome."

"Thanks," said Tito. "It was a solitary effort."

Her fear of being driven seemed to have disappeared, at least when Tito was the driver. He drove Jenna and Halley to his parents' house. Juan was outside with some of his grandsons, the smaller ones, filling trash bags with leftover debris from the Fourth of July party.

"Go on inside, Halley," he said. "Rose will put you to work. She already put me to work. We've got a party to get ready for."

"Looks to me as if you're still recovering from the last party," Tito said.

"Recovering?" his dad scoffed. "There's nothing to recover from. And when it's time to throw a party, it's time, whether you're ready or not, so you better be ready."

Inside the house, Rose was seated at the dining table with the other two grandsons, the one who'd ridden the bull and another one who looked about ten years old. They were working with stacks of brightly colored papers, cutting them into designs.

"Hey, Halley," said the bull-riding grandson in a surprisingly deep voice.

"Oh, hi, David," said Halley. "I didn't know you were going to be here today."

Judging from her carefully casual tone, Jenna was pretty sure this wasn't true. No wonder Halley had been so quick to suggest that she stay with Tito's parents this evening.

"Come on in!" said Rose. "We're making *papeles picados* for Eddie's birthday party. You can help, Halley. I've heard how artistic you are."

David pulled out the seat next to him at the table, and Halley sat down.

"What are *papeles picados*?" she asked.

"It means punched papers," said Rose. "It's a traditional Mexican folk art. They're used in lots of different celebrations—weddings, quinceañeras, Christmas, Easter, Day of the Dead. You can hang them up individually, or string a bunch of them together and make a banner."

She held up a hot pink rectangle with scalloped edges and a cutout flower design surrounded by hearts and stars and swirls.

"Cool!" said Halley, picking up an X-Acto knife. "Bye, Mother! Bye, Tito! Have a good time!"

"Uh, goodbye," said Jenna. "Remember…"

"I know, I know," said Halley without turning around. "All the usual rules apply."

It was a happy family scene, Rose and the boys and Halley sitting around the table, busy with paper and cutting tools. But a prickle of doubt kept Jenna from thoroughly enjoying it. She had kept herself and Halley free from entanglements for a year and a half. Now they were forming connections—not just to Tito, but to his family, and Gillian and Kevin, and Susana and Roque. Jenna's own budding friendships with Annalisa and Eliana and Lauren were quickly gaining momentum. The three of them had been almost as excited as she was about putting together her outfit for tonight. It was nice. But it was also risky.

"All the usual rules?" Tito asked as he and Jenna walked back to the Cadillac hand in hand.

"What?" Jenna asked.

He jerked his head toward the house. "What Halley just said."

"Oh, right. Yeah, you know. Just standard stuff. But I think I might need to add to the rules if she's going to be spending time around that nephew of yours. What is he, fifteen?"

"Who, David? He's thirteen. He's just a big kid. And my mom has very definite standards of propriety and isn't shy about enforcing them, so don't worry."

Jenna didn't answer. She looked over her shoulder at the house.

Tito stopped walking, and gently pulled her to face him. "Hey," he said. "I'm serious. My parents are good people. They won't let anything happen to Halley."

He looked so earnest and decent and kind, and also fantastically handsome.

She sighed. "It isn't that I don't trust them. It's just—I've been solely responsible for her for so long now. And the world is a dangerous place. There are so many things that can go wrong. I can't possibly even predict them all, much less make any sort of effective defense against them. I know worrying doesn't accomplish anything, but…" She trailed off.

"But it doesn't change the way you feel," Tito said.

"Exactly."

"I get that. Look, you can check in as often as you like. And if at any point in the evening you want to come home, we will—even if it's while we're still on our way to San Antonio."

She laid a hand against his cheek. "Why are you so good?"

He chuckled. "Honestly? I'm so happy to

be with you that I'm willing to take you on almost any terms."

"Wow," she said. "That's quite a confession. Are you sure it's safe to tell me that? I might take advantage."

He covered her hand with his own, moved it to his lips and kissed it. "I think I can trust you," he said.

TITO HAD ALWAYS loved the River Walk—the old architecture, the stonework, the winding course of the blue-green water opening upon vista after vista of balconies and bridges and tall old trees. Now he was seeing it through Jenna's eyes, and falling in love with it all over again.

It was a warm evening, but the water always seemed to have a cooling effect, even at this level tucked away below the main part of the city, and the big live oak and bald cypress trees provided plenty of shade. Flagstone-paved pathways curved around sparkling fountains and big flowerbeds bursting with tropical plants, bright and bold with big glossy leaves and extravagant blooms. Restaurants and coffee shops spilled out of their walls into patio seating with tabletop umbrellas. River barges sailed down the waterway, looking like children's toys in their candy tints of turquoise and yellow, pink and red, with elaborate designs cut into their sides.

Jenna twined her arm through his and gave it a squeeze. "Oh, I love this place! It's so vivid. There's so much color and life everywhere you turn."

"I thought you'd like it. I do, too. I love living in a small town, but it's nice to come to the city once in a while."

"Yes. It seems strange that I've never been here before after living in Limestone Springs for a year and a half, but…well, you know."

Tito did know. She'd felt more comfortable staying home where things were familiar and secure. But she was here with him now, while Halley was with his family. It was a profound expression of trust from someone in her situation—even if she had already checked in with Halley several times since they'd driven away.

"You should see it at Christmastime," he said. "The lights, the caroling…"

She gave him a flirty glance. "Are you

asking me out? Is that going to be our third date? Christmastime on the River Walk?"

A sharp jolt of joy shot through his chest as he laid his hand over hers. "Oh, I expect our third date to be a lot sooner than Christmastime," he said.

"Good," she replied. "So do I."

She pointed at a passing river barge. "Those boats look like those punched papers your mom was making for Eddie's birthday party," she said. "When is his birthday, anyway?"

"The ninth, but the party won't be until later in the month. Gives everyone a chance to rest from the Fourth of July."

"And when's your birthday?"

"The tenth. Day after Eddie's."

"That's less than a week away. Have you got any plans?"

"Dinner with the family. I'll make sure to get you an invitation."

"Yeah, you'd better. Maybe that'll be our third date."

"Unless I can convince you to go out with me again before then."

She squeezed his arm again. "You might be able to do that. So where are we eating tonight?"

"You tell me. I didn't make a reservation. We're early enough to beat the main dinner rush, and I thought you'd like to look around and choose a place yourself. All the menus are posted outside the entrances."

They took their time, walking hand in hand alongside the water, occasionally crossing a bridge to get a closer look at what was on the other side.

"Ooh," said Jenna, scanning the menu of Boudro's Texas Bistro. "Prickly pear margaritas, tableside guac, shrimp and grits. Let's eat here."

Tito chuckled. "This is exactly the place I thought you'd choose."

She looked almost startled. "Really? Why?"

"I don't know. It just felt like you, somehow. Sort of traditional and hip at the same time."

"Wow. I had no idea I was so transparent."

"Maybe I'm just very observant," said Tito.

"Oh, I know you are. Should we eat inside or out?"

"Whatever you prefer, my lady."

She thought a moment. "Inside, then. We can take a little break from the heat and then walk around outside some more after dinner, when it's cooler."

Tito could see all the heads turning their way as they followed the hostess to their table. He felt his chest swelling with pride. *That's right*, he thought. *She's with me.*

The interior of the restaurant was deliciously dim and cool. They were seated beside a rough limestone wall. Candlelight glimmered on the glassware and shone on the polished dark wood of the table.

Over prickly pear margaritas, Jenna picked up her phone and did some rapid typing. She waited a moment, watching her screen, then relaxed visibly and smiled.

"Everything all right with Halley?" Tito asked.

She darted a guilty glance across the table. "I'm sorry. I'm being rude."

"Not at all. I told you, I don't mind. So how are things going at Casa Mendoza?"

"Well, it sounds like Halley's having a great time. They've had their dinner, and made about a bazillion of those picado papers, and now they're going to play board games."

She smiled down at the text again. "You

know, it's easy for me to forget that Halley needs social interaction, because she's such an introverted kid. Most of the time she's fine with a book and some drawing paper, but she does have *some* social needs. Being around your family is good for her."

Tito's own phone lit up. He checked it and said, "Oh, look. My mom sent pictures."

He leaned across the table with his phone so Jenna could see and scrolled through images of Halley and his nephews holding up finished *papeles picados*. The two of them hunched close together, their heads almost touching, laughing over the pictures.

"Thanks for being so understanding about all this," Jenna said.

"It's no problem," said Tito. "I get it. You just want to protect your child."

The white-shirted waiter returned with a wheeled cart, loaded with avocado and citrus fruit, tomatoes and peppers, garlic and red onion, and fresh cilantro. He chatted with them as he sliced and chopped, juiced and mixed.

Jenna scooped up some guacamole on a chip and took a bite. Her eyes rolled back in her head. "Oh my gosh. This is so *good.* I love my adopted state."

"It loves you too," Tito said before he could stop himself. Jenna looked a little flustered, but he thought he saw a tiny smile.

Toward the end of the meal, Jenna got a text. As she read it, her brow furrowed, and she said, "Hmm."

"What's up?" Tito asked. "Is it Halley?"

"Yes. She says your brother Johnny and his wife are trying to set a date to take their boys to Schlitterbahn early next week, and they want to know if we want to come along with Halley."

Her clear green eyes met his across the table. "What is Schlitterbahn, anyway? I hear people talk about going there, but I don't know what it is."

"It's a water park in New Braunfels. Going there is one of the few outdoor activities that are actually fun to do in South Central Texas in July. Really gorgeous place, fed with unchlorinated water straight from the Comal River, and covered with hundred-year-old trees. It's got slides, tube chutes, wave pools, the works. Even a swim-up bar where you can get a Coke or a bottled water or a glass of wine."

"That sounds amazing. Is it big?"

"Pretty big, yeah. But it's not hard to keep a group together."

Jenna took a deep breath and said, "Let's do it."

Tito set down his fork. "Seriously?"

"Yes. If we can manage to get the same day off from work, and coordinate with Johnny's family."

"I don't think that'll be a problem," said Tito, privately resolving to call in every favor owed to him by the staff of Tito's Bar and Lalo's Kitchen, and maybe add some bribery if necessary.

"Great!" Jenna gave him a sly smile. "So that'll be our third date."

"Yeah. A water park with my brother and his wife and a bunch of kids."

Jenna's smile broadened. "Sounds perfect."

"Yes, it does," said Tito.

## *CHAPTER THIRTEEN*

TITO STOOD BEHIND the bar, looking out over his establishment in that way he had, alert and watchful, spick-and-span in his black and white, with his head held high and his eyes roving to and fro. Every line of him spoke of his pride and affection for this place.

Jenna took out her phone and snapped his picture.

He turned to her, and his expression softened into a smile.

"What are you doing?" he asked.

"I'm taking a picture of my handsome boyfriend," she said.

His smile brightened, as if being called her boyfriend—and handsome—had made his day. He was so tender and responsive to praise. He really had no idea how much he was valued, by her and everyone else around here.

Suddenly, her thoughts and feelings came

together in an idea so perfect that it took her breath away.

"Something wrong?" Tito asked.

"No, nothing's wrong," said Jenna. "I just realized there's something I have to do."

She hurried back to the restaurant and started typing on her phone. Could she pull this off? She didn't have much time, but she didn't have to do it alone.

Her first text was to Luke. He replied within seconds.

That's a great idea. Just tell me the day, and put it on the calendar, but in code.

Next she texted Tito's mother, and Lauren, who had a photography business and the necessary technical know-how, and Anna-lisa, who'd known Tito all her life, and Eliana, who really knew how to bring a project together.

Within minutes, the Events calendar for Lalo's Kitchen was marked with a new item on the tenth of July, under the cryptic name of "private party."

But that was all she had time for right now. Clint called in sick for his evening shift, and

Lalo's Kitchen got slammed with a dinner rush that started early and ended late. Jenna didn't have another chance to work on her plan, or see Tito, until well after nine, when he sought her out.

"Hey," he said. "I have to leave, and I don't know when I'll be back."

"Why? What's wrong?"

"Well, there's this neighbor of my parents', Mrs. Gibson. She's going out of town tomorrow to visit her grandson in Denver, and my mom agreed to take care of her cats while she's away. So my mom went over this evening to get the key to the house, and meet the cats, and see where Mrs. Gibson keeps the cat food. And she found Mrs. Gibson all freaked out because she doesn't have her boarding pass for tomorrow. Her grandson booked the flight for her online and had all the flight information sent to her email address, but it's been so long since she checked her email that she was logged out. She couldn't remember her password, so she had to reset it. And now her printer won't communicate with her computer, possibly because she's had her router replaced since the last time she printed anything, and…you get the idea."

"If she gets the app for the airline, she won't need a physical boarding pass," Jenna said.

"She has a flip phone."

"Ah. Of course."

"Anyway, my mom's been there for I don't know how long trying to sort things out—she spent an hour just clearing the pop-ups and malware from Mrs. Gibson's browser—and she's all done in, so she's asked me to come and take over. I don't know how long I'll be. So the upshot of all that is that I've asked Garrett to close for me tonight."

Jenna reached up and smoothed his hair back from his forehead. "You are such a good man."

Tito shrugged philosophically. "Well, Mrs. Gibson was my kindergarten teacher, and she was very good to me the time I stepped right in the middle of a fire-ant mound on the playground and got stung all over. It's the least I can do."

She gave him a quick kiss. "Aw. Try to get some rest tonight. Remember we're going to Schlitterbahn tomorrow."

"I remember. I'll meet you here at nine in the morning."

They'd planned their trip for a weekday to beat the crowds, and this time there'd actually been enough time for a quick shopping trip for something to wear. Jenna and Halley now had new swimsuits, bags, cover-ups, the works. Halley was doing her best to act cool, but Jenna knew how excited she was. She'd been ecstatic when Jenna had actually agreed to visit such a big public place without raising more than a few security concerns.

Jenna smiled as she cleared a table. Things were happening that she hadn't believed possible even a few weeks ago. She felt as if a whole new world were opening up to her, fresh and bright and full of promise.

TITO SAT AT a small table on the back patio of Lalo's Kitchen, wearing his swim trunks and a black-and-white T-shirt that had an image on the front of Søren Kierkegaard in sunglasses, the sort of thing people gave as gifts to relatives who'd majored in philosophy. He had a lot of nerdy T-shirts in his closet upstairs, but he rarely had a chance to wear them anywhere other than to the gym, or to bed.

But today was different. Today he was taking Jenna and Halley to Schlitterbahn, which he hadn't visited since he was a kid. As soon as Jenna got back from the bank, the three of them would get into his Cadillac and drive to the water park for a day of recreation.

They'd planned to meet Johnny and his family here and caravan to New Braunfels. While Jenna was making the deposit for the restaurant, Halley was in the break room, working on some chalkboard art. Their bags and towels were behind the counter at Lalo's, ready to go.

The breakfast rush had cleared, leaving him alone on the patio. It was pleasant here, in the semi-enclosed outdoor room closest to the back door, with the sunlight filtering through the grapevine canopy overhead and bees buzzing around the blossoms in the flowerpots. He was a little sleepy from his late night helping Mrs. Gibson, but everything had come out all right, and he'd arranged an Uber to take her to the airport and seen her safely inside the car. It was pleasant to sit in the shade now, and watch the dragonflies flit around on the grapevines, and anticipate the day to come.

He leaned back in his chair and shut his eyes. It felt strange to be going on an outing like this with Johnny's family. Johnny was the oldest of the Mendoza brothers, and the only one who'd married and had kids so far, but now here was Tito with a girlfriend who had a twelve-year-old niece. Maybe, just maybe, Tito would have himself a ready-made family soon.

Footsteps approached. Tito opened his eyes and saw a man rounding the corner of a vine-covered wooden post, looking around as if he wasn't sure he was in the right place. The guy was wearing sunglasses and had his long blond hair pulled back in a ponytail, and he looked to be around Tito's age. When he saw Tito, he stopped short, and a wide grin spread over his face.

"Are you Tito Mendoza?" he asked, in a tone filled with something like awe.

"I am," said Tito.

The guy walked over to the table and stuck out his hand. "Wow. This is such an honor. I've heard so much about you, and about your bar. You know, you're something of a celebrity in the craft bar community. My name's Jordan, by the way."

"Good to meet you, Jordan," Tito said as he stood and shook hands. He was inclined to like Jordan, with his firm handshake and sensible opinions.

"So I guess this is the back patio of Lalo's Kitchen, right?" Jordan asked.

"That's right. And the bar is right next door."

"Well, the patio is gorgeous, with the trellises and the stone walls and all the plants. It's a perfect indoor-outdoor space. I saw the pictures in that article in *Texas Monthly*, but they don't do it justice."

"Oh, you read that, did you?"

"Yeah. Read all about how you transformed the bar after you inherited it from your uncle, and then developed the restaurant next door. You've really put Limestone Springs on the map."

"Wow, thank you. That's nice of you to say so."

"I'm not just saying it to be nice. It's the truth. I live in Austin, and I don't get to come out this way very often, but today I had some business in Seguin County, and I couldn't pass up the opportunity to zip on over to Limestone Springs and see Tito's Bar and Lalo's Kitchen in person."

"Well, go on in," said Tito. "The restaurant is still serving breakfast."

"I will. I'm going to have one of Abel's omelets, relax, watch a game, wait for some people to call me back. Then at eleven, when the bar opens, you can make me one of your signature cocktails, and I can try some of those locally brewed craft beers."

"Actually, I'm not working today. But the other bartenders will take good care of you."

"Oh." Jordan's face fell. He looked genuinely disappointed. "That's too bad. From what I've heard, half the reason people come to Tito's Bar is Tito himself. Sure I can't change your mind? I'm a good tipper."

Tito shook his head. "Afraid not. I'm spending the day with my girlfriend and her kid."

It was the first time he'd called Jenna his girlfriend out loud, and the words filled him with pride.

"Oh, I see how it is," said Jordan in a teasing tone. "Have you been seeing each other long? Is it serious?"

His friendly interest warmed Tito through. "We've only just started dating," he said, "but I've known her for over a year, and… well, she's really special."

"I'll bet. How old's the kid?"

"Twelve."

"Twelve," Jordan repeated, slowly nodding. "That's such a fun age."

"Yeah, it really is. So how long are you going to be in town? Any chance you could come back to the bar tomorrow? I'll be working then."

"Possibly," said Jordan. "I'm not sure how long my business in this area is going to take. A lot of it depends on other people."

Tito chuckled. "I hear that. Here, let me get you a menu."

He walked over to the wall-mounted rack near the back door and took out a menu.

"Thanks," Jordan said. Then he took off his sunglasses, revealing a pair of startlingly blue eyes.

It wasn't just the memory of Chase's mug shot that made everything click into place. Those were Halley's eyes, too. Tito hadn't noticed the resemblance when he'd first seen Chase's picture, but he saw it now.

He froze with his fingers still gripping the corner of the menu that Jordan—Chase—now held in his hand. Chase met Tito's gaze with those oddly bright blue eyes. His smile didn't fade, but something shifted.

"While you're making up your mind," Tito said in as natural a tone as he could manage, "how about if I go inside and get you some merch? We've got some nice T-shirts and hoodies. Plenty of coozies, too. On the house."

It was the best he could come up with on the spur of the moment. All he could think was that he had to reach that glass door ahead of Chase and bolt it shut, and call the cops, before Chase made it inside.

"That's kind of you, Tito," Chase said. His voice sounded as smooth as ever, but Tito could hear the menace beneath the veneer of charm. "But it's a mite warm out here in the sun. I'll come inside with you and see for myself what good things you've got hidden away inside behind that door."

He made a move to step past Tito, but Tito blocked him, placing himself between Chase and the door. No way Tito could get through the door himself, now that Chase was forewarned, without Chase coming through as well. The door was equipped with a damper that caused it to close slowly and gently, to prevent it from slamming shut and possibly breaking the glass. The best Tito could do now was to stand his ground and keep Chase and himself on this side of the door for as long as possible.

They stood, braced and still, inches apart, like two dogs sizing each other up before a fight. Chase was several inches taller and strongly built, probably a good twenty pounds heavier, but Tito had gotten the better of far bigger men in the past. He knew how to handle himself. Unfortunately, so did Chase. Tito could tell by the way he carried himself.

Amusement flickered in Chase's face. "Now, Tito," he said softly. "Don't go starting something you can't finish, or getting involved in things you don't understand. Be reasonable, for both our sakes."

"Reasonable?" Tito repeated. "Is it reasonable to come halfway across the country to terrorize a child?"

A look of cold rage washed over Chase's face. "Kirsten's *my* child," he said. "Kayla took my baby girl away from me. And I'm going to get her back, whether you like it or not."

Light footsteps came hurrying up. Over Chase's shoulder, Tito saw Halley rounding the wooden post at the corner, just as Chase had done minutes earlier.

"Mother just texted. She's on her w—"

Her words cut off and her mouth dropped open as she saw her father.

"Halley, get inside!" said Tito.

There wasn't time to say more. A blinding pain exploded in his head and everything went dark.

## *CHAPTER FOURTEEN*

AT 9:00 A.M. IT was already a scorcher of a day, perfect for water slides and wave pools with Halley and Tito. The bright morning sunlight dazzled Jenna's eyes as she stepped out of the dim coolness of the bank. With the morning's deposit made, all she had to do was walk back to the restaurant and put the money pouch away, and they could be on their way.

"Jenna?"

It was Annalisa, in a black pencil skirt, sleeveless blouse and high heels.

"Annalisa! Hi! What are you…"

The question died on her lips as she saw the look on Annalisa's face.

"I came to find you," Annalisa said. "I… I don't know how to tell you this, but—"

The ground seemed to drop away from Jenna's feet. "Tell me," she said. "Is it Halley?"

Annalisa nodded, her chin trembling.

"She—oh, Jenna, I saw a man put her in his car and drive away. I tried to reach her, but I didn't make it in time. Jenna, I'm so sorry."

It had come at last, the thing Jenna had been dreading for so long, and now it didn't seem real.

"Did you call the police?" She heard herself ask in a voice that didn't sound like her own.

"Yes, right away. They're coming to Lalo's. Luke said you'd gone to the bank, so I went after you. I didn't want to tell you on the phone."

Annalisa took her arm and started leading her down the sidewalk toward the restaurant, as if Jenna were injured or infirm. The sharp clicking of Annalisa's heels mingled with the shuffles and slaps of Jenna's new mint-green flip-flops. Halley had a new pair too, pink, with little white flowers on the soles.

It was a short walk from the bank to the restaurant. The bell in the front door of Lalo's Kitchen jingled cheerfully as Annalisa opened it and Jenna walked through.

Tito was sitting in a booth at the back of the room. Veronica stood beside him, her hand on his shoulder, holding a white towel to his chin. Coby Kowalski was pacing nearby, in uniform, speaking into his radio.

"… Caucasian female, age twelve. Blond hair, blue eyes, approximately four feet ten inches tall and ninety pounds. Last seen wearing blue jean cutoffs and a yellow T-shirt."

Jenna pressed both hands to her mouth. Then she balled them into fists and put them back at her sides. Panic was a luxury she couldn't afford. She had to put away her fear, lock it inside a drawer in her mind, and do what had to be done.

Tito raised his head and locked eyes with her across the room. His face looked all wrong—hollow-eyed, and with a swollen, misshapen jaw.

Annalisa steered her toward the back of the room. Jenna let herself be led. Her legs were shaking now, but she made it to the booth and sat down across from Tito. There was blood on the white towel and on the front of his black-and-white graphic T-shirt. The restaurant's first-aid kit stood open on the tabletop, stuffed with gauze pads, ice packs and a variety of bandages.

"How long ago did it happen?" Jenna asked.

"I don't know," said Tito. "A couple of minutes, maybe? I don't know how long I was out."

"You were knocked out?"

"I found him out on the back patio," said Veronica. She looked white and scared. "I heard him yell, and Halley was screaming. She was gone by the time I got there, and Tito was lying there with blood all over him."

Tito took the towel from Veronica and scowled down at it. "I'm fine," he muttered.

"It was about five minutes ago," said Annalisa. "I was taking some documents to my car when I saw the guy forcing Halley into the trunk of his car."

A hot surge of anger flared in Jenna's chest. "The trunk?" she repeated, her voice sharp. "He put her in the *trunk*?"

"She did not go quietly," Annalisa went on. "She yelled and screamed and fought him every inch of the way, Jenna. She almost got free, too."

"Did anyone get the license plate number?" Jenna asked. "Or the make and model of the car?"

"I'm pretty sure it was a Ford," said Annalisa. "Maybe a Taurus? It was gray. I remember the license plate started with XXL—that part stuck in my mind—but I don't know what came after that. I'm sorry."

Coby had just put his radio back on his belt and now joined them at the booth. "It's a 2005 Ford Taurus, gray, with a small dent in the driver's-side door and Arkansas plates, plate number XXL 94R," he said. "Assuming that it's the same car that's been parked on this street off and on for the past two days, with a thirty- to forty-year-old white male inside. I saw it yesterday and the day before, and something about it just struck me wrong, so I made a mental note."

A cold, heavy weight settled in Jenna's stomach. Chase had been watching Lalo's for *two days*? And she hadn't even *noticed*? How could she have been so careless?

But she already knew the answer. She hadn't noticed because she'd been so happy with her new romance. She'd let her guard down—and now Halley was gone.

Coby pulled up a chair, sat down at the end of the booth and took a pencil and pad of paper from his belt. "Jenna, do you know who this man is?"

Jenna took a deep breath. "His name is Chase Latimore. He's Halley's father."

"Her father?" Coby repeated.

"Yes, but his parental rights have been terminated."

"Is he your ex-husband? Current husband?"

She shook her head. "Ex-brother-in-law."

Coby's pencil came to a stop.

"I'm Halley's legal guardian," Jenna said.

"Not her mother?" Coby asked.

"No. Her mother was my sister, Kara." Jenna looked down at the table. "Kara was killed in a car accident a year and a half ago. Chase was the driver. He was high on meth at the time."

"He went to prison?"

"Yes, for felony DUI. He was a repeat offender, so…"

Coby paused while he caught up on his note-taking, then asked, "Where was he incarcerated?"

"Green Rock Correctional."

"Virginia?"

"Chatham, Virginia, yes. He got out almost three weeks ago."

She heard the words coming out of her mouth, a bit jerkily at times, but coherently.

"Did the accident take place in Virginia?" Coby asked.

"Yes. Rocky Mount."

Coby pocketed his notepad.

"Okay. I'll pass this on to my superiors, and they'll get in touch with authorities in Virginia so we can get an AMBER Alert out as quickly as possible."

"Thank you," said Jenna. She'd been serving Coby burgers and beers for months now, joking around with him. She'd never dealt with him in his law enforcement capacity before. Now she felt humbly grateful for his calm competence.

He got to his feet, took up his radio again and walked away.

Veronica was still standing beside the booth, listening, her eyes round. Now she asked, "Can I get anyone anything? Something to drink?" She looked at Tito. "I'll activate one of these ice packs for your chin."

Tito shook his head. "No, that's okay."

"You really ought to at least get a bandage on it," said Veronica.

"I'm fine," Tito said shortly.

"Go ahead and bring them a couple of waters, please, Veronica," said Annalisa.

Veronica nodded and walked away.

Annalisa turned to Jenna. "Is there anyone you'd like me to call for you?"

There was no one to call but Jenna's mom. All at once, Jenna longed to go to her and lay the whole nightmarish situation at her feet, the way she'd once brought her skinned knees and torn doll dresses, and let her fix everything. But Jenna wasn't a little girl anymore, and her mother wasn't the same confident, energetic thirty-year-old that Jenna remembered from her childhood. Jenna could just see her, all alone in her house in Rocky Mount, going about her day, ignorant of the horrible thing that had just happened. She'd already been deprived of her husband and youngest daughter, with her only remaining relatives now accessible only through an electronic screen. She couldn't take any more tragedy. She just couldn't.

Then Jenna saw Halley's canvas beach bag with the big pink hibiscus printed on the side, lying in a heap on the counter behind the booth. A rolled-up beach towel, blue with yellow polka dots, peeked out at the top, along with a bottle of sunscreen. A floppy straw hat was tossed on top.

The tears came then, in an abrupt, violent storm. Halley had been so excited this morning, packing her bag, braiding her hair and then taking it down and braiding it again, and securing the ends with pink elastics. Now she was trapped in a car, scared and possibly hurt, with a father who'd been nothing but terror and grief to her.

Annalisa rubbed Jenna's shoulder and made soothing noises, and Tito silently pushed the napkin holder across the table to her. Jenna grabbed a fistful of napkins and held them to her face.

"I'm going to call Luke and Eliana," said Annalisa. "And I ought to let my boss know where I am. I'll be back soon."

Jenna didn't answer. She just kept sobbing into her wad of paper napkins.

*The police will find her*, she told herself. *They'll get her back.*

They had a lot of things working in their favor, including an actual cop who'd made note of the vehicle and its license number. Highway patrol would set up roadblocks, or something. Chase would be caught, and be sent back to jail, and Jenna would get Halley back.

But Chase wasn't like other people. He didn't give up, even when he had no chance of success. He just kept going, no matter what it cost him, no matter who got hurt.

She wanted Tito to come over to her side of the booth and put his arm around her, and tell her everything would be all right. But he just sat there across from her, saying nothing, staring down at the bloody towel in his hands.

Veronica came back with their waters. She set the glasses on the table and melted away again. Jenna blew her nose and gulped some water.

She glanced across the table at Tito, turning her attention to the swollen bruise distorting the clean line of his jaw beneath the neatly trimmed beard.

"Wh-what did he do to you?" she asked.

His shoulder twitched up in a shrug. "Uppercut to the chin. Classic sucker punch. I should have seen it coming, but I didn't."

He looked at her then with haunted eyes. "I'm sorry," he said.

She understood now. Tito was ashamed. That was why he wasn't comforting her. He thought he didn't have the right.

"It's not your fault," she said.

"I should have known better. He played me. Came up to me on the back patio, pretending to be an out-of-towner visiting the restaurant and bar. He knew all about me, and the renovation, and the menu. Acted like he was my biggest fan, and I fell for it. I didn't recognize him until he took his sunglasses off. I saw his mug shot after you looked it up on my phone that day. He clearly knew Halley was inside. From what Coby said, it sounds like he'd been watching the place for a while. I don't know what his plan was."

"He didn't have one," Jenna said with conviction. "He was only getting the lay of the land. He was never one for thinking ahead. He just plunges in. And if an opportunity presents itself, he takes it, and figures out the rest as he goes along."

"Yeah, that sounds about right," said Tito. "By the time I figured out who he really was, it was a little late in the game, and he was already several steps ahead of me. I knew I didn't have time to get inside to protect Halley. All I could hope to do was to keep Chase from going through the glass back door to get to her. I never expected her to come out the other way."

"Which other way?"

"From Luke's office, I think. He has that door that leads to the outside."

Jenna let out a groan. "Oh, right. Yes, I texted her from the bank and asked her to go in there and check something for me."

She took her phone out of her pocket, opened up her text thread with Halley and scrolled through, as if the words might hold some clue that would help her get Halley back. The whole exchange looked so innocent and hopeful now, filled with anticipation for their upcoming day at the water park, the words interspersed with emojis of yellow suns and water droplets.

She set the phone down.

"You should go to the hospital," she told Tito. "You've been concussed."

"I'm fine. I don't even have a headache."

"You don't know that you're fine. You could have brain damage. Head injuries are nothing to mess around with."

"I know. I'll go later. After…"

He didn't finish, but she knew what he'd been about to say. *After Halley's found.* As if it were that simple. Another few minutes, a half hour tops, and she'd be back, and life could go on as it had before. Until then, everything else had to be put on hold.

But how long would it take? And what if it never happened? Jenna had learned by now that things didn't always turn out fine in the end. They hadn't for Kara. Chase had seen to that. And now Chase had Halley.

She shook her head. They *would* get Halley back. They had to. It was only a matter of time. And after that…

After that, what? Chase would go to jail, assuming he was caught. But he'd gone to jail before, and gotten out, and somehow managed to track Jenna and Halley down.

How had he done it? Jenna had worked so hard to shut the door so firmly on the past that she and Halley would never have to see Chase again. But she hadn't done all that she could have done, not by a long shot. And over the past few weeks, she'd let down her guard. She'd listened to that soft, soothing voice that had told her it was okay to relax once in a while, that she didn't have to maintain constant vigilance, that she and Halley could have normal lives, with friends, and fun, and parties, and love. Somewhere along the way, she'd messed up, and Chase had taken advantage of that. He'd found the chink in their armor and exploited it, like he always did.

All of which raised a very disturbing question. Once she did have Halley back safe and sound, what new lengths of precautions and safeguards would Jenna have to go to in order to keep her safe?

## *CHAPTER FIFTEEN*

NOT MANY MINUTES had passed since Chase had tossed Halley into the trunk of the Ford Taurus, but it felt as if a long time had gone by. Annalisa soon returned to Lalo's, as she'd said she would, along with Claudia, her boss. Johnny showed up with his wife and kids, ready to go to the water park, and stuck around after learning what had happened. As word of Halley's abduction spread, more people trickled in. Tito's parents came.

Tito was reminded of the time just after the bad storm a few years back when the restaurant and bar had become gathering places for the community. He'd kept busy then, passing out food and drink and trying to encourage people. Now it was Luke who was feeding everyone, while Tito was being treated as a victim of the crisis. He sat there in his booth, useless—as useless as he'd been when Chase had gotten the drop on him and taken Halley.

Coby reported that the local police had been in touch with authorities in Virginia and Arkansas. They'd learned that the car Chase was driving had been reported stolen in Little Rock. Other than that, no progress had been made.

Tito kept thinking about that time when he'd worked with Halley on self-defense. He'd shown her how to break the most common holds, and even given her some pointers on how to escape from the trunk of a car, should she ever find herself stuffed inside one.

*But don't let it come to that*, he'd told her. *All your energy needs to be focused on not being put into the car to begin with. Have you ever seen how a feral kitten acts when it gets picked up? It goes all out, twisting and clawing and yowling and biting. Be like that. Be a little cat.*

From what Annalisa had said, Halley had done everything he'd told her to do, but it hadn't been enough. He hadn't told her that a kidnapping victim's chances of survival plummeted once the victim was inside the abductor's car.

If Tito had been vigilant this morning, Chase never would have had a chance to get hold of Halley to begin with.

He writhed at the memory of himself swallowing Chase's lies, being taken in by his flattery. How could he have been so gullible? He, Tito Mendoza, who prided himself on his people-reading skills, had been thoroughly bested by a small-time lowlife criminal. True, he'd never met the guy before that morning, and the long hair, spiffy clothes and dark sunglasses had gone a long way toward altering his appearance from the mug shot Tito had viewed weeks earlier on his phone's screen. But Tito had known of Chase's existence, his cunning ways, his penchant for violence. He'd known, because Jenna had told him, that Chase was a people-smart charmer. Jenna was the smartest, most capable woman he knew, and Tito had seen how much she feared Chase. He should have been on his guard.

But he hadn't. Chase had gotten to him by appealing to his vanity, and now Chase had Halley and there was nothing Tito could do about it.

The words *chances of survival* kept swirling through his mind. He wanted to believe it wasn't a question of survival. Chase was Halley's *father*. Surely he wouldn't hurt her. But Tito couldn't make any assumptions based on the behavior of normal people. And even if Chase's intent wasn't to harm Halley, he was reckless enough to hurt her without meaning to, through drug-impaired driving or sheer thoughtless stupidity. He'd already proven that.

Had Chase been high when he was smooth-talking Tito on the back patio of Lalo's Kitchen? Was he high now? There was no way to know.

Where were Chase and Halley now? How many miles had they traveled in that Ford Taurus, and in which direction, and at what speed? Tito didn't know any of those things. He'd never felt so powerless in his life.

He was still sitting across the table from Jenna in the back booth. They didn't have much to say to each other, but they'd stayed there, waiting, drawing comfort—at least Tito was—from their nearness.

A cell phone's ringtone went off. Everyone turned toward the sound. It was Coby Kowalski's phone. The room went quiet as Coby picked up and said, "Yeah?"

Tito and Jenna reached for each other's hands across the table. The silence grew and stretched as Coby stood motionless and expressionless with the phone to his ear. Jenna's hands gripped Tito's with white-knuckle intensity.

Coby let out a breath. His eyes shut. What did that mean? Good news or bad?

"Thanks," he said. "I'll pass that along."

The entire crowd seemed to be holding its breath. Coby opened his eyes and ended his call.

"She's safe."

A great sigh went through the restaurant, like a gust of wind. Across the table from him, Jenna drew a quick ragged breath and dropped her head onto their clasped hands.

"Where is she?" Tito asked.

"At the Foxes' place with Kevin and Gillian and Kevin's dad. We have officers at the scene. She's about to be transported to the hospital."

"Hospital?" Jenna repeated. "What's wrong with her?"

"I don't have any details about her condition, except that it's not considered life-threatening. Also, the suspect has been apprehended. He's on his way to the police station."

Jenna let go of Tito's hands and stumbled to her feet, looking dazed and bewildered, as if she'd just woken up. "Okay, okay," she said. "I've got to go to the hospital. Where's my purse?"

"You're in no shape to drive yourself," Tito said. "I'll take you there."

"Oh, no," said Annalisa. "Neither one of you is fit to drive. I'll drive both of you, and while Jenna is with Halley, Tito can get himself a brain scan or something. Two birds, one stone."

HALLEY HAD LOST one of her new pink hair elastics. Her hair had come unbraided on that side, giving her a lopsided appearance that would have been funny under other circumstances. She had scrapes and scratches on her face and limbs, her new T-shirt was torn, and her new cutoffs were stained with spots of what looked like motor oil.

But she was safe, and suffering no worse injuries than what would be expected from escaping from the trunk of a moving car on a state highway. Jenna drank in the sight of her. She felt that she could never get her fill of looking at Halley.

"Tito told me how," she said, bright-eyed with excitement on the exam table in the emergency room, her swollen wrist secured in a splint. "There's a cable on the driver's side that you can pull, if it's that kind of car. You have to feel around under the carpeting and cardboard paneling and stuff until you find it. Then you yank it toward the front of the car, and the trunk opens up."

Jenna spared Tito a quick flash of a smile, and he smiled back. He was sitting on the other side of the exam table. He hadn't gone for his own examination yet. He'd insisted on seeing Halley first.

"Smart girl," he said.

She *was* a smart girl, and a brave girl. But things could have just as easily gone another way.

Over the course of the day, details came to light, and the story of Halley's abduction and escape took shape like a mosaic, pieced together from Halley's own recollections and various enthusiastic witness accounts, as well as from the grudging statement given by Chase himself. Coby Kowalski briefed

Jenna in a small meeting room at the hospital, using an official-sounding voice and diction that she'd never heard him use before today.

"To the best of our knowledge," said Coby, "this is what happened. After securing Halley in the trunk, the suspect headed east on Highway 281, where he got stuck behind a farm vehicle which we believe to have been a John Deere cotton harvester, traveling at a speed of twenty-five miles per hour. The driver of the farm vehicle did not pull onto the shoulder, and the highway was busy enough at that time of day to make passing difficult. The suspect, whether out of concern for the welfare of his child in the trunk of the car, or because he didn't want to get pulled over, elected to keep in his lane and tailgate the farm vehicle in hopes that it would move over. Eventually the farm vehicle slowed down in preparation for making a right turn. While this was taking place, Halley was searching for the release cable in the trunk of the car. She found it and pulled it. The trunk popped open and she exited the vehicle."

Jenna shuddered at the thought of Halley jumping out of a moving car onto a state highway. Even at a speed of twenty-five miles per hour, it was dangerous—but not as dangerous as staying in the trunk of Chase's car.

"The motorist behind the suspect was also traveling at a reduced rate of speed," Coby went on. "She witnessed Halley jumping out of the trunk and immediately applied her brakes and slowed to a stop. She then witnessed Halley roll into a bar ditch, get to her feet and begin to run."

*Yeah, I'll bet she did*, Jenna thought, tears pricking her eyes. She could just see Halley, with her broken wrist and skinned knees, adrenaline coursing through her little body, temporarily numbing her to pain as she ran with all her might—in flip-flops, no less.

"The motorist called 911 from the shoulder," said Coby. "She saw the suspect's vehicle swerve off the road, where it collided with a concrete culvert near the junction of 281 and Ripke Road. The suspect then exited his vehicle and pursued Halley on foot. Halley recognized the home of Kevin Fox and his daughter Gillian and headed toward it."

The property was conspicuous enough,

Jenna knew, with its big, ramshackle house and overgrown field filled with defunct farm machinery.

"Kevin and Gillian were both outdoors with Kevin's father, Ray," Coby continued. "They had been working all morning on getting an old tractor into salable condition and had heard nothing of Halley's abduction. By the time Halley reached them, she was incoherent and out of breath, but Ray and Kevin were able to figure out the essentials of the situation. The suspect was still pursuing Halley at this time. Ray took the girls inside the house, locked the doors and armed himself with a shotgun. Kevin removed a rifle from his truck and began walking toward the suspect."

"*Kevin* did that?" Jenna asked.

"Yes," said Coby.

"Kevin Fox?"

"That's correct."

Jenna sat back in her chair, stunned.

She liked Kevin well enough from her interactions with him at the restaurant and bar, and when they'd carpooled together to get Halley and Gillian to and from horse camp, he'd been punctual and responsible with his end of the deal. But he was so unkempt and bewildered-looking, and a part of Jenna had judged him for that. And here he'd stalked out to meet an unknown miscreant, firearm in hand, to protect her child.

"Did Chase have a gun too?" she asked.

"Yes," said Coby.

"Did Kevin shoot him? Did he shoot Kevin?"

"No. While they were still some distance from each other, a neighbor of Mr. Fox's observed the suspect pursuing Halley. The neighbor ran down the suspect, tackled him from behind and secured him with two lengths of baling wire. He and Mr. Fox then disarmed the suspect and remained with him until police officers arrived on the scene to take him into custody."

Jenna slowly shook her head. To think that Chase had a gun on him all along—

"At this time," Coby continued, "it is unknown whether this weapon was stolen, or provided to the suspect by a friend or family member, or recovered from a private stash. But even if the weapon was not illegally obtained, merely having one in his possession and transporting it was a clear violation of the suspect's parole."

"One in a long list of violations, I would think," said Jenna. "Assault, stealing a car..."

"Driving while revoked, driving without insurance," Coby added. "And, of course, kidnapping is a federal offense, as well as a state crime in Texas."

Jenna let her breath out in a big puff of air. Then she asked, "What does Chase say? How did he track down Halley and me? I—I took a lot of precautions to keep him from finding us."

Coby nodded. "It appears that shortly after his release from prison, Mr. Latimore was shown a video of a barn raising which you and Halley attended. You aren't visible in the video, but Halley is. To date, this video has had over twelve thousand views."

"A video?" Jenna repeated blankly. "Someone took a video of Halley at the barn raising?"

"Halley was not the main subject of the video, but she is visible in it long enough to be recognized. Someone within the suspect's circle of acquaintance viewed the video in connection with a building project he was undertaking. He noticed the resemblance to Halley and mentioned it to one of Mr. Latimore's relatives, who identified Halley from the video and passed it along to the suspect. Mr. Latimore was able to locate the Vrba Equestrian Center through an internet search. He then obtained a large amount of cash from a source which has yet to be determined and took a series of buses west. Upon reaching Arkansas, the suspect stole a car. He then drove to Limestone Springs, where he rented a hotel room and spent several days observing the downtown area. In the barn raising video, Halley was wearing a T-shirt bearing the logo of Lalo's Kitchen, which was also listed as one of the businesses providing food for the event. Once the suspect started keeping an eye on the place, he observed you and Halley in the company of Tito Mendoza. It's believed that he did not have an overarching plan but merely waited for an opportunity and improvised."

Jenna dropped her face in her hands. After all the pains she'd taken—the new home, the carefully crafted new identities—Chase had found them through some video on the internet that she hadn't even realized had been taken. He'd staked the place out for days, and she'd never noticed, because she'd had her heart and head filled with Tito. Months of effort and vigilance, wasted. No matter how long Chase went away for this time, it could never be long enough. He'd get out one day, and come after Halley again.

The knowledge wrenched her heart. The more she came to know this place, the more she saw to love. The history, the landscapes, the people. Mostly the people—especially one of the people. But none of that mattered.

Limestone Springs wasn't safe for her and Halley anymore.

## *CHAPTER SIXTEEN*

TITO WAS PEELING off his Kierkegaard T-shirt when Jenna's ringtone went off on his phone, startling Bunter, who was curled up on the bed near the phone. A tremor of pleasure passed through Tito's heart at the sight of her picture on the lit-up screen. He quickly stepped into his jeans and pulled them up before answering.

"Hey," he said.

"Hey. Where are you?"

"Home. The hospital let me leave after my scan. But I'm just here long enough to change clothes. I've been in swim trunks and a bloody T-shirt all day, and I was ready for a change. Where are you, hospital or police station?"

"Hospital. The police came to me for my interview so I could stay near Halley."

"How is she?"

"Sleeping, finally. They had to give her

a pediatric cocktail for sedation. I'm in the hallway outside her room."

"Poor kid. How's the arm?"

"Fractured at the scaphoid, which I've just learned is one of the tiny bones in the wrist. She's got a cast on it now. Apparently the fracture is in the part of the scaphoid bone that has a good blood supply, which helps with the healing."

"Glad to hear it."

"Yeah. How about you?"

"Grade 1 concussion. No caffeine or alcohol, no driving or electronic devices, until I'm cleared for them. Ibuprofen for pain."

He could hear the smile in her voice. "You're on an electronic device right now, you know."

He walked over to his closet, flipped through his shirts and took out the dark blue button-down that Jenna liked. "Yeah, well, I won't tell if you won't. I'll meet you back at the hospital in a few minutes."

"I thought you said no driving."

"Johnny gave me a ride home. He's waiting for me downstairs."

"Oh. Well, don't bother coming back. Stay home and get some rest."

"I don't need to rest. I barely have a headache."

This wasn't entirely true, but he could cope with the pain.

"You had a brain injury. You need to rest."

"I'm not leaving you to deal with all this alone. I want to be with you."

"Well, I'd rather you didn't come, okay?"

Tito slowly laid the shirt on the bed. "What's wrong?"

Jenna's voice rose. "What's wrong? I have a child who was abducted and thrown into the trunk of a car by her criminal father, with physical injuries and a fresh load of trauma to add to all her previous trauma."

Tito didn't answer. He didn't say what he was thinking, which was that Halley was free now, that things could have ended much worse, and that they had much to be thankful for. That was all true, but didn't negate anything Jenna had said. And there had been something almost hostile in her tone, as if Tito were the enemy, which gave him an uneasy premonition about where this conversation was heading.

Then her tone softened. "I'm sorry. You didn't deserve that. You've had a hard day too, and you've been very good to Halley and me. If it wasn't for you, Halley wouldn't have known how to escape from the trunk of a car, and…well, thank you—for that, and your friendship, and just everything."

Tito's knees gave way. He sat down on the edge of his bed and waited.

Jenna sighed. "There's no good way to say this, so I'll just say it. We're leaving, Halley and I, as soon as she's well enough and I figure out where we're going to go."

"You can't be serious," Tito said.

"I'm dead serious. We can't stay here. Limestone Springs isn't safe for us anymore."

Tito ran a hand through his hair and clenched a handful of it. "Jenna, Chase is in jail. He's not going to be set free to go on his merry way. He's going away for a long time."

"So what if he is? He'll be released again, maybe early if he keeps his nose clean. He might even escape. He's crazy enough for anything, and smart, and cunning, and charming, and quick on his feet—not to mention that he's got a whole family tree's worth of crazy relatives who aren't above kidnapping her themselves. I've got to take

Halley somewhere that he can never hurt her again."

"Jenna, no. Don't do this."

"I have no choice. You heard how he tracked us down. Through that video at the barn raising. That was all it took. I let my guard down and this was the result."

"You can't prevent things like that from happening! It isn't possible, no matter how careful you are. Not in today's world. Isolating yourself won't keep you safe. Stay here, and let me help protect you and Halley."

"Yeah, well, we've seen how well that worked this time."

Tito's hand dropped to the mattress with a soft thud. He was too stung to reply.

"I'm sorry," Jenna said in a different tone. "I didn't mean that the way it sounded. I know how tough you are. I've seen you in action at the bar, throwing out drunks. But Chase is a special kind of crazy. People like you and me will always be at a disadvantage dealing with people like him, because people like him don't operate according to ordinary logic. We can't possibly predict all the bizarre things he might do."

"All the more reason why you shouldn't

try to deal with him on your own. Your problem is that you've been taking care of everything by yourself for so long that you've forgotten how to trust anyone else."

"Don't tell me what my problem is. This is my responsibility and my decision to make."

"And your decision is to keep running? How long can you keep that up? It's time you stopped running and made your stand."

Jenna's voice rose. "Make my stand? How? He took her, Tito. He picked her up and threw her in his car and drove away."

"And she got away from him," Tito reminded her.

"Then he'll escalate next time. Do something more extreme." She let out an impatient sigh. "Look, there's no sense in arguing about it. My mind is made up. And I've got to go now and get back to Halley." She paused. "I'm sorry it has to be this way, Tito. I really am."

He could hear the tremor in her voice. He opened his mouth to say something, anything to stop her, but before he could get a word out, she said, "Goodbye, Tito," and hung up.

He slowly lowered the phone to his lap

and looked down at the empty screen. Then he lifted his head and saw himself in the mirror, slumped over, shirtless, blank-eyed, his chin still misshapen from its encounter with Chase's fist and his hair standing on end.

A hoarse meow made him turn. Bunter had crept onto his blue shirt and was busy depositing black and white hairs on it. Tito gently removed him, picked up the shirt, brushed it off and hung it back in the closet.

His head was starting to ache now, and there was a weird tense soreness in his neck and jaw. He thought suddenly of Halley when he'd visited her in the ER, before he'd had his own exam. While Jenna was talking to a nurse, Halley had looked at him with tears glistening on her lashes and said, *Thank you for teaching me how to get out of a locked trunk, Tito. I'm sorry my dad hit you.*

He'd smiled at her and said, *Halley, you have nothing to apologize for. None of this is your fault.*

*I know*, she'd said. *But he's still my dad.*

True enough, he'd thought, looking at those bright blue eyes, so much like Chase's.

She'd glanced at Jenna, then said, so quietly he almost didn't hear her, *I wish you were my dad.*

*I wish that too*, he'd replied.

But wishing didn't make it so.

## *CHAPTER SEVENTEEN*

JENNA BROUGHT HALLEY home that evening, along with several pages of care instructions and an appointment card for a follow-up doctor's visit. Halley went to bed early. Jenna stayed in the living room, fully clothed, too keyed up to go to bed. She picked up a book, read the same paragraph over and over without comprehending a word of it, laid it down, scrolled mindlessly through her phone for a few minutes, picked up the book again, laid it back down and got up to check that all the doors and windows were locked.

She fell asleep on the sofa around midnight. An hour or so later, she woke to the sound of Halley screaming in her room. Jenna toppled off the sofa, barked her shin on the coffee table and stumbled down the hall to find Halley, alone in her room, sitting up in bed and staring straight ahead at nothing. Jenna took Halley into her arms, and Halley clung to her like she hadn't done since she was a little girl. Halley didn't say anything—Jenna wasn't sure she'd even woken up—but her cries subsided, and within minutes her eyes were shut and her breathing was soft and regular. Jenna crawled under the covers with her and stayed there for the rest of the night, sleeping fitfully and waking at every sound.

In the morning, she crept out of the room and started making breakfast preparations. She was setting the table when Halley emerged, heavy-eyed and rumpled in her old sleep shorts and oversize T-shirt with Tweety Bird on it, with bandages over her knees, scrapes on her legs and the pristine white plaster cast on her wrist.

"Good morning," Jenna said brightly.

"Morning," said Halley.

"How's the arm?"

"All right. Hurts a little."

"Do you want to take something? I've got ibuprofen right here. The liquid kind, so you don't have to swallow a pill."

"Not now. Maybe later. What are you making?"

"Pancakes with blueberry compote. Your favorite."

She was pushing too hard. She'd have been okay if she'd stopped after the first sentence. Halley didn't have to be reminded what her favorite breakfast was.

Halley gave her a wan smile as she took a seat at the kitchen bar. "Thanks."

"I didn't start cooking them yet," Jenna went on. "Well, I did make the compote, but not the pancakes. I just mixed the batter. That way you can have the pancakes fresh and hot off the griddle."

The sound of her voice was chirpy and annoying in her own ears. She needed to stop talking, now, or Halley was going to clam up.

She forced herself not to speak another word until the first batch of pancakes was done. "There wc go," she said. "Now I'll just take these to the table and—"

But Halley had already picked up her plate from the table and brought it over to the bar. "I can just eat here," she said. "Will you hand me the pan with the compote, please?"

"I'll ladle some on for you," Jenna said.

"That's okay. I'll do it myself."

Jenna handed over the pan, and Halley spooned some compote onto her stack of pancakes. Jenna stood a moment, uncertain, before fetching her own plate from the dining table and bringing it to the kitchen.

She filled her plate. Now what? Should she eat at the bar with Halley, or would that be hovering? Maybe she should eat at the table. But wouldn't that be weird, the two of them eating in two different places? Seemed like anything she did at this point was going to be awkward.

She ended up eating in the kitchen, standing with her hip against the counter and wondering how she was ever going to survive Halley's teen years if things were this difficult now. Was it really just seven hours ago that Halley had gratefully accepted comfort from her like the small child she used to be?

Halley was halfway through her pancakes when she glanced at the time on the kitchen clock. "It's late," she said. "Don't you have a breakfast shift?"

"Oh, I'm not working today," Jenna said. "We're staying home and watching movies all day, whatever you want to watch. And we'll snack on popcorn and chips like a couple of couch potatoes."

Halley thought about this. For a moment things hung in the balance. Jenna held her breath. Had she struck the right tone, or was she trying too hard again?

Then Halley smiled. "That sounds perfect," she said.

Jenna smiled back. "Good. You need to take it easy and get your strength back, so you might as well enjoy yourself, right?"

"Yeah. Hey, we should invite Tito."

Jenna hesitated a little too long before saying, "Tito can't come."

"Why? He isn't working, is he? He needs to rest, too."

"Actually, he's supposed to avoid screen usage while his concussion heals."

"Oh," said Halley. "Well, we don't have to watch movies. We can do something else. Maybe play some board games. His parents have some good ones."

"Tito isn't coming over," Jenna said.

"Why?" Halley asked, in a tone that indicated that she had a pretty good idea of what was coming and didn't like it.

Jenna sighed. "I didn't want to tell you this way."

"Tell me what?"

Silence. Then Jenna steeled herself and said, "There's no point in my seeing Tito anymore, because you and I aren't staying in Limestone Springs."

Halley's mouth dropped open. "We're moving? What for?"

"Because the whole point of coming here in the first place was to get away from your father and his family. Now that he's found us, this place isn't safe for us anymore."

"I thought he was going back to prison."

"I certainly hope he is. But he already went once, and he got out, a whole lot sooner than we thought he would. That could happen again."

Halley's pupils dilated, swallowing up the blue of her eyes, and her face went white. For a moment Jenna thought Halley might faint.

She reached across the kitchen counter, grabbed Halley's hand and held it tight. "You don't have to be afraid. I won't let him hurt you again."

Halley jerked her hand away and stood

up. "Stop it! Stop treating me like a baby. I don't need you constantly taking care of me and telling me what to do."

"I'm not treating you like a baby, Kara, I just—"

Halley actually stamped her foot, like a toddler throwing a tantrum. "I'm not Kara! I'm me. And I'm not a little kid anymore. I can look out for myself. I got myself out of the trunk of that car, and I don't think you're giving me enough credit for that."

"How can you say that, honey? I'm proud of you for what you did."

"That's the first time I've heard you say so."

"Well, I am. You were brave and smart, and you kept your head in a horrible situation. But you were also very lucky. That big tractor thing that slowed down the traffic, the fact that you were on that exact stretch of road close to a house you recognized, the fact that Kevin happened to be at home and outside—not to mention that weirdly athletic farmer who chased after your dad and knocked him down. Without all those things being in place, this story could have had a very different ending. I'm not trying to devalue what you did. I'm just saying that next time, it might not be enough."

"Maybe it wouldn't have to be enough if we had other people on our side. You aren't the only person who can do things, you know. Other people can be smart and strong too, and they can help us. People like Tito, and Gillian's dad, and that really fast farmer, and Tito's family."

She squared her jaw and glared at Jenna head-on with those bright blue eyes so eerily like Chase's. "Tell me you didn't already break up with him. Did you? Tell me."

"I—I—"

The bright blue eyes filled with tears. Halley didn't look like Chase anymore. She was just herself, a twelve-year-old girl, serious and precocious, but still a child.

She turned and stormed off to her room and slammed the door, leaving Jenna alone in the kitchen, staring at Halley's half-eaten stack of pancakes.

She planted her hands on the counter and hung her head. She was shaking all over, and her stomach was tied in knots. How had she managed to make such a mess of things? All she wanted was to keep Halley safe. Was that so wrong?

She stood there, staring down at the countertop, until her hands steadied and her stomach settled into a dreary calm. Then she took a deep breath and ambled slowly through the dining room, all the way to the back window.

And there was Tito's building, just visible through the limbs of her neighbor's pecan tree. Was Tito inside his apartment right now? Sleeping? Reading? Petting his cat? Thinking of Jenna? Feeling as miserable as she was?

Halley's accusations rang in her ears. Was it really just arrogance that made her take all the responsibility on herself? Tito had said pretty much the same thing. Maybe they were right. If she had told the truth right from the start in her new community, she would have had a lot of people looking out for her and Halley. If Coby Kowalski had known about Chase, then his cop instincts would have made the connection between Halley's recently released ex-con father and the suspicious-looking vehicle parked downtown for several days in a row. Tito might not have gotten hurt, and Halley might not have been taken. Jenna's secrecy hadn't protected Halley or herself. It had only made them more vulnerable.

She rested her forehead against the glass. Something was pulling her, gently but firmly, like an invisible line stretching from here to that old downtown building, connecting her heart to Tito's.

She stood up straight, then walked down the hallway and knocked on Halley's door.

She heard Halley let out a heavy sigh, then ask, "What?"

"Can I come in?" Jenna asked.

"Yes."

Halley was lying on her bed with her back to the door. Jenna sat down on the edge of the bed. She started to reach for Halley, then drew back her hand and said, "I'm sorry."

Almost before the words were out, Halley had spun around and wound her arms around Jenna's neck and was crying into her shoulder. "I'm sorry too. I shouldn't have been so mean."

Halley's hair was tickling Jenna's face. Jenna smoothed it back.

"You weren't mean," she said. "You were right."

Halley sucked in a quick breath of air and pulled back to look Jenna in the face. "I was?"

"Yes. I was trying to do everything on my own, and I can't. It's too much. I'm not strong enough or smart enough to handle it all."

"You're the smartest, strongest person I know," Halley said, her voice quavering. "You gave up your old job and your old house, and got new names for us, and moved us away from my dad and all the other Latimores. I know you didn't have to do all that, and I'm glad you did, I really am. It's just... it's hard sometimes, knowing you did all that for me. It's like I took everything away from you, and now I have to be enough to make up for it."

Jenna laid a hand against Halley's cheek. "Oh, Halley, you're already enough. You don't have to earn my love. You're mine. You hear me? Nothing will ever change that. I'm sorry if I've put too much pressure on you. I guess I'm just afraid of making a mistake. I have to keep you safe."

Halley sniffled. "It isn't only about me

being safe, though. You're afraid I'll turn out like my mom—or my dad."

Jenna wanted to deny it, but she couldn't without lying.

"You're right," she said. "I guess I am afraid of that sometimes."

"Well, you don't have to be. I remember what it was like when I lived with them. I'm not going to make those same mistakes."

"Okay," Jenna said. "I believe you."

And she did. Of course, Halley would make different mistakes. But there was no help for that, and no sense in trying to predict what those mistakes might be and head them off.

"And speaking of mistakes…" Halley gave Jenna a reproachful look.

"I know," Jenna said. "I messed up."

There was no need to be more specific. They both knew they were talking about Tito.

"Do you think you can get him back?" asked Halley.

"I don't know," said Jenna. "I hope so."

"You *have* to. He's perfect for you."

Jenna smiled. "He is, isn't he? He's really special."

"Call him," said Halley. "Tell him you

were wrong and that we're not moving away after all."

"Not so fast," said Jenna. "I haven't actually said we're not moving away."

Halley gave her a sly smile. "Then say it now."

Jenna chuckled. "Okay. We're not moving away. We're staying in Limestone Springs."

Halley squealed, and hugged Jenna so hard the bed bounced. "Now call Tito and tell him you're sorry. Where's your phone?"

"I think it's in the kitchen. Halley, wait!"

But Halley had already bounded off through the door and down the hall.

"Careful!" Jenna called. "Do you want to break your other arm?"

Halley came skipping back and dropped Jenna's phone on the bed in front of her.

"Call him," she said. "Do it!"

Jenna picked up the phone and clicked into recent calls. Tito's number was right there at the top. She could call him right now, just as Halley said, and tell him she was wrong and she wanted him back. And maybe that would be enough for him. But it wasn't enough for her. She wanted to give him more. He deserved more.

Halley stared at her, eyes shining. "What are you waiting for? Go ahead!"

Jenna laid the phone back down. "I have a better idea," she said. "I've been planning a sort of surprise for Tito for a few days now. Something to show him how special he is to me, and to the whole town. I sort of forgot about it after—well, you know, everything. And I don't have much time to pull it together."

"Maybe you don't have to do it all by yourself," Halley said.

"Maybe I don't. In fact, I've got one of the smartest, most capable people I know, right here in this house with me."

Halley grinned. "Then let's get to work."

## *CHAPTER EIGHTEEN*

One of the bedrock principles of self-defense, Bart had told Tito years ago, was not being around to get hurt. This included defensive moves, like blocking, deflecting and dodging, but it went deeper than that. Whenever possible, you had to prevent a situation from developing or escalating to a point where a punch or kick was thrown in the first place. You had to think ahead, and predict different ways an encounter might go, and be ready to respond—and also keep yourself away from compromising situations, whether that meant staying out of dark alleys in sketchy parts of town, or defusing conflicts before they turned violent.

Tito had taken the lesson to heart. In the years since he'd taken over the bar and started acting as its bouncer, he'd de-escalated a lot of situations, and he'd never once had a surly drunk actually land a blow on him.

But Chase had knocked him out cold with a single punch. A child had been taken by force, and Tito, with his years of training and experience, hadn't been able to do a thing to stop it. As Bart used to say, all the knowledge and skill in the world wouldn't do a bit of good if you didn't put them into practice.

And that was the thought that kept nagging at him now. He'd known better, but he'd still gotten hurt. Just like he'd known better than to believe he and Jenna could have a future together, but had fallen for her anyway. It was the same old story he'd seen playing out all his life. Whatever it was that made a woman want to stay with a man for the long haul, he didn't have. His wounded pride hurt more than his concussed head, but less than his broken heart.

He lay stretched out on his unmade bed, with his feet on the floor and his arms spread wide, staring up at the ceiling. Once in a while he eased his mouth open, slowly and cautiously, trying to work the soreness out of his jaw.

It had been a long day. His mother had brought him food and fussed over him for half an hour or so before taking off again, saying that she had a busy day ahead of her.

*Try to get some sleep*, she'd said. *You need to rest and heal.*

She hadn't even mentioned the family birthday dinner scheduled for the following evening. Jenna and Halley were supposed to come, but of course that wasn't going to happen now. He'd been dreading telling his mother that, because she would want to know why, and he wasn't ready to talk about the breakup to anyone, especially his family. They all liked Jenna so much. But the fact that Rose hadn't even mentioned the dinner was almost worse. Was it possible she'd forgotten it? Had it been eclipsed by the plans for Eddie's big celebration later in the month?

Rose had at least wished Tito a happy birthday, but almost as an afterthought before breezing out his door. It was all very dissatisfying and strange.

He hauled himself to his feet and started ambling around his apartment for what felt like the millionth time that day. No movies or TV or electronic screens of any kind, the doctor had told him, and no reading either, even from an analog book. Well, what else was there to do? It wasn't as if he could go for a hike. He was pretty much stuck indoors resting until he was cleared for regular activities, but resting wasn't very restful without books or movies, at least once you felt well enough to be out of bed. He'd tried an audiobook, but it couldn't hold his attention. He'd tried listening to music, but every song he heard had some sort of memory of Jenna attached to it now. He'd already taken two naps today, and he could only pet the cat for so long.

It would be different, of course, if he had company. Someone to talk with and be quiet with. Someone to ask how he was feeling and maybe bring him a glass of juice. But he didn't. He was all alone, with nothing to do but wander aimlessly around, and think, and feel.

This must have been what it was like for Uncle Tito after his wife left. No one to talk to about it, and no one he wanted to talk to at all except the one who'd gone away. Nowhere for the pain to go. Nothing for it to do but swell and grow until it was ready to burn its way out of his chest.

He went into the kitchen, took down a glass and poured some bourbon. He wasn't supposed to drink alcohol while recovering from his head injury, but he had to get some relief. They hadn't even given him any good painkillers, just told him to take ibuprofen or acetaminophen, neither of which could do a thing for the worst pain of all, this feeling of loss that was like a physical ache in his soul.

He picked up the glass, swirled it, set it down, stared a few moments into the amber-colored liquid and picked it up again.

Uncle Tito stared solemnly at him from the photo on the fridge, telling him not to do it, that it wouldn't help, that once he started he wouldn't be able to stop, and once the alcohol wore off he'd have a hangover to deal with, and the thing he'd been trying to bury would still be there, staring him in the face, bigger and stronger than ever.

He set the glass back down, picked it up, set it down, picked it up…and poured the bourbon back into the bottle.

He walked to the living room. Bunter lay in his usual spot on the windowsill, surveying the downtown area. He flicked an ear back when Tito knelt beside him but didn't turn around. Tito stroked the cat's smooth back and gazed in the same direction, at the patch of metal roof just visible through a gap in the trees. Was Jenna there right now, making plans for her next move? Where would she take Halley this time?

If only she would call, and say she'd been wrong, that she'd changed her mind and wanted to be with him. He'd been straining his ears all day, listening for her ringtone, occasionally checking his phone to see if he'd somehow missed a call from her.

His phone was lying on the coffee table right now. He was about to pick it up and check it again when the chime of an incoming text message went off.

He spun around in a clumsy sprawl, nearly whacking his head against the coffee table in his haste to reach his phone.

The message wasn't from Jenna. It was from Lalo.

Never in his life had Tito been more disappointed to hear from his cousin. And the content of the message did nothing to change that feeling.

I need to ask you a favor, it said.

Tito stood a moment, staring at the screen, before typing, What is it?

It's kind of a big favor, Lalo replied.

Tito let out a heavy sigh. He was not in the mood for this. He stood watching the dancing dots, waiting to find out what the favor would be. Maybe Lalo had locked himself out of his office again and needed to borrow Tito's keys. That wasn't a very big favor, but maybe he felt bad about disturbing his freshly concussed cousin who was supposed to be resting.

I need you to come downstairs and tend bar.

"What?" Tito said out loud. He typed, Why?

It's a long story, Lalo answered. But you know we've got that private event booked at the restaurant tonight, and the people want an open bar. Eric was scheduled to work but he called in sick, and Garrett has car trouble.

"Are you kidding me?" Tito asked his phone screen, louder this time. Eric and Garrett had jumped at the chance to work this event, presumably expecting good tips. The servers at Lalo's had been quick to volunteer as well. All of which had worked out really well, since he and Jenna both wanted off that evening. Jenna had said she was going to take Tito out to dinner for his birthday, just the two of them, in advance of the birthday dinner with Tito's family.

Well, that wasn't happening now.

*Jenna can tend bar*, Tito thought. But Jenna was home with an injured and traumatized child.

He paced around the living room, seething. Why were things like this always happening to him? Why was he always the one who had to take up everyone else's slack?

Maybe he would just say no. He had every right to. He'd given enough hours of his life to that bar.

But it was his name on the sign above the door. And he'd already rested for the 24 hours the doctor had recommended. At this point, in all honesty, an evening of work would be a pleasant change.

I'll be there in ten minutes, he typed.

Great! Lalo replied. See you downstairs.

No mention of the fact that Tito had suffered a brain injury the day before while trying to prevent a kidnapping, or that today was his birthday. Not even a simple thank you.

Tito started to exit from the messaging app, but the dancing dots appeared again, followed by a new message.

Be sure to wear your gold tie bar. This is a classy event.

It took Tito longer than usual to get dressed. Everything felt like a huge effort. He sat on the edge of his bed for a good five minutes, unable to summon the energy to button his shirt.

But he did it at last and made his way downstairs, ready to slip into his place as the guy handing out alcohol, unseen except as part of the background.

The bar seemed unnaturally quiet as he walked down the hallway. Maybe they were still setting up for the event, or maybe the guests hadn't started arriving yet.

But when he entered the room, he saw that it was already packed with people. Tony and Alex Reyes were there, along with their wives and kids. Annalisa and her boss Claudia. Mad Dog McClain and the entire volunteer fire department. The Reyes brothers and their families. Luke and Eliana. Bart. Lalo.

Coby Kowalski. Abel from the kitchen. Kevin Fox with his daughter, Gillian, and his dad. Susana Vrba and Roque Fidalgo from the equine center. Eric, looking perfectly healthy, and Garrett. Tito's own parents and brothers.

What the heck? What was happening here? Just what was this event, and why hadn't he been invited?

Everyone was facing him, and smiling at him, no doubt relieved to see that the serving of alcohol would go on as expected. Someone had set up a long buffet table, with plates, flatware and chafing dishes of food neatly laid out.

Standing at the end of the table, in a mango-colored dress, was Jenna, with Halley at her side. Her eyes met Tito's. He saw her take a deep breath.

Then he saw the banner hanging overhead, painstakingly made of *papeles picados*, each letter a sheet in itself, spelling out *Happy Birthday Tito!*

There was no shout of *surprise*, no throwing of confetti or blowing of noisemakers. Just a familiar loud laugh ringing out, followed by, "You ought to see your face right now, Rigoberto! Come on in, birthday boy, and join the party."

And then his mother's arms were around him, and she was kissing him on the cheek and saying, "Happy birthday, baby!" More people hugged him, or shook his hand, or clapped him on the back.

Lalo grinned as he gripped his hand. "I had you going there, didn't I, cousin? Asking you to come in and work when you were supposed to be taking it easy. You fell for it, too!"

"I can't believe you didn't figure it out!" said Garrett. "We were planning this party right under your nose, on your actual birthday and everything. But Jenna said you'd never suspect it was for you, and she was right."

"Jenna said that?" Tito asked.

"Oh, yeah," said Lalo. "The whole thing was her idea. She's been planning it for days."

Since before she'd broken up with him, then. And now she was following through with it. Why? Out of duty, or friendship, or something more? Why didn't she come over to him right now? He wanted her to, and at the same time he was terrified of what she might say if she did.

Then Lalo started clinking a spoon against a glass. Once the room had quieted down, he held the glass high.

"We're here tonight to honor Tito Mendoza," he said. "Tito is my cousin, business partner and sounding board. I know I'm not the easiest guy in the world to work with—" lots of agreeing murmurs from the crowd "—but believe me, I'd be a lot worse without Tito to give me reality checks and help me think things through. This place, Lalo's Kitchen, this is my dream. And that man right there—" he pointed at Tito "—he's the one who made it happen. I never could have raised the capital on my own to get a place with as good a location as this one. Being right next door to an established bar, connected to it by a pass-through, gave Lalo's Kitchen a head start and credibility that can't be overestimated. I wouldn't be where I am today without Tito. He took his uncle's legacy, and he made it into something more. So let's all raise a glass to him. Happy birthday, Tito."

"Happy birthday," the crowd said, and drank.

Eddie went next. He was looking his best,

well dressed, hair perfectly styled, grinning hugely.

"I remember when this guy was born, just one day after *my* fourth birthday," he said, his eyes sweeping the crowd. "Yeah, that's right. Our birthdays are one day apart! Can you believe that? I don't know what my mother was thinking!"

He paused for the crowd to laugh, which it did.

"I didn't get much of a party that year, with a brand-new baby in the house squalling all day and all night," he continued. "Lots of people came over to drop off food and take a look at him, and you know what they told me? They told me how cool it was that I'd gotten a new brother for my birthday. Well, I didn't think much of *that*. I already had three brothers. What did I need with one more?"

He looked at Tito, and his toothy grin softened into an affectionate smile. "I couldn't have been more wrong. Tito is one of a kind, and my life is richer for knowing him. Happy birthday, little brother. Here's to many more years of separate birthday celebrations for me and you."

"Hear, hear!" Tito called out above the laughter and cheering.

Then Tito's father said, "Quiet down, everyone. My turn."

Holding his stein of beer, he faced his youngest son head-on across the room and spoke in his usual bellow.

"This is a very special occasion, y'all. This is the first time my boy Rigoberto has had a proper birthday party since he was fourteen years old! Can you believe that? He told his mother and me that he didn't like parties, and I believed him. But I might have been wrong about that."

He paused to rub his jaw, then went on, "There might actually be a lot of things about this son of mine that I don't understand. He's kind of a hard one to figure. He's always been his own man. It takes a lot of courage to be different, and Tito's one of the best and most courageous men I know."

He raised his stein high. "Happy birthday, *huerco*!"

The rest of Tito's brothers toasted him as well. Javi gave his toast over FaceTime via Annalisa's iPad, live from West Texas, beer in hand.

Even Marcos Ramirez gave a toast. He was Tony Reyes's brother-in-law and a man of famously few words. He and his wife and son came to the restaurant and bar regularly, but Tito didn't know him very well, despite having gone to high school with him. After graduation, Marcos had joined the Marines. He'd only moved back to Limestone Springs a few years ago. Marcos didn't drink alcohol, so that glass he was holding probably held turmeric ginger tea.

Marcos took a deep breath and squared his shoulders. "I, uh, I'm not one for public speaking, but I'll do my best. There was a time in my life, not many years back, when I was at a crossroads and not sure what to do. Tito had some words of wisdom for me that pointed me in the right direction, and I've never forgotten that, though I don't think I ever thanked him for it. He and I didn't know each other all that well, even though we went through high school together and graduated the same year. I see now that that was my loss, and I'm glad and honored that Tito is my friend today."

He raised his glass. "Here's to you, man. Happy birthday."

Tito was touched. He didn't even remember ever giving Marcos any advice.

The toasts kept coming. Tony Reyes gave one, followed by Mad Dog McClain, chief of the volunteer fire department, and Coby Kowalski. All of theirs made reference to that late-summer storm a few years back, when Tito and Lalo had provided free food and drink to first responders and to people whose houses had suffered damage.

And then Tito's heart seized up, because it was Jenna's turn.

She stood straight, head high, looking very determined, a little nervous and unbelievably beautiful. Halley watched from nearby, her face shining with excitement.

The crowd quieted down. They'd yelled out some good-natured cross talk during some of the other toasts, but everyone seemed to want to pay close attention to whatever Jenna had to say.

"I think everyone here knows me," she said. "I've been living and working in this town for about a year and a half now, and I've served beer and burgers to most of the people in this room. As recent events have probably made very clear, Halley and I came to Limestone Springs to get a fresh start, away from a dangerous man and some bad history. But what you don't know, what I haven't yet told anyone, is how I chose Limestone Springs in the first place."

She spoke formally, as if she'd planned in advance what she was going to say. She cleared her throat.

"The Texas part was an easy decision," she said. "My father once spent some time here as a young man and often spoke fondly of it. He always wanted to go back one day but never got a chance. And I knew I wanted to live in a small town. It felt safer, somehow. So I Googled best small towns in Texas, and wouldn't you know, Limestone Springs made everyone's top ten."

She tucked a long curl behind one ear. "I liked the look of Limestone Springs, with its prosperous small businesses and beautiful old downtown buildings. I liked the fact that the town had an annual persimmon festival, with a parade and carnival rides and a dance, and a Persimmon Queen and a Persimmon Court, and vendors selling crafts and pastries and jams, and even a guy who put on a persimmon suit and walked around glad-handing the crowd and posing for pictures."

Several people laughed. Jenna laughed too. Then her expression turned serious again.

"And then," she said, "I saw an old news video about how the people in the town came together to help each other after a late-summer hailstorm. Some of the video was actually shot right here inside Lalo's Kitchen and Tito's Bar. Tony was in that video. You were great on camera, Tony, talking about the community's neighborly spirit and generosity. You even teared up a bit when you said how grateful you were that no one had been seriously hurt."

She turned the full force of her gaze on Tito. His heart was pounding now.

"But what really caught my eye," Jenna said, "was the guy in the background, quietly handing out food and drink to firefighters and volunteers and people who'd been displaced by the storm. A slender guy in a crisp white shirt and black vest, with a gold tie bar, and a little Clark Gable mustache that made him look like a film star from a bygone and classier era."

A surprised murmur rose from the crowd.

"That's right," Jenna said sheepishly. "I basically traveled fourteen hundred miles to meet a cute guy I saw on the internet. That sort of thing is usually not a smart move, and in general, I don't recommend it. But in this case, it worked out pretty well."

The crowd laughed but quickly subsided, clearly eager to hear more, as was Tito, who could hardly believe what he was hearing. Was it possible? Could it be true? Had Jenna actually come to Limestone Springs because of him?

"So I came here, and got a job at Lalo's," Jenna said. "I got to know Tito, and found out that he was even better in person than he was on that news video. But I didn't really put down roots here, because I didn't trust anyone enough to share the truth about myself and where I'd come from. That was a mistake, and I want to do better now."

Her chin trembled. Tito swallowed hard over a lump of soreness in his throat. The room was dead silent.

"But enough about me," Jenna said briskly. "We're here tonight to celebrate Tito Mendoza—son, brother, boss, friend, confidant, and so much more." She raised her glass. "Happy birthday, Tito."

"Happy birthday, Tito," the crowd chorused.

Then Juan's voice called out, "Enough with the speechifying. Let's eat!"

## *CHAPTER NINETEEN*

IT TOOK A while for Tito to make his way to Jenna. He had a whole succession of people to get through, all of whom wanted to shake his hand, wish him a happy birthday and tell him how much he and his bar had meant to the community, and to them personally, over the years. It was very gratifying and heartwarming, of course. He'd never realized how much of an impact he'd managed to have on the town, and hearing it made his heart swell. But it took time. And while he was listening and smiling and nodding, another part of him was yearning after Jenna in her mango-colored dress, beautiful and out of reach.

When he finally got free, he had a brief moment of panic because he couldn't see her anymore. Had she left without even speaking to him?

Then suddenly there she was in front of him, holding out a glass.

"Hey there," she said. "I thought you could use some sustenance. It must be thirsty work, getting toasted by half the town."

He took the glass from her, his fingers brushing hers. "Thanks," he said.

"It's just juice," she said. "No alcohol for you."

He sipped it just to have something to do. He didn't even know if he was thirsty anymore. The juice was mango, like her dress.

An awkward silence fell. There was so much Tito wanted to say, but he couldn't seem to get the words from his brain to his mouth, and Jenna looked anxious.

"I got you a present," she said. "Do you want to open it?"

"Sure," he said.

She led him through the crowd to the bar, and he followed, keeping his gaze fixed on her smooth golden head. Eric and Garrett were busily pouring beer and mixing drinks. And on the bar top was a black box topped with a gold bow.

He set down his juice, opened the lid of the box—

And there was his uncle, looking out at him from a black-and-white photo with a white mat and a gold frame. Uncle Tito was standing behind the bar as it had looked in the eighties, his head held high, gazing out with the watchful expression that Tito remembered so well.

Tito lifted the picture out of the box. "Is this the pic that's on my fridge?" he asked.

"Yes. Your mom gave me the negative."

There was something else in the box, beneath a thin sheet of cushioning foam.

Another picture. Same size, matching frame, also in black-and-white. It was the photo Tito's mother had taken of Tito and his uncle together at the bar.

Tears pricked his eyes. His uncle looked so *young*. So did he, for that matter.

He laid the two pictures side by side on the bar top. "These look amazing," he said.

"Yes, they do," said Jenna. "But are you sure there isn't anything left in the box?"

Sure enough, there was one more framed photo under another sheet of foam. This was an image he'd never seen before. It showed just him, standing behind the bar as it appeared today, with the antique mirror behind him. He had the same upright posture and vigilant expression as his uncle. He'd never seen the resemblance so clearly before now.

It was a good picture, too, probably the best picture he'd ever seen of himself.

"Where did this one come from?" he asked.

"I took it," Jenna said. "Remember?"

And suddenly he did remember. It was the day after the Fourth of July party and his and Jenna's first kiss, when everything had seemed so fresh and full of hope. He remembered seeing her at the pass-through, holding her phone pointed at him, smiling at him. *I'm taking a picture of my handsome boyfriend*, she'd said.

A rush of heat flooded his face and neck.

"I got Lauren Reyes to edit the photos for me," Jenna said.

"She did a great job," said Tito. "The black and white gives them a nice vintage vibe. And the gold frames are perfect."

She smiled. "They look like the Johnnie Walker label," she said. "They look like you."

He let out a shaky laugh. Memories washed over him—of the day when they'd assigned all the liquor bottles to the people they most resembled, and all the other times they'd closed together.

He managed to get control of his voice long enough to say, "They're beautiful. Thank you. Thank you for all of this. The party and…everything."

She shrugged. "I had a lot of help. Everyone was happy to pitch in. They just needed someone to give them the idea. They really love you, you know."

*And you?* The question was right there, in the air between them, so plain that he didn't need to ask it.

Jenna spoke in a rush. "Tito, I'm sorry for what I said before, and for all the ways I've held out on you and been less than truthful with you. I was only trying to protect Halley, but I should have realized that I can do that better with you than without you. Everything is better with you than without you."

"So…you're not leaving?" Tito asked.

It seemed unlikely that she was still planning on leaving after she'd just told her story to a roomful of people, but he had to hear her say it.

"I'm not leaving," she said. "You were right. It was arrogant of me to take so much on myself, to think I was stronger on my own and that I was the only one who could take care of Halley."

"It wasn't all arrogance," Tito said. "You've been carrying a heavy load for a long time, and you don't want to make a mistake. That's only natural. And it isn't everyone who'd take on the responsibility of raising their sister's child. I've never heard you speak a single complaint, or a word of regret for the life you left behind. You're the strongest woman I know, Jenna."

She smiled. "Thank you, Tito. That means a lot. But a lot of it really was arrogance. Halley pointed that out to me in no uncertain terms when she found out I was planning to move us away from Limestone Springs. So did you. You were both right, and I was wrong."

"Thank you," said Tito. "That couldn't have been an easy thing to say."

"It wasn't that hard," said Jenna. "I'll admit to any number of character flaws if you'll take me back."

A LOOK OF soft wonder washed over Tito's face. Jenna saw him swallow.

"Take you back?" he repeated in an incredulous voice. "As if there could be any question of that."

Then he laughed, a wonderfully rich laugh, and said in his wonderfully rich voice, "Come here."

He reached for her, and she came to him, resting her cheek against his chest. She felt it expand as he took a deep breath; she felt the rapid beating of his heart and inhaled the clean starchy scent of his shirt.

"You know," he said, "you could have just called and told me you were staying. You didn't have to be so dramatic with the party and everything."

She squirmed. "I know. Maybe I was wrong to wait. But I wanted to do something special for you, to show you how special you are—to me, and to the whole town."

He held her tight for a moment longer. When he finally pulled back and looked at her, his eyes were shining. Slowly, gently, he lowered his face to hers and kissed her.

Someone cheered, but Jenna didn't open her eyes. She just held on to Tito as surges of joy went off like fireworks inside her head.

SHE DIDN'T LEAVE Tito's side for the rest of the evening. He kept her hand tightly clasped in his as if afraid she'd slip away if he let go. They made the rounds of the party together. People smiled at them in an approving sort of way. Some of them said, "It's about time." And quite a few of them said words to the effect that if Chase ever tried to take Halley again, or harassed Jenna in any way, or so much as dared to show his face in Limestone Springs again, he would have a whole town's worth of angry Texans to deal with. By the time the party wound down, Chase's mug shots—the Virginia one and the new one taken a few days earlier at the Limestone Springs police station—had been posted on the *do not serve* group text and circulated to various other local businesses.

Halley appeared to be having a great time. By the end of the evening, her cast was full of signatures, including a *David M* in bold black letters.

Susana and Roque came by to pay their respects.

"I'm going to go ahead with those barrel-racing lessons," Susana said. "I could do Halley and Gillian in a class together if you're interested—after Halley's out of her cast, of course."

Jenna glanced at Tito and smiled. "That sounds great," she said. "Why don't you go tell her right now?"

She did. Jenna and Tito watched as Halley's eyes lit up. Her squeal of delight carried across the room.

It wasn't even 9:30 p.m. when the guests began to make their goodbyes. Jenna had seen to that ahead of time.

"I didn't want you all worn out," she said. "Don't forget, birthday boy, you're still recovering from a head injury, and you need your rest."

She and Tito walked outside together to send Halley on her way to her first ever sleepover at Gillian's house. They lingered awhile, thanking Kevin for everything he'd done to protect Halley. By the time they went back inside, the food was cleared away. The benches and chairs were upside down on the tables, and Clint and Veronica were mopping. They'd already worked pretty far back, and the middle part of the floors were starting to dry in streaks.

Jenna took off her strappy shoes and

tiptoed across to the bar, and the music-streaming cellphone.

"No indie pop tonight," she said. "Just a playlist of old love songs for slow dancing. Plenty of Journey and Guns N' Roses for me, and sixties and seventies stuff for you."

Tito slipped his own shoes off. "I thought the party was over," he said.

"This is the party after the party," Jenna replied.

Jenna held on to Tito, swaying to the music, and let her mind drift and wander. A Bee Gees cover band was coming to New Braunfels. She would take Tito to the concert as a surprise. She wanted to take him to Virginia, too, to meet her mother. She'd look at the schedule tomorrow and figure out some dates. She wanted the trip north to happen sooner than later. Why not? Chase was locked up again, and would be for a long time. There'd be a trial to deal with at some point, but with as many crimes as he'd racked up, and as many credible witnesses as their side had, she was confident that the charges would stick.

They had so much to do, so much to look

forward to. Lots of wonderful things seemed possible just now. She felt as light and buoyant as if she could fly.

* * * * *